Wild Kat

Wild Kat

Lydia Joe Cates

Byron,
Thanks for your interest in my book.
Enjoy... Sequel coming up!
Warm Wishes,
Lydia Joe Cates

Writers Club Press
San Jose New York Lincoln Shanghai

Wild Kat

All Rights Reserved © 2001 by Lydia Joe Cates

No part of this book may be reproduced or transmitted in any form or by any means, graphic, electronic, or mechanical, including photocopying, recording, taping, or by any information storage retrieval system, without the permission in writing from the publisher.

Writers Club Press
an imprint of iUniverse.com, Inc.

For information address:
iUniverse.com, Inc.
5220 S 16th, Ste. 200
Lincoln, NE 68512
www.iuniverse.com

This is a work of fiction. The characters and events described in this book are imaginary, and any resemblance to actual persons, living or dead, is purely coincidental.

ISBN: 0-595-17523-6

Printed in the United States of America

For my first born and most demanding critic, who encourages with delicate aggression and persuades with velvet gloves. Her singular devotion has renewed my confidence with grace.

Epigraph

All we like sheep have gone astray; we have turned every one to his own way; and the Lord hath laid on him the iniquity of us all.
 Isaiah 53:6

Foreword

Lydia Joe Cates's debut novel, Wild Kat, is not only a romantic adventure, but a statement about inequality and injustice in the late 1800's. The author's affinity for the American Indian led her to explore a common ground between Kiowa Chief Great Eagle and the white woman, Katherine Stone. Equality for women is specifically addressed through Katherine's youthful determination. A better understanding of mankind as a whole evolves through each character's willingness to understand and compromise with a culture other than their own.

The book is a delightful afternoon read by the fire and conveys the age old message of love conquering all.

Wild Kat is my lifetime friend, Joe's, voice. Katherine is her nature. The book is an escape to the reality of yesterday and a promise of understanding through education for tomorrow.

Ruth Kesler Berrier, EdD

Acknowledgements

Gratitude to my editor and publicist, Lindy, whose sense of humor sustains me through long hours of dedication to detail. To my husband, Charlie, who provides and guides me with state of the art tools to hone my profession…and understands that writing comes before laundry. Moreover, I express my genuine appreciation to the brilliant pathologist, Dr. James Makar, Jr., for mapping my way through cyberspace with the patience of Job. With earnest admiration, I thank the Vaughts; David, graphic artist extraordinaire and Jennifer, writer/producer/director who challenges me daily. Ultimately, I thank God, my family and my closest friend and confidante, Ruth, who believed in me even when I did not.

EDITORIAL METHOD

Edited by Lindy C. Makar

Chapter One

◯

Light illuminated dormer windows in the early morning darkness. A passerby might imagine two yellow eyes protruding from the head of an enormous black cat instead of the large, comfortable old farm house.

Katherine Stone slipped out of her nightgown and reached for her new dress. She had turned eighteen the day before, which was good enough reason to be enthusiastic, but uppermost in this redhead's mind was the adventure that was about to begin. It was a journey that would take her away from a life that had become meaningless and just plain boring.

Although Katherine loved her parents and two brothers, she felt detached, frequently wondering if she had been born to the wrong family. The spirited girl had lived with this peculiar feeling most of her life. Her self imposed sentiment fed a wild streak, causing her family their share of grief. Wild Kat…that's what they called her…and concealing her uninhibited side from the civilized world was out of the question, at least in Kat's mind.

A soft glow from the kerosene lamp added an intense sparkle to her copper colored eyes. She was a slender mite, not skinny by any means, but willowy with the good fortune of being well endowed. Kat slipped on her dress and a heavy woolen cape, both the color of red wine. Glancing around the familiar room for the last time, she felt only a tinge of sadness. Her thoughts were suspended as her youngest brother bellowed from the other side of the oak plank door.

"Kat!"

Wild Kat

"What is it, Bobby?"

"Mama says git a move on; Papa's gittin' itchy."

"Coming!"

Katherine quickly braided her waist-length hair into one long rope, flipped it over her shoulder, donned her bonnet and spoke to her image in the mirror.

"Everybody thinks I'm daft, but the good Lord gave me an imagination and I intend to make use of it."

Kat stared into the mirror more intently now. One last time, she thought as she closed her eyes. When she opened them the image of a tall stranger, shrouded in a vaporous fog, stood behind her. He was naked except for a breechcloth, which her fantasy provided for privacy's sake. His feet were shod in uniquely beaded Indian moccasins.

He spoke in a soft, sensual tone. "You are quite beautiful, Katherine."

"I don't think much about things like that." She blushed and added, "But you're the most beautiful man I've ever seen."

He smiled openly. His teeth, touched by the lantern's glow, glistened as pearls and darkened the sheen of his princely bronze skin. "You seem as innocent as a redbird, but I sense a part of you that is yet to be tamed."

A light of comprehension flickered in the girl's eyes. "Maybe. I only know that Katherine must die before Kat can begin to live." She shook her head as if to clear her vision. "I'm going away. I can't bear the thought of never…"

His wide lips softened and winged into an ingratiating smile. "We will meet again, Katherine." The stranger backed away from her and dissolved into the gossamer mist from which he had appeared.

"Katherine Stone! We're leaving!"

"Coming, Mother!" With one last wistful glance at the empty mirror, Kat gathered up her skirts and raced to the family wagon.

Sam Stone, heavyset and solemn with a face full of freckles, sat rigid on the driver's bench. His wife, Bess, ten years younger, sat beside him cloaked in gray wool. The color enhanced the strands of silver threading through her dark chestnut hair. Although forty, she still had a youthful, attractive face that framed dancing copper eyes. It was obvious that she had gifted them…as well as a lively spirit…to her daughter.

Bess turned to face Kat and detected that familiar faraway gleam in her eyes. "Well, missy, are you daydreaming again?"

"No, Mother, I'm not! I've decided to take my looking glass even if I have to sit on it all the way to Fort Riley." Poised to jump off of the wagon, Bess Stone's voice grabbed her and held on.

"Oh no you're not, young lady! We don't have room for one more sack of grain, much less another piece of furniture. When we get to Fort Riley, Papa'll buy you a new mirror that's not cloudy for lack of silver."

Sam slapped the horse's reins and glanced over his shoulder with a smile. "Are you in this world or another, Katherine?" It seemed that his little girl had blossomed into a woman overnight.

"My mind isn't wandering, if that's what you mean, Father. Why can't I drive our other wagon? God knows I'm old enough…and good at it too."

Bess turned and glared at her. "You're a lady, Katherine. I'll thank you not to use the Lord's name for selfish chatter."

Todd, the eldest son, ambled toward them after opening the gate. His pale blue eyes glistened, as did his rusty hair set afire by the rising sun. He edged his lanky frame to the side of the road and glanced sideways at Kat.

"Hope you don't mind me driving the other wagon instead of you, Sis."

"I **do** mind! But we mustn't forget I'm a lady." Katherine's tone oozed sarcasm as she studied Todd with mixed emotions. He was twenty, older than his years and as domineering as hell.

Todd's freckled face wrinkled into a grin. He was proud of Kat, but she had such a reckless nature. She required special looking after. He had appointed himself her keeper years ago and had found it a burden at times.

* * *

Wild Kat

Great Eagle gathered the buffalo skin tightly under his chin. Although he and his hunting party were camped in a copse of pines around a raging campfire, his body ached with cold. His heart ached as well. It had remained an empty shell that only the intimacy of a woman could fill since his beloved wife, White Doe, had died of the fever two years before. Since that time his feeling of incompleteness plagued him daily. In recent weeks his masculine yearning…the bodily need with which all young men either pleasure or suffer…was slowly awakening.

The campfire crackled, spitting showers of sparks from the hole with each surge of the wind. Great Eagle nestled deeper into his blanket and thought of a dream…a vision…that manifested itself in the form of a young woman with eyes the color of cinnamon. Who was she, this flame-haired girl whose lovely face and tinkling laughter had dominated his ethereal, disjointed mind tremors for the past few months?

The Indian chief sank into slumber, hoping that the vision would appear again.

*   *   *

It was the first day of March, 1865. The Stone family joined a wagon train headed for Fort Riley, Kansas to stake their claim for free land. They had no way of knowing what misery and grief awaited them. By journey's end their lives would never be the same.

At the edge of a small settlement known as Kindly, Texas, Sam and Todd Stone took their place in line with eight other wagons. Bess smiled at her husband and said, "Well, what are you waiting for Sam? Go sign us up. Your dream is about to begin."

He jumped down from his perch and looked up at her. A startling blue eye winked under a brown wide-brimmed hat as he turned and made his way to the head wagon.

Lydia Joe Cates

Muscular Deke Stiles, the wagon master, had a face that resembled a hunk of roughly carved wood. A smile softened his craggy appearance.

"You the wagon master?" Sam asked.

"That I am. You must be Sam Stone." Deke's voice sounded as scratchy as rocks rolling around in a wooden bowl.

"That's me all right. The only stock we're taking besides our team is a milk cow, six goats and one saddle horse."

"I'll make a note of that. Now we'd best get moving." Deke folded his makeshift desk and shoved it into the lead wagon. He then mounted his bay mare, pulled a red bandanna out of his hip pocket and mopped his sunbaked face. A beefy hand waved his black western hat in the air as he bellowed, "Wagons hooooo!"

Chapter Two

After the wagons had circled for the night, a group of young men gathered at the campfire with a purpose. Kat hid behind a water barrel and listened with envy. Her resentment began to mount as they planned the hunt. She would be in that group if men could accept the fact that those with lace on their drawers were not without skills.

A husky man about Todd's age stood in the center of the circle giving instructions. A born leader, Lincoln Sheffield brushed his dusty blond hair from his forehead and motioned for the young men to follow.

Kat snorted angrily as she slipped from behind the barrel, hiked up her skirt and climbed into the wagon. She dropped down on a sack of grain and swore. The gloomy interior did nothing to cheer her and she was not in the mood to help the women set up their cooking circle. A smile crossed her face as she idly gazed at Todd's clothing sack. She grabbed the bag and dug out an old pair of his overalls.

"I'll show those arrogant bastards how to shoot."

Lincolns's umber eyes sparkled with enthusiasm as he noted the eager faces surrounding him. "I see a new man has joined us. What's your name, partner?"

Kat was wearing a wide brimmed hat that brushed her eyebrows. She lowered her voice to a manly pitch and said, "Just call me Jack, Mr. Sheffield.

"And call me Linc. Have you done much hunting, Jack?"

Lydia Joe Cates

"This'll be my first time on the trail, but I can shoot." Kat shyly dropped her head and rammed her hands in her pockets.

Bess Stone smiled as she watched the hunters saunter into the woods. She quickly made a sling out of her apron and filled it with potatoes and onions for the community stew. Irish lass, Callie Forsythe, hailed her.

"'lo there, Bess."

Bess waved and waited for the Forsythe woman to catch up. She admired Callie's coal black hair and milky complexion. A comely woman in her prime, Bess thought, but hard living on the trail had a way of cheating a woman out of her looks.

In a thick Irish brogue Callie asked, "And where might Katherine be this evenin'?"

"In the wagon. She asked to be excused from helping at the supper pots, complaining of a headache."

"Too bad. If ye'll take me contribution to the circle, I'll just be peekin' in on the darlin' girl."

Bess nodded, but by the time she reached the fire, Callie came running back, her skirt flung over her arm to keep from stumbling. "Katherine is nowhere to be seen. Do ye suppose she might be takin' a walk alone?"

Bess frowned. "She knows better. Sam cautioned her this morning that we're knee deep in Indian territory now and she's to stay close to camp."

* * *

Now in the heart of the woods, Linc raised a hand and pointed a finger to a pile of brush. "Over there," he whispered. "Cottontails." He glanced at Kat. "Stay here, Jack. Todd and I'll flush the rabbits out."

Kat crouched and waited. A peculiar feeling engulfed her as she glanced over her shoulder. There was nothing unusual about the scene…only a dead tree trunk embedded in thick brambles. She

Wild Kat

discarded the foolish idea that she was being watched and focused her attention on Linc. When the two boys poked their gun barrels into the brush pile rabbits hopped in all directions. Kat raised her shotgun, took careful aim and felled the first one.

The hunt ended with a dozen animals bagged and Kat taking the honors for shooting three of them. As the weary young men began to meander back to camp, a lone Indian waited until Katherine faded in the distance. He then stole away unseen from behind the old dead tree trunk where he had observed her during the hunt.

Todd had not paid any attention to the new boy until they started back to the wagon train. He snatched the hat from Katherine's head and remarked, "You know, Jack, you look a lot like my sister!"

Kat's braid tumbled down her back. Seething with anger, she grabbed the hat and slapped her brother with it. "Damn you, Todd Stone! Why'd you have to give me away?"

Ignoring her, Todd latched onto her shirt sleeve. "You're going back to camp, Sis. Don't try that anymore or I'll tell Papa you've been swearing again."

Nose in the air, looking past Todd as if he were a stump, Kat shook herself free. She picked up her sack of rabbits and stomped past him.

Bess and Callie were breathless as they combed each wagon for Kat. The men had already organized a search party. They were ready to leave when Bess stopped them. "Don't bother, gentlemen! I see our Wild Kat being escorted back to camp by her brother."

Bess's forehead crimped as she watched Todd nudge Kat along at a steady lope. It was not the first time she had observed such an unruly scene. Exasperated, Bess wondered if she had ever known Katherine at all.

✴   ✴   ✴

Lydia Joe Cates

After supper the fiddler struck up a lively tune. Although the nightly chill had set in, people began to leave their wagons and feet began to shuffle in the direction of the music. The musician's pregnant wife, Josie, clapped her hands in time to the music while their toddler daughter danced.

"Come on now," Josie called out to the crowd around the campfire. "Don't be bashful, we might as well enjoy ourselves tonight and let tomorrow take care of itself."

Kat pouted in the shadow of the wagon. As if her brother's humiliating treatment had not been enough, she'd had to suffer a heated parental chastising too. She continued to watch the dancers, unaware that her father was standing beside her.

"How's the headache, Katherine?"

She looked down. "I didn't really have one."

"I'm well aware of that, young lady. In time you'll be glad you're a woman. God gave you many gifts, Katherine. Take advantage of them."

"I'm trying!" Kat changed her tone and smiled. "Two-step with me, Father?"

Sam grinned. "Why, I'm honored, Miss Katherine." With that he swept his daughter onto the dirt floor.

Linc Sheffield squatted on his haunches, warming his hands at the campfire while admiring Kat's feline grace as she danced. Mustering his courage, he stood up and tapped Sam on the shoulder. "May I borrow your partner, sir?"

Sam smiled. "I'm willing, Linc, if the lady is." He stepped back and bowed.

Kat dismissed the day's grievances by rewarding Linc with a dazzling smile. "My pleasure, Mr. Sheffield."

"Linc. Remember?"

Wild Kat

A waltz lilted on the breeze of the clear April evening as Linc proudly clasped Kat's tiny waist and swung her around Mother Nature's dance floor with ease.

"I've wanted to talk to you before now, Katherine, but I'm lacking in courage when it comes to a woman like you."

"What do you mean?"

"You are everything a man could ever want."

Kat thought of her phantom in the looking glass. Having loosened her braid, she tossed her luxuriant flowing hair with a smile. From a short distance Sam noticed that his daughter did indeed, know how to use her feminine wiles when the time was right.

Inadvertently caught up in the dance, Kat leaned closer and fingered the hair on the nape of Linc's neck. His ears grew hot from the innocent fondling. He cleared his throat and said, "Katherine, I seriously doubt that your father would approve of us dancing so close."

Amused by his sober look, she moved away. "Is that better?"

"Yes and no." He gave her a sickly smile and breathed somewhat easier.

As the music ended they strolled into the shadows of the firelight. Linc caught her hand in his and pressed it to his lips.

"That was nice. Why did you do it?"

"I guess it's because you're such a good shot," he teased. "How did you learn to fire a gun like that?"

"Father taught me to shoot when I was eight, but I learned to ride a horse when I was three."

"What I'm getting at is this, Katherine. It's good to know how to handle a firearm, but women should use one only in an emergency."

"Huh! You sound just like Todd."

"It's a fact. A gun belongs in a man's hands."

"You're like all the rest, Linc. You just can't stand the thought of a mere female being able to shoot, or do anything else like a man," she retorted.

"Not true, Katherine."

"Would you have invited me to go along on the hunt if you'd known I was a woman?"

"With a bunch of men? Definitely not!"

"I'd hardly call your hunters a bunch of men. Goodnight!"

Linc stared after her, excited by the flare of her temper that challenged the crackling fire. He shook his head to clear it, stifling an arousal that he'd been fighting all evening. The air was crisp so he decided to walk, an unsatisfactory solution to rid a man of his masculine urge.

*   *   *

For weeks the weary travelers had followed an eastern route bordering the Kansas River, also known as the Kaw. They had begun to work their way in a northerly direction where the Kaw emptied into the Missouri. On the new course an abundance of chipped arrowheads and colorful bird feathers were discovered along the way. Deke examined a broken staff and other telltale signs that answered their unasked questions.

The train had entered virgin territory where the Pawnee, Osage, and Kansa roamed the vast plains. A scattering of Kiowa had wandered south from the great northwest and had continued to grow in number.

In late summer a treaty would be signed at Fort Riley, Kansas, giving the Indians their original right to hunt and fish the land freely without interruption from the government. So far, the Indians had remained compliant. Even so, the men on the wagon train now rode with their rifles and shotguns visible and within easy reach.

Bobby began to squirm restlessly. "I'm hungry, Papa, when're we gonna stop and eat?"

"We won't be resting until sundown, Bobby. The jerky's right satisfying. Grab a hunk and start chewing; that'll take the edge off your appetite."

"I don't want none," Bobby grumbled. "I wanna ride Old Blue."

Wild Kat

"Todd needs her now. He's scouting with Linc. Now stop your whining."

It was near sunset when Deke signaled with a blast on his powder horn for the train to make a circle. After a short meeting the men went back to their wagons. Sam and the Irishman, James Forsythe, walked to Sam's wagon where their wives waited.

Brimming with curiosity, Bess asked, "What did Mr. Stiles say?"

"Deke lagged behind the train late this afternoon looking for Indian signs at the edge of the woods. He ran across a dead campfire about an hour ago. It was still warm."

"There'll be no sleepin' tonight," Forsythe added, turning to his wife. "Come along sweet Callie. Our instructions are to be takin' a quick meal at our wagons. We'll then be startin' out again."

Bess frowned. "You mean we have to travel at night?"

Sam nodded. "Deke thinks we're being followed. If it's Indians we can't take a chance on getting bottled up in Rattlesnake Canyon. We'll be safer moving at night." Sam smiled. "Don't look so worried, my dear, the wagon master knows what he's doing."

Bess jumped down from the wagon's tail-gate. She began to shout orders to her family before she touched the ground. "Todd, you and Bobby go to the creek for water. Kat, get the leftover biscuits out of the tin and start slicing some salt pork while I relieve Annie. We can all do with some fresh milk."

"You've always got to milk Annie when there's a crisis, Mother." Kat laughed nervously, rejecting the possibility of danger lurking nearby. That strange feeling of someone watching her still lingered.

Clearly impatient, Bess said, "You know as well as I do that the poor cow would be dripping and nigh to busting if I waited until morning. Get busy, Kat!"

Lydia Joe Cates

Bess rushed to the back of the wagon where the cow was tied and set the bucket under her swollen bag. She had gripped an udder firmly in each hand and was just finishing up when Deke steered his bay in her direction.

He tipped his hat and dismounted. "Can I help you, Miz Stone?"

"I'm near done, Mr. Stiles, but we'd be proud if you'd sup with us."

"Why I'd be grateful, ma'am."

Deke shoved his hat back and yanked a soiled bandanna from around his neck to swab his face. As an afterthought he ambled to the other side of the wagon and spit out a plug of chewing tobacco.

"Excuse me." He chuckled, showing a pleasant grin. "When I bit off that plug I wasn't expecting an invite to supper." Deke held out his hand for the milk pail. As he took it he could not help noticing the glow surrounding Bess as she smiled.

"Let's wash up for supper," she urged.

Deke nodded as an unexplained feeling of melancholy settled over him like the sun going behind a cloud. Bess was a desirable woman, no denying that. He watched her as she lowered a hinged board attached to the side of the wagon and set out tin cups brimming with warm milk. For no logical reason, her actions gave him comfort.

"Supper's ready," she announced as everyone gathered around the makeshift table ladened with the modest fare.

Deke talked a lot, which was unusual. Bess seemed to have a way of putting people at ease, more so than any woman that he had known since his deceased wife. His stoic face was a sight, but it did not fool Bess Stone. She picked up on the nostalgia reflected in his watery gray eyes and guessed that the friendly, robust man was a lonely soul.

After the meal Deke stepped away from the wagon and blew twice on his powder horn. The families gathered and waited for Stiles to speak. "Our plan to travel through Rattlesnake Canyon tonight is for two reasons. If the dead fire hole I stumbled onto this afternoon belonged to Injuns, then we might have company before long."

Wild Kat

He studied the troubled faces staring at him. "Settle down now; it might be a hunting party. That's what I'm counting on. Chances are they'll avoid the narrow canyon and stick to open land to make better time…'specially if they have fresh meat. Now I know that's a lot of **ifs**, and the next quarter mile might be a little nervy, but we'll make it just fine."

Deke's confident tone was rewarded with nods. "One more thing. No lanterns. We've got a full moon shining bright enough to get us through the passage. Any questions?"

Linc spoke up. "Sir, I've heard rumors that the Indians this far north are friendly with the troops at Fort Riley and the neighboring communities. Is there any truth to that?"

"That's right, Linc. They're minding their own business because of the Rights Treaty coming up this summer. That's probably why we haven't run into any of the scalawags so far. Now we'd best get rolling. We need a couple of volunteers to act as spotters at the other end of the canyon. Any takers?"

A burly Swede by the name of Borg Larsen raised his hand and walked forward. James Forsythe joined him. Deke gave orders to signal with a dove call when they reached the other end. Not more than ten minutes passed before the coo of the bird penetrated the still night.

The passage of darkness gaped like a huge mouth as the wagons were swallowed into its shadows. They immediately encountered an uneven rocky surface. Gritty, crunching noises split the air as the wagons, one by one, began to sway into the opening.

*   *   *

Three miles away, in the woods south of the wagon train, Kiowa Chief Great Eagle and several of his braves leaned close to the fire pit. The night had taken on a chill. They were hungry and their mouths watered as a tender doe roasted over a bed of coals.

Lydia Joe Cates

Low, angry voices of the men mingled with the hissing of the meat's succulent juices dripping into the fire. Great Eagle spoke to all the braves, but addressed one in particular. "Although we have hunted in the same path as the wagon train, we dare not consider a raid, Howling Wolf."

"The wagons look rich, Great Eagle. I have seen many sacks of grain, barrels of flour and fine horses."

"It would be taking a foolish chance, my brother. I will soon go with the chiefs of our neighboring nations to sign the treaty. Do you want the white man to keep what rightfully belongs to us?"

"No! But it is wrong not to take what we need. The others agree with me."

Great Eagle squatted before the meat, carved a slice, tasted it and groaned with pleasure. "Eat. There is no more to be said."

The sullen braves gathered around the spitted animal and began to devour its tasty flesh, grunting their approval. The chief sat apart from the others deep in thought. A quick attack for supplies would satisfy his men. As for himself, he had only one goal in mind…the young woman with hair the color of flames. He knew that she rode in the wagon behind the lead wagon. **She is my vision. I must have her.**

Having made his decision, the chief stretched and sauntered to the circle of men. "I have reconsidered. We will continue to follow the wagon train and, when the time is right, attack swiftly. We will take what we need, defending ourselves only if we are fired upon."

Amid cheers Howling Wolf asked, "Why have you changed your mind, Great Eagle?"

The chief ignored him. "After we have rested we will pick up the white man's trail again."

*   *   *

Wild Kat

Deke tailed the last of the train into Rattlesnake Canyon and swore as a rear wheel of the fiddler's wagon struck a large boulder. Dangerously loose, the wheel shimmied wildly and spiraled to the ground. Deke galloped to the head of the train and began working his way back, leaving a brief explanation in his wake.

"Whoa! The tail wagon's lost a wheel." As he turned he made a quick stop and called for Sam Stone. "Sam, go get the Swede at the other end of the canyon. We need his muscle."

Sam found the spotters a quarter of a mile away. As he neared, gasping for breath, he managed a faint signal and received one in return. The Irishman whispered loudly, "I'll be hearin' yer name!"

"Sam Stone! A wheel's off one of the wagons. Larsen's to go back with me. We need his weight."

Without further explanation the large man picked up his feet and flew as if he were as light as a cloud instead of two hundred and fifty rock-solid pounds.

"I've got a feeling the Injuns won't figure we'd go through the canyon with the wagons," Deke remarked to the fiddler as they began repairs. "But I've always been a cautious man where redskins are concerned. We'll still keep a sharp lookout. Treaty or no. This night I'm more than a trifle skittish."

"Listen! Did you hear that, Mr. Stiles?" said a boy standing at Deke's elbow.

"What'd you hear, son?"

"A whippoorwill. Sounds like a helluva big bird."

Stiles listened for a moment, then edged closer to the youngster and whispered, "I don't hear a thing." In one swift motion he plucked the boy's hat off his head. "I thought so. Get yourself back to your wagon, Miss Kat, before your Mama finds out."

"How the hell did you know it was me, Mr. Stiles?"

Deke grinned. "I've never seen a boy shaped like you, even in overalls that don't fit. Now get along or I'll have to tattle on you. By the way, Miss Kat, watch your language."

Katherine took a couple of steps and stopped abruptly when she heard a weak voice calling for help. "Hear that, Mr. Stiles?" She bolted and ran, skimming up the rocky canyon wall with several men following.

By the time the wagon master reached Kat, Linc was standing beside her on a rock ledge looking down at a small figure huddled in her arms. "I've got a hurt child," she called out. "Give me a hand."

Deke lifted the seemingly lifeless form. "Please help me," the small voice painfully cried out. "My arm hurts…am lost." The child went limp.

Agitated, Deke stepped up his pace as he made his way down the rocky incline. He slowed when he reached the edge of a stone shelf. Sam waited on a boulder below and relieved him of the small burden.

As the handful of men dispersed, Linc clasped Katherine's arm. "Come along, Jack, I'll walk you home," he teased.

"Your humor is boring, Mr. Sheffield. I don't have time to poke along."

"I didn't ask you to take a stroll with me. I offered to take you back to your wagon."

Guided by the luminous moon, Linc vaulted to a flat rock below and extended his arms to Kat. "It's not far. Jump! I'll catch you."

Without hesitation she stepped off the ledge and landed in his arms. He held her a few seconds thinking about what lay ahead of them. What if the Indians attacked? What if he never saw her again? Summoning all his courage, Linc's grip tightened around her as he kissed her soundly on the lips.

She wanted him to kiss her, but she had not counted on such a show of ardor. The whole thing left her weak and sagging against him for support.

He chuckled. "You've never been kissed before, have you, Kat?"

Her answer was indignant. "Of course I have!"

"Don't fly off the handle. I find your lack of experience refreshing."

"Refreshing! Lack of experience! Is that so?" She twined her arms around his neck with languid grace and kissed him with abandon.

He was glad that she could not see his rosy face…or the uncomfortable bulge in his pants. He made an attempt at humor and said, "I never expected to be kissed by anyone answering to the name of Jack."

Kat's laugh was cut short by the anxious tone of Bess's voice. "Katherine, is that you?"

"Yes, Mother, we're coming."

"Who's that with you?"

"Linc Sheffield."

Still warm from their brief encounter, he ached for more time with Kat, but he did not want to fall in Mrs. Stone's estimation. After all, she happened to be the mother of the girl he intended to marry.

CHAPTER THREE

Sam hurried alongside Bess. "This child's a boy about the age of Bobby near as I can tell."

Bess was uninterested in the sex of the child. "Put him on the bed in the back of the wagon and clear the tail-gate for working room."

Deke stationed himself a few yards from the Stone's wagon. Seconds later Bess caught sight of him and called out for help.

"What can I do for you, Miz Stone?"

"We need some light and a fire, Mr. Stiles. The boy's arm is broken. It looks like a wigwam, bones sticking up and all."

"Then a fire it'll be. I'll get a bottle of sour mash out of my wagon for dulling the pain."

While a group of men draped extra ducking over the wagon top to conceal as much light as possible, Deke hurriedly built a fire a short distance from the tail-gate. The task completed, the wagon master got out of the way, leaned against a boulder and bit off a plug of tobacco. He buttoned his jacket to ward off the cold and was contentedly chewing when he felt a slight tremor underfoot. Following his first instinct he fell to the ground and put an ear to the cold, hard surface.

"Horses," he muttered. "A herd of them." Agile for such a big man, Deke jumped to his feet and ran to the Stone's wagon. Bess and the Swede's wife, Lissie Larsen, were working on the injured boy. "Miz Stone!"

Bess whipped around at the sound of alarm in Deke's tone. "What's wrong, Mr. Stiles?"

Wild Kat

"Trouble!" he exclaimed as he kicked dirt on the fire. "Blow out the lantern!"

"Whatever for?"

"Just do it, ma'am. Stay in the wagon until you hear from me. I'm going to warn the others."

He immediately rounded up those within sight and issued instructions. He then headed back to the end of the train, relieved to see that the wheel had been repaired.

"Where are you going in such a hurry, Deke?" Sam asked.

"To find you. Larsen's gone back to join Forsythe at the other end of the canyon. I want you to go tell them that horses are headed this way. They could be wild, or they might be toting redskins. Either way, tell them to take cover where they are and stay put. You stay too, Sam. You can't make it back before they get here."

The men readied their firearms and crawled under the wagons to wait. As Deke neared the Stone's wagon he heard the actual sound of the horse's hooves in the distance. The moon had dropped behind the wall of the canyon, leaving the area in total darkness. Thankful for the cover, Deke stopped and scratched on the canvas.

"Miz Stone, Sam's at the far end of the canyon. I'll stay here with you and the boy."

Bess opened the flap and whispered, "I won't say we're not glad to have you, Mr. Stiles."

"Lay flat on the floor board between the grain sacks. And keep that youngun quiet! I'll be under the wagon if you need me."

"Don't worry about the boy. He's out cold from Lissie's paregoric. She wouldn't hear of using your sour mash whiskey."

Deke smiled inwardly as he slid behind a wagon wheel and lay down on his stomach. His adrenaline flowed as fast as the pounding hooves rolling like endless thunder across the prairie.

As the noise grew nearer, the gait of the animals slowed. Deke heard the horses pass the mouth of the canyon and stop. He barely breathed, giving thanks for the absolute darkness and praying that the moon would not reveal the tracks they had made upon entering the passage.

A hand touched his shoulder and Deke grabbed an arm with phenomenal speed. "It's me, Deke…Sam…I thought you might need me so I came back."

"Gawdamighty! Don't ever do that again. I came near to throttling you."

Sam wondered if he would still be alive after one of the rugged man's so called throttlings. He quietly crouched beside the wagon boss and nudged him when an unfamiliar voice drifted through the canyon.

"We will rest here for a time." Great Eagle tossed a blanket over his shoulders and dropped to the ground beside a small fire. "Our return to the village will be triumphant; our hunt went well."

Several braves grunted with approval, talking among themselves about the approaching raid.

"Gawdamighty! They're beddin' down."

"What can we do?"

"Nothing. We'll have to wait them out and hope they leave before daylight."

Sam shook his head slowly. "I have a feeling they know we're here."

The two men listened and watched as the Indians began to settle down. "Probably Kiowa. They're thick around these parts. I count a dozen in all. They've been on a hunt all right, just look at the game tied on their pack horses."

"Yeah, I hope they're headed home." Sam shifted his position and the movement sent a shower of small pebbles rolling across the path. Sweat trickled down the back of his neck; the cool breeze had become as sweltering as a midsummer's night.

Wild Kat

Deke tensed and held his breath when Great Eagle glanced in their direction. The Kiowa chief stood motionless for a few moments, listening, then shrugged and went back to the fire.

An hour or more passed without incident. All was quiet except for the clicking of the crickets. Deke had begun to nod when a rustling of activity jarred him into full consciousness. The Indians were breaking camp. After smothering the fires they mounted their horses and thundered away as quickly as they had come.

Deke nudged Sam as he moved from under the wagon and prepared to build another fire. "They're gone! I wonder how much longer our luck's going to hold?"

Sam shook his head as he lit the lantern. Bess and Lissie Larsen had not yet set the boy's broken arm. "God only knows. I just hope we get out of this canyon without incident."

Bess finally finished dressing the child's arm. "Lissie, you can douse the fire now."

Short, blue-eyed Lissie was as blond and robust as her Swedish husband. She smiled and wiped her hands on her apron. "Glad to help out. I'll say goodnight now."

Deke ambled to the back of the wagon and took Lissie's arm. "Here, let me help you down, Miz Larsen. I'll take care of that fire. You go on back to your family."

"Is that you, Mr. Stiles?" Katherine asked.

"It's me, sure enough. How's that boy, Miss Kat?"

"He's sleeping. We'll know more come morning. Do you think those Indians will come back?"

"Naw, we were lucky. To my way of thinking they were just resting a spell after a good hunt."

Bess stuck her head out of the wagon and motioned to Deke. "Come inside if you'd like."

Lydia Joe Cates

She scooted closer to the boy, tucking the blanket in around his small form. Until that moment little thought had been given to his appearance. "Mercy! Would you look at this?"

Katherine was about to jump down from the tail-gate when the sound of her mother's excited voice stopped her. "He's an Indian, Mother, didn't you notice?" Kat's eyes scanned the dark-skinned boy with interest. "He couldn't be much older than Bobby."

Bess raked the long sable colored hair back from the child's forehead. "Lissie and I were busy and it was too dark to notice anything but the little fellow's arm." She stared at Deke.

His smile turned into a smirk as he fingered the beads and tiny bells on the detailed shirt hung over the tail-gate. "Looks like we could have us some trouble, Miz Stone."

"You told me that he spoke a few words after Kat found him; was it Indian gibberish?"

"Naw, English. He asked for help, then passed out."

Kat gazed at the boy's moccasins. "I recognize those beads."

Deke chuckled. "I doubt that, Miss Kat, unless you've had some dealings with the Kiowa. That's their handiwork for sure."

With a gleam in her eye Kat remarked, "And he could speak English…hmmm."

Her mind raced back in time to her treasured mirror. A fleeting image of the handsome stranger rose to the surface of her memory. She was certain that the intricate design on his moccasins were identical to those of the injured boy. She felt that there was a connection between the two. Sadly, she had learned from experience that no one would listen to such prattle. Prattle indeed, she mused. Energy depleted, she reeled and fell into her father's arms.

"Are you ill, Katherine dear?"

"No, Father. I'm exhausted."

Wild Kat

"I'll take you to the other wagon." Sam carried her to bed and kissed her on the forehead. "You're still my little girl, Katherine." He crawled out of the wagon and found Deke waiting. "Are we ready to move out?" Sam asked.

"Yep, it's time. Is Miss Kat sick?"

"No. She has a spell like this once in a while when she's had too much excitement. She'll be fine by morning."

Sam went back to his other wagon and closed the tail-gate after Bess climbed in beside the sleeping child. He leaned into the lantern light and observed the boy for a moment, then shifted his gaze to Bess. "He's a bad omen, my dear. I can feel it right down to my toes."

* * *

James and Callie Forsythe caught up with Deke before he gave the order to roll. "I say, Mr. Stiles, would ye be allowin' James and me to be takin' care of the boy?"

"Well now, that's real nice of you, Miz Forsythe. As far as I'm concerned he's all yours." Deke thanked the childless pair and left, still worried about the safety of the wagon train community.

The Irish couple went directly to Bess and told her about their conversation with Stiles. Bess agreed and turned the child over to them. Once inside their own wagon Callie told James, "I'll just be lyin' down beside the child keepin' him warm, me dear."

The Irishman was pleased about his wife's interest in the boy. "Ye do that, sweet Callie. And be takin' good care of the both of ye."

Callie smiled back. "Ye know I will, me darlin'."

James had climbed onto the drivers bench when he noticed that Deke had dismounted. The big man lay prone with an ear flattened to the ground. James groaned. "I don't mind tellin' ye, Deke, that I'm hopin' yer just bein' cautious."

Lydia Joe Cates

"That's exactly what I'm doing, James. The ground's as quiet as the night." He mounted his horse and trotted past each wagon, silently setting them in motion. A blast on the powder horn would be too risky.

After a while Callie poked her head through the canvas and spoke softly. "James, we'll be callin' the boy Matthew. 'Tis a fine Christian name, don't ye think?"

"Aye, but what if his Indian name is more to his likin'?"

Her green eyes twinkled happily as she answered. "Then we'll be callin' him whatever he's choosin'!" An amusing thought occurred to her. "It'll be quite a laughin' matter if we're pressed to learn the Kiowa dialect with Irish brogues such as ours."

James nodded with a smile and directed his attention to the team. His dark, bushy eyebrows rose slightly. He could not help wondering what a dull life he would have led without sweet Callie. A chuckle parted his lips. He had fallen in love and married her in Dublin ten years ago. They had almost given up hope of having children of their own. Now, he reflected, Callie was willing to settle for an Indian boy who was surely as old as their marriage.

* * *

An hour before daybreak Great Eagle and his hunting party returned to the mouth of Rattlesnake Canyon. "We will give the wagon train a few more hours to enter open land before we attack. They do not suspect that we know where to find them."

A smile teased the corners of his mouth when he saw the eagerness on the faces of his braves. Outsmarting the white man had always given him pleasure. The chief raised his hand and said, "Patience, my brothers."

* * *

Wild Kat

By midmorning the wagon train had crossed over the Kansas border into Bonner Springs, a small settlement marked on the wagon master's map. Hoots and shouts of delight invaded the silence. More than one soundless prayer floated toward heaven as the drained travelers began to circle at the edge of the hamlet.

The Indian boy, dubbed Matthew for the moment, opened his eyes and blinked. He was disoriented and frightened. Suddenly he blurted out, "I am the son of a Kiowa Chief and a white woman." He spoke in flawless English.

Awakened from twilight sleep, Callie bolted upright. "James, me dear, were ye listenin' with both yer ears?"

"Aye," he mumbled, guiding the team behind Sam Stone's wagon to complete the circle. "Whooooa, ye black devils! We're done." He dropped the leather straps and crawled into the back with Callie and the young Indian. James studied the boy for a moment. "Would ye care to be tellin' us about yerself, son?"

Matthew moved his arm and winced. His lips began to quiver and moisture welled up in his eyes, limpid black pools still brilliant from the paregoric Lissie Larsen had given to him. "My father is Kiowa Chief Great Eagle. My mother was a white woman…a school teacher…known to the Kiowa as White Doe. She died of the fever two winters ago."

"So that's how yer knowin' such fine English," Callie added. "How did ye wind up in the canyon alone, darlin'?"

Matthew sighed as his eyes rolled back in his head and closed. James and Callie waited for him to gather the strength to go on. He finally continued. "Young Squirrel and I were hunting. We separated and lost our path. I had been wandering for days when I fell off of the cliff. Did you find my friend or my pony?"

"No, son, we found nothin' but ye," James said.

Tears spilled over. "I hope my friend is alive. Perhaps he found my pony and took him back to our village."

"I'm bettin' that's what happened, me dear. Will ye be takin' a wee bit more broth?"

"Yes. I am hungry."

Callie's heart filled with love. She drummed up enough courage to call him by his new name. "Ye speak the English language with a bit of a flair, Matthew."

Instantly alert, a frown knit the boy's raven brow. "What did you call me?"

"Matthew. But only fer the time bein'." Callie smiled sweetly, smoothed back his hair and noticed that his forehead was damp. No longer feverish, she thought.

"My name is Sleeping Rabbit. That is the name I was given; that is the name I answer to," he stated flatly and closed his eyes. He was thinking about the disappointment he had just perceived in the motherly woman's expression. The name she had given him must be important to her. He opened his eyes and studied Callie with a discerning eye before he spoke. "You can call me Matthew…if you like it that much."

"Thank ye, me darlin'."

James put his arm around his wife, observing lashes spiked with tears. "He's a thoughtful lad I'm thinkin'. Agreein' to the name of the son ye someday hope to bear."

"Aye, me dear, a wee miracle in a way."

Callie left Matthew in James's care while she went in search of Deke. She found him resting by the campfire. "Can ye be sparin' me a minute of yer time, Mr. Stiles?"

"Something wrong with the boy, Miz Forsythe?"

"No, sir. His fever broke and he's sleepin' peacefully." Callie reiterated the boy's story about his family. "I thought ye ought to be knowin' sooner than later."

Deke mopped his face and neck with a ragged bandanna while he digested the information. "Gawdamighty, that's all we need; a Kiowa

Wild Kat

Chief's son on the wagon train. I've heard of Great Eagle. He's a proud cuss and a whale of a fighter. He won't give up until he finds his son. God help us then."

"What can we be doin' about it?"

"All I know is we'd best keep our eyes open."

Gossip scattered like leaves in a whirlwind. Word coursed through the wagon train that the injured boy was the son of Kiowa Chief Great Eagle. Deke blasted a note on his powder horn to signal an emergency meeting.

"We're going to double back a few miles and head due north. It'll be a loss of time, but if my calculations are right we'll have a few days before Great Eagle reaches his village and discovers his son's missing. The boy told the Forsythes that his father was on a hunting expedition. I suspect it was him resting with his braves last night. Anybody have a better idea about what we should do?"

The Swede spoke up. "You got us this far, Deke; we're willing to do whatever you say."

"Thanks for your confidence, Borg. Then our plans are made," Deke needed all the support that he could muster. The responsibility he felt for the small community fed his growing anxiety. As the wagon train pulled out of the circle and headed north, he smelled trouble.

*   *   *

By dusk they had reached a bend in the river where Deke saw a likely place to camp. He sounded his horn and shouted, "Time to rest!"

After dark, spirits unexpectedly soared. Bellies were stuffed with squirrel stew and pan biscuits. Children played their usual giggly game of tag while the adults milled around and chatted about their dilemma. Conversation ended abruptly when the fiddler began to saw away at a sprightly tune.

Lydia Joe Cates

Bess was scrubbing out the big iron stew pot when Sam clasped her hand. "Come on, my dear, I'll show you that I haven't forgotten how to sashay and bend gentle at the waist."

Bess wiped her free hand on her yellow apron, smiling. "It'll be a pleasure, Mr. Stone." Taking his arm, she laughingly two-stepped with her husband to the center of the ring.

Borg and Lissie Larsen trotted in behind them. Lissie spied Deke and signaled to him. "Get a partner, Mr. Stiles, and join us," she chirped, prancing as high as her short legs would allow. Her fair hair, braided and wrapped around her head, gleamed in the firelight as if she had a halo.

Deke waved. His eyes strayed to Bess Stone. He thought she looked as fresh as a mountain daisy and scolded himself for coveting another man's wife. He bit off a generous plug of tobacco as he walked away muttering, "Chewing'll have to do, you old fool."

Linc kept an eye open for Kat and finally found her lounging across a grain sack in the shadows of the wagon. "Good evening, Kat."

"Evening," she said with disinterest.

"I figured you'd be in the middle of the hoe-down."

She sighed loudly. "I'm tired of dancing in the dirt and I'm sick of eating the same stew every night. My rump is worn out from jostling in the wagon all day…and that's just the beginning."

Amused, yet sympathetic, Linc smiled. "The moon's full. How about a walk down by the creek?"

Kat tossed her head and stared blankly into space. "Might as well. There's nothing else to do."

He took her arm as Todd hurried over to them leading Bobby by his suspenders. "Where're you going, Sis?" he asked, yanking at his little brother as though he was a calf on a rope.

"Quit it, Todd!" Bobby yelled.

Wild Kat

Todd yanked again. "Mama says you have to go to bed and I'm supposed to tuck you in." Todd shot a look of disapproval at Kat and growled, "Where're you going?"

"Linc and I are going for a walk, Nosy Poke."

"Mama says not to leave camp after dark."

"Mama says, Mama says," she mocked. "Damn it, Todd Stone! When are you going to let me grow up?"

"Yeah!" Bobby chimed in. "Quit your bossin', Todd."

Todd flushed. "Shut up, Bobby! Somebody around here needs to show some sense."

"You shut up or I'll tell Mama you peed off the tail-gate this morning and all three Larsen girls seen you."

With a face as red as a ripe tomato, Todd jerked hard on Bobby's overall straps. "You're not telling anybody anything. As for you, Sis, I'll give you one more chance to stop cussing."

Linc, struggling to keep a straight face, broke in. "Katherine will be safe with me. Go on and take care of your little brother."

Strolling in the midst of the high sage grass, Linc slid his arm around Kat's shoulder and squeezed. "You're shaking. You cold?"

"A little." She smiled up at him and draped her arm around his waist. Maybe if she acted more like a woman she would feel more like one.

She was doing it to him again, thought Linc. Flapping those long lashes at him with her pouty lips poised for a kiss.

✯   ✯   ✯

Across the stream, hidden behind a dense thicket, Great Eagle and Howling Wolf watched Kat and Linc with interest. Howling Wolf turned to his chief. "Is she the woman you want?"

Great Eagle's eyes narrowed. "She is the one."

Lydia Joe Cates

As time passed, Howling Wolf became bored and sleepy. He returned to camp, leaving the chief to observe the scene in solitude.

*   *   *

The fiddler's melody floated toward the couple as they meandered beside the stream. The creek played its own tune gurgling over the rock-ribbed bed. "I like listening to the water splashing. Don't you, Linc?"

"Uh-huh. I like hearing you say my name too."

"You do?" Kat's spirits lifted and she brazenly asked, "Would you like to kiss me?" After it was out of her mouth, she could not believe that she had asked such a question. It wasn't that she did not like Linc. She did, however, have somewhat of an invisible barrier that stood in the way of her emotions and sapped any real feeling of pleasure before it began.

Kat knew that there had to be more. Somewhere deep inside of her there was supposed to be a magic fountain. At least that's what she had overheard from the gossip at her mother's quilting parties back home.

Linc viewed her lovely profile in the moonlight. "You can't imagine the effect you have on me, Kat."

"To be perfectly honest with you, Linc, I wish I didn't; it seems that something is missing."

Agitated. "I don't understand you, Katherine. One minute you're a woman and the next, a little girl. I don't think you know what you want."

Linc knew what he wanted and took advantage of the moment. "See if this makes a difference." His lips sought hers and began to move. Slowly at first, before blossoming into what he termed a full-fledged buss. More surprising to Kat than Linc, she issued a tiny whimper of delight.

When he became more demanding she tried to push him away. "Stop it! Please!"

Wild Kat

Caught up in the passion, his grip turned brutish as he pulled her down to the ground and grabbed hold of her breast. "Don't tell me you don't like this, Katherine," he murmured against her lips.

Kat pushed and shoved, oblivious to the fact that they were being observed. Great Eagle's attention heightened as he strained to see the tussling taking place in the high grass. Once Kat's husky voice wafted toward him, but the distance between them was too great for him to recognize that she was grappling with Linc. The Indian crept closer to the stream and stood behind a tree.

The couple was near enough to camp for Kat to be heard if she screamed, but she already knew what the outcome would be. Unfair as it was, she would be blamed for everything. The woman always was.

Linc slipped his hand under her dress and tried to untie her underpants. "Be still, Kat! I'll show you what's missing."

"No you won't, you bastard!" She struggled to her feet, gathered all her strength and slapped him hard across the face. "Don't ever so much as look at me again, you damned fool!"

Stunned, Linc instantly became contrite. "Katherine, I'm sorry. I don't know what came over me. Please forgive me!"

"I think not! Now get out of my way."

Great Eagle was amused. Such spirit in one so small delighted him. Sensing fear in Kat's tone, he was ready to spring to her assistance. When a harsh voice landed on his ears he stepped back into the shadows.

"Sis! Sister!" Todd yelled.

"Oh Lord, it's your brother."

Kat grinned. "Over here, Todd," she screamed.

Linc was panting with excitement. "Please, Katherine, don't say anything. I promise it'll never happen again."

She ignored his plea and finished rearranging her clothes as her brother came into view. "Sis, you've been gone too long."

"Katherine hasn't done anything wrong," Linc offered lamely.

"Yeah, well, you're sure out of breath for somebody who's just been gazing at the moon."

"Oh shut up, Todd. I...I'm glad to see you."

Kat swished her petticoats as she turned and left the two standing alone. Dumbfounded, Todd absently scratched his head. "Now what was that all about?"

A wave of relief swept over Linc as he exclaimed, "Women! Come on, Todd, we'd better get back to camp.

Chapter Four

The wagon train headed out at dawn. Deke felt that a skirmish with the Indians was fading away with each new sunset. He reasoned that they would not risk losing the treaty for a raid.

Luck ran out in the early afternoon of that day. Kiowa Chief Great Eagle and his band of hunters appeared on the horizon whooping and hollering. While his ears sputtered and crackled from the assault, Deke shouted orders to circle the wagons. He was astonished by the volume of his own voice.

As they completed their circle Deke whirled around. He was startled by the imposing figure of a muscular, radiantly painted savage wearing an eagle feather in his headband. The plume, Deke knew, was the sign of a chief.

The warrior's steed gracefully pranced in the midst of the melee as the Indian raised his staff and slashed venomously at the air. The horse instinctively reared on its hind legs as the redskin screeched, "Whoooeeeyah! Eeeyah! Eeeyah!" The terrifying sound faded with the Indian's disappearance on the horizon.

Deke recovered from the earth-shattering performance and waved his arms at the Swede shouting, "Where's Todd and Linc?"

Larsen shook his head and bellowed, "Hunting!"

Bess squatted beside Sam and loaded the guns. As he dropped an empty rifle in her lap she shoved a live one into his outstretched hand. Taking careful aim, he wounded a Kiowa stealing Deke's team of horses.

Lydia Joe Cates

Wiping sweat from his eyes, Sam watched two of the marauders break away from the others and head toward the woods.

One Indian had the fiddler's pregnant wife, Josie, and the other carried her tiny daughter in the crook of his arm. Sam stood up to fire and instantly keeled over, an arrow embedded in his shoulder.

Bess screamed. "Help! Over here!"

Larsen heard her cry and ran toward the Stone wagon in a zigzag pattern to dodge the deadly arrows. He finally threw himself on the ground and rolled the remaining distance to where Sam lay. Larsen grimaced. "Don't look, Bess, I'm going to pull the arrow out of his shoulder."

The Swede clutched the shank of the arrow with one hand while he pressed against the flesh with the other. Sweat drenched the giant man as Sam moaned his way into oblivion. "It's just as well he passed out; I'm going to have to burn it to stop the bleeding."

Katherine and Bobby lay on the floor of the wagon when a sudden chill swept over Kat. She draped a cloak around her shoulders and settled back down. Pummeled by the horrible whoops, a bizarre feeling of excitement overpowered Kat and her curiosity exploded.

"Bobby, stay down!" she commanded as she got to her feet.

"Mama told us to stay put."

"I'm not going anywhere. I just want to see what's happening."

Kat had parted the flap no more than an inch when Bobby heard her scream. A muscular arm the color of snuff shot through the canvas, seized her around the waist and dragged her across the closed tail-gate onto a huge sorrel horse.

Kat's howls dissolved in midair, the breath crushed from her as they galloped into the afternoon sun. She recovered immediately and shrieked until she was hoarse. "Let go, you damned bastard! Let me go!" Immediately she felt an arm with amazing strength reach around her waist and yank her upright.

Wild Kat

A constant stream of screams and curses flowed from her mouth. Each time the Indian's grip tightened as though her midsection was being squeezed in a vise. Choking for air, she managed one more proclamation. "You'll burn in hell for this, Indian! God'll punish you if I don't get a chance first."

The Kiowa released her and grabbed her braid at the neck. Bouncing fiercely she shook her head, trying to pull her hair free. Kat's terror stricken voice had become a pathetic whisper. Not once did she realize that the wagon train had faded from sight…that the countryside was racing past them at a staggering speed.

* * *

Bobby's rabid yells rousted Bess from under the wagon. She clawed her way on hands and knees to get to him. "Mama! Papa! They got Kat! A painted Indian stole Kat!"

He was crying now, no longer the man he claimed to be, and fell into the safety of his mother's arms. Bess shoved him under the wagon where Sam lay unconscious and crawled in after him.

"We'll have to wait here, Bobby, until some of the men are free to move your papa," she soothed while rocking him in her arms.

Bess peered at the horizon splattered with trails of dust settling against the sun. The Indians had left as swiftly as they had come, taking with them her only daughter. She covered her face with her hands and tried to convince herself that what she had just witnessed was an illusion.

In her soul she knew that she might never see Katherine's laughing face again. Unable to suppress the panic gripping her heart, she gave way to the tears so foreign to her nature.

"Anything I can do, Miz Stone?" Deke asked as he knelt beside her.

His voice unheard, Bess stared. Deke wished he could smooth the wisps of graying brown hair away from her tear-stained face. "I'd like to help, Miz Stone. Are you all right?"

Her vacant look disappeared when he spoke again. "Thank you, Mr. Stiles," she softly said and turned her attention to Callie, who was bandaging Sam's shoulder wound.

"Sure'n the Indians abducted Katherine, Mr. Stiles."

"Gawdamighty!" Filled with empathy for Bess, he fought the urge to take her in his arms. His feeling for her had sneaked up on him like a predator. Quiet and hungry. He knew it was foolhardy and fruitless, so he focused his attention on the misery around him.

Several bodies lay on the ground. Each face stirred up a memory of sorts and Deke wondered if the bloody heathens would return. "Gawdamighty," he uttered again as he checked for any sign of life in the ruins.

"What's that you say, Deke?"

"Nothing, Larsen. We'd best bury our dead."

Surveying the rubble, Stiles shook his head vigorously declaring, "I don't see any way to salvage enough to travel on. Supplies gone. Horses stolen. Then there's the loss of three wagons beyond repair."

"You think the redskins got ahold of Linc and Todd?"

"I wouldn't even make a guess." He nodded in the direction of the fiddler laying face down in the dirt, an arrow buried in the middle of his back. "The bastards took his wife and little girl."

Several of the wagons were miraculously untouched. With a trace of irony in his tone Deke said, "I see the Forsythe's wagon was spared. Wonder what those gawdless animals would've done if they'd known one of their own kind was inside it?"

Deke finally tore himself away from the pathetic sight to look for James and Matthew. He found them sitting on the ground in a daze. Callie had stayed to help Bess tend Sam's shoulder wound. Deke

Wild Kat

stooped down and examined Matthew's injured arm trussed neatly in splints made from wooden butter paddles.

"Your arm's looking fine, son."

A frown corrugated the child's forehead and hostility evolved as he glared at James, then leveled his eyes on Stiles. "I apologize for my people. I hope that someday there will be a better understanding between the white man and the Indian, but how can I help if you refuse to let me return to my family?"

Amazed by the boy's wisdom, Deke asked, "How old are you, Matthew?"

"Ten, sir."

"Sounds like your mama taught you the difference between right and wrong."

"And my father too," he said defiantly. "When I am a man I will walk his path proudly."

Deke nodded and smiled. "I'm sure you will."

"I heard the cry of my people today. I want to go home."

"We'll be talkin' more about that later, Matthew," James interjected.

Stiles slowly straightened up and asked, "Tell me, son, what kind of sound would make you yearn for home?"

The child threw back his head, took a deep breath and screeched, "Whoooeeeyah! Eeeyah! Eeeyah!"

His hearing momentarily impaired, Deke slid a kerchief out of his hip pocket and mopped his sweaty face. "I heard it too, Matthew." As Deke walked away he mumbled under his breath, "But it didn't make me the least bit homesick."

✶ ✶ ✶

Lydia Joe Cates

Early that evening Deke stopped by the Stone's wagon. With the Swede's help, the two men moved Sam to a mattress. "If you're set for the night, Miz Stone, Larsen and I'll be getting on. There's graves to be dug."

Bess nodded. "Thank you, Mr. Stiles. We won't be needing anything more tonight."

For a lucid, fleeting moment Sam opened his eyes and grasped Bess's hand. "You must be an angel." He winked a startling blue eye and slept again.

She drenched the flour sacking with water and placed it on his fevered brow. "There now, you're going to be just fine," she crooned, consumed with grief over Katherine's abduction, Todd's disappearance and having to bear these traumas alone.

*   *   *

Wishing it was a bad dream, Katherine slowly opened her wind-whipped eyes. The Indian's muscled chest bore into her back. His arms and thighs crushed her, reminding her that she was, indeed, awake.

Aching from the incessant bouncing, she relaxed against his chest long enough to catch her breath. In answer, he ground his thighs into her hips. She groaned, unable to control the movement of her head lolling on his chest as if it were a ball.

Through such turmoil, she could still think with clarity. Uppermost in her mind was escape. They had to stop **some** time. She felt the Indian's grip on her tighten and was amazed at his ability to abuse her body and execute such excellent horsemanship simultaneously.

As they reached the edge of the woods, Great Eagle unexpectedly slackened his hold on her and slowed his elegant sorrel to a walk. "Guo-la-te!" He roared and the stallion came to a halt. A whimpering sigh escaped Kat's lips as the Indian relaxed his hold, allowing her to breathe freely again.

Wild Kat

"You're a mean sonofabitch!" she hissed. "A thieving, murdering, ornery…"

She pivoted to get a glimpse of her captor and severed her words. The sight of his red and white streaked face reduced her fury. Kat calmed herself. "I think the sound of my voice may have angered you, so I'll say what I damn well please, but in a pleasant tone."

The Indian's black velvet eyes scoured the trees. He seemed to ignore her, but the twitch at the corners of his thin lips suggested amusement.

Kat's brain roiled with terrifying visions of what he might have planned for her once they reached their destination. She had heard horror stories about the redskins treatment of their captives. She shivered and silently prayed for her safety.

As they approached the tree line, a bird's song caught her attention. It was a whippoorwill's call. Guo-la-te stilled, waiting for his master's command. The savage tightened his lips against his teeth and returned the signal.

Two Kiowa braves appeared from the dense thicket. The fiddler's wife, Josie, rode behind a pot-bellied man. Her little girl, in a state of shock, rested in the crook of the other Indian's arm.

Short hairs on the back of Kat's neck prickled. She remained motionless and gave no indication that she recognized the prisoners. Hoping that Josie would follow suit, Kat soon realized that she had no cause to worry. The fiddler's wife, like her child, floated in a murky haze.

Although Kat kept her head turned away from them, the marauders did not escape inspection out of the corner of her eye. They were more hideously painted than her captor. As the men spoke with their leader, their appraising eyes strayed to Katherine. She wriggled nervously under their scrutiny. The fear that she might be traded to the pot-bellied savage in exchange for the fiddler's wife petrified her. She was aware that Indians favored Josie's blue eyes and yellow hair.

"We will meet at the clearing, my brothers," Great Eagle told them in the Kiowa tongue.

"We waited only to tell you, Chief Great Eagle, that we will not stop to rest. We go to our village to prepare for your return."

"As you wish, Howling Wolf."

Kat's head pounded as she tried to make sense of their conversation, but the pain mounted and convulsive tremors enveloped her body. Out of control, she plunged forward and was arrested by two large hands grasping her shoulders.

The chief leaned close to her ear, whispering in his native tongue, "Is your courage waning, Flaming Hair?"

Unable to decipher one word of what he had said, but hearing a softer tone, she thought he was being conciliatory. Maybe she still had a chance. A chance for what? She didn't know. Holding her in place with his powerful thighs, they moved deeper into the piney woods. After riding another hour or so, Kat felt the need to relieve herself.

"Stop, Indian, I have to pee."

He gave no sign of understanding and continued to stare straight ahead. Uncomfortable and irritated, Kat belted his hard body with an elbow. "Please stop. I need..." She turned her head and looked him in the eye. She blushed while slowly enunciating each word. "Privacy. Pee. Make water. Surely you can see that I'm miserable."

Great Eagle drew back on Guo-la-te's reins and they came to an abrupt halt. His eyes took on a curious gleam. Although he had seen her hair glimmer like flames in the moonlight, he had not see that her eyes, in the sunlight, sparkled like fire. The Indian stared, fascinated.

As she opened her mouth to protest again, the chief jumped down and pulled Kat with him. As soon as she hit the ground her legs turned to rubber; she fell and lay sprawled on her face. The smell of moldy leaves and damp earth clung to her nostrils. Her eyes filled as he seized her cape and yanked her upright. She imagined herself a puppet with more than one broken string.

"Come," he said in English. "Make water." He led her to a clump of bushes where Kat hastily squatted, noting that he had planted himself on the other side of her makeshift privy.

Ignoring her embarrassment, she quickly relieved herself. She acknowledged his meager English while rearranging her clothes. "So you **do** know a few words of my language."

"Make water. We go."

"I'm hurrying." Her eyes had become accustomed to the growing darkness and her vision was good enough to see that the Indian had moved a few yards away. He was inspecting a patch of berries at close range. A spark of her old courage flickered. She took a step in the opposite direction. When Great Eagle made no sign of moving she took another step, then another. All at once she broke into a run, caring little about where she was going as long as she got away.

The undergrowth was horrendous. She stumbled. Spiraling to her knees, she picked herself up only to step into a sink hole and twist her ankle. As Kat scrambled to her feet, tentacles of briars tore at her skirt, ripped her petticoats and tripped her. She hobbled on.

Struggling to breathe, Kat stopped and listened for some sign of pursuit, but there was only silence. Encouraged, she resumed her flight and collided with the Indian. She screamed as he snatched her up and tossed her over his shoulder. He made no attempt to be gentle as he carried her back to the horse.

"I must have lost my way," she offered meekly.

"We go," he roared, shaking her roughly before he flung her across Guo-la-te.

Great Eagle mounted behind her and trotted to a clearing where more braves waited. When the procession started again, Katherine drew an exaggerated breath as he positioned her between his thighs and tightened his arm around her. She felt a ripple from his stomach as if he were chuckling. Merely wishful thinking. She knew it was fury that prodded the Kiowa.

The chief's sleek stallion, sure-footed enough to carry them through the living tangles of wilderness, led them to their eventual camp for the night.

Kat fought to stay alert. Sleep would seem weak in his eyes and she wanted to appear strong. Her will to remain awake began to evaporate as she listened to the distant rumbles of thunder, a noise that had affected her like a sleeping potion since early childhood. Prospects of a storm increased with jagged streaks of silver carving an uneven trail through the tree tops. Soon an exhausted Katherine relented and slept against the hard bed of the Indian's chest.

Drops of rain filtered down through the trees forming a fine mist. Katherine's eyes blinked open when the drizzle dampened her face. She was so weary by this time that she was unable to think of anything other than stretching or moving about freely.

Great Eagle stopped as if he had sensed her thoughts and raised his hand for the others to halt. They had come upon a small clearing. The entourage dismounted and four more braves joined them. They grunted some sort of greeting and removed the blankets from their horses.

Kat's gaze leaped to each painted face, searching for the renegades who had snatched Josie and her daughter. They were gone. Great Eagle lifted her from the horse and dragged her under a tree. "Stay," he growled as he settled her against the trunk.

Tears tumbled down Katherine's cheeks as she twisted into the fetal position and pulled her filthy cape tightly around her. She closed her eyes to shut out the grotesque images building fires and fell asleep.

Sometime during the night Kat stirred, conscious of the Indian standing over her. She was prepared to gaze upon the savage's war paint again, but was amazed by his freshly washed face. No more than thirty,

Wild Kat

his obsidian eyes were set wide apart. His nose was straight...finely chiseled...unlike most of his people. Katherine's appraisal continued along the strong jawline and lingered momentarily at his thin, sensual lips. She searched her memory. She had **seen** this man.

Luring her out of her reverie, Great Eagle pointed to a fresh bed of pine and cedar boughs spread with a colorful woven blanket. She smelled his cleanness as he pushed her ahead of him.

"Stop jabbing me, Indian, I can see the bed," she said in her newly adopted lilting manner. She detected an aura of enthusiasm in his demeanor, as if he were pleased with her improved attitude.

Kat shucked her cape, spread it over the blanketed branches and removed her shoes. Snuggling between the folds, she addressed him. "You didn't have to go to the trouble to make such a big bed.

The Indian cocked his head as if he were trying to comprehend her statement.

"I know you don't understand me, but the pine is springy and surprisingly comfortable." Soon her aching body began to slacken as she slipped into the coziness of her own private cocoon.

Sleeping lightly, she awakened again to the low voices of the braves who sat around the campfire. Great Eagle stood and stretched. He said something that created a few snickers as he reached for more food. Kat lay on the pine pallet listening to the constant rumbling of her stomach. Didn't the heathen know that she was starving? Maybe he did, she decided, as he approached her with his hands full.

The Indian carried a hunk of roasted meat speared on a stick and a catalpa leaf filled with a pasty mixture. "Eat!" he encouraged as he placed the leaves on the bed and set a bark bowl beside her containing fresh water.

Katherine's voice was tranquil as she said, "I see you finally remembered your guest, you sonofabitch."

Great Eagle's expression was passive as he held up two fingers and scooped it through the mush, demonstrating to her how to eat. Famished, Kat ate and drank with no regard to manners. The Indian watched her, fascinated that such a small creature could consume so much food before he'd had time to sit.

"This is the best meal I've had since we left home," she gurgled, unaware of meat juices trickling down her chin. He removed a large leaf from his waist band and wiped the drippings away, then poured the remainder of the water over her hands. Kat thanked him and glanced toward the brightly glowing fire. All were sleeping.

"Sleep." he said as he sat down on the opposite side of the bed and removed his moccasins.

Kat stiffened when he lifted the cloak and slid in beside her. "Wait just a damn minute, Indian, I'm not used to sleeping with anybody." She pointed to the campfire. "Go sleep over there!" He remained immobile. "I know you understand **go** and **sleep**. Go to your brothers…braves…or whatever they are!"

She backed down when she saw the firelight reflected in his icy stare. The uneven beat of her heart quickened as she eased down beside him, certain of what he had in mind. She thought for a moment. He was too huge to fight. She could not **talk** him out of it. He did not know enough English to understand. Begging was out of the question! Reconciled, she began to relax and mumbled under her breath, "Thank God he's clean."

Still deep in thought, Katherine reviewed the events of the past few hours. The Kiowa chief had not treated her too badly so far. Handled her roughly, yes, but nothing devastating had happened. Maybe he would eventually free her. In many ways he seemed different from the rest.

She risked turning her head ever so slightly and was relieved to find him asleep. Arms folded across his chest, he was as still as a tree leaf on a windless night.

Wild Kat

The storm had subsided. Lulled by the low timbre of receding thunder and the heat radiating from the Indian's body, Kat's eyelids began to droop. Instead of the horror she had expected, warmth spread over her and sleep finally came.

* * *

Sunlight sifted through the lacy foliage overhead and a bird warbled his morning song as Kat yawned and stretched her arms heavenward. A pneumatic freshness hovered in the atmosphere…the kind of airiness that comes to the wilderness and stays long after a rain has evaporated. She yawned again, plucked a small bough of cedar from the sleeve of her dress and made an attempt to roll out of the bed. The revelation that Great Eagle had not tried to molest her during the night gave her an abundance of hope as well as a reason to be puzzled.

Discovering that she was alone, she scrambled out of her pine and cedar boudoir to find the nearest clump of bushes. When she emerged, Great Eagle waited on the other side of the thicket with his back to her.

"I'm not going anywhere," she grouched.

An angry scowl fluted his forehead. Although he said nothing, his look suggested that she harness her belligerence. The chief handed her several pemmican cakes made from meat paste mixed with berries. She devoured one without stopping. "Delicious!" Very little could ruin Kat's appetite.

Impatient to get back to his village, he took her arm. "We go."

"We go," she mocked and wearily followed him to Guo-la-te. Never releasing her hand, he mounted and hoisted her onto the animal's back. Spent before she started, she placed her hands on his shoulders and dryly remarked, "We go, we go, we go!" This time she received a prickle of a laugh and recognized it as such.

Each night and day were the same. They rode from dawn to dusk, pausing long enough to fill their water pouches at a stream or to relieve themselves. At first Kat refused to drink from the Indian's canteen of buffalo hide. She gave in after realizing that Great Eagle would not stop at any of the plentiful streams along the way unless the container was empty.

Cantering along late one afternoon, the full impact of what had happened completely unnerved her. Kat began to tremble, sobs took over and racked her small frame. Squawking at the top of her lungs, she grabbed the horse's reins and jerked them before the Indian could stop her. Guo-la-te reared, but seemed to know how far to go without unseating them.

After the horse's abrupt landing, Great Eagle twisted Kat around to face him and shook her vigorously several times. A series of wild screams followed. With a masked expression of pain, he lashed her across the face with the back of his hand, stunning her into silence.

Kat crumpled against him snubbing like a child. His first impulse was to comfort her and, without thinking, he gently stroked her hair. Suddenly aware that his braves were watching, he pushed her away and tugged her auburn locks before releasing her.

Howls of approval somewhat eased the chief's chagrin. When they finally stopped for the night Kat remained sullen, disturbed by Great Eagle's mock cruelty. She slid off of the horse, landing on her backside. Ignored by all, there she stayed.

Great Eagle glanced at Kat intermittently as he worked. It seemed as though he was trying to settle something in his mind. She nonchalantly observed his attention toward her. After a lengthy deliberation, the Indian strode purposefully to his men. When he finished speaking, the braves tossed their blankets on their horses and rode out of camp.

Kat watched them go with mounting trepidation. Had the chief resolved to make her his own? If so, what difference did it make to a heathen whether his braves were there or not? She was confused again.

Crouched by the fire, Kat watched Great Eagle lead his horse to a nearby stream. His eyes never left her while the animal drank his fill.

Wild Kat

After tethering Guo-la-te to a low tree branch, he sat near Katherine. Eyes averted, he handed her a deer skin pouch containing pemmican.

Starving as usual, Kat began to chew, but the taste of the rancid jerky made her gag and she tossed it aside. His face became expressionless as he commenced gathering branches. Although the bed was his primary interest, Kat noticed that he was picking something from the smaller trees and bushes at the edge of the forest. She was also aware that he was keeping her in his sight at all times.

Her thoughts ran rampant with worry. No longer able to contain herself, she broke the heavy silence. "Sending your brothers away so you can be alone with me won't do you any good, Indian.

He did not look away from his task until the bed was finished. Leading her by the arm, he said, "Sleep now."

"Where did you learn those few words of English?"

Disregarding her, he reiterated, "Sleep now."

Not to be outdone, she harped, "I guess you picked up the English from the other poor white people you captured. Tortured. Or killed."

Silence.

Throwing all caution aside, she proclaimed, "You're nothing but a bloody, murdering sonofabitch!"

Grasping her arm, he jabbered with inclement severity. Katherine imagined his voice sounded very much like God's when He was angry. As Great Eagle flung her onto the branches, she kicked as high as her leg could reach and managed a blow to his knee. He glared with doubled fists ready to strike if she made another attempt, but making note of the fear in her eyes, composed himself.

As if nothing had happened, he removed his moccasins, buckskin pants and shirt. He stood before her with only his breechcloth in place. Eyes cast downward, Kat whispered, "Please let me go."

"No!" Great Eagle shook his head adamantly.

Kat gritted her teeth and stared into oblivion. The moon crept from behind the clouds and its glow escaped through the lacy tree branches. She could see him clearly now. As the shifting winds patterned inane ripples of quicksilver over his smooth brown face, his countenance softened. His eyes caressed her with such tenderness that her heart began to hammer against her rib cage. She found herself wishing that he had taken off his breechcloth too. Curious to see a man's naked body, she was sure that Great Eagle's would be nothing short of perfection.

What would her mother say if she could hear her musings? Kat's own reaction was one of absolute shock. It left her wondering how she could stoop so low as to be attracted to a heathen.

The chief continued to study her, unnerving her all the more. She had to change the mood. A new approach was in order. She reached for the pouch of grapes and deer plums which he had picked earlier in the day and popped a grape into her mouth. "Ummm, good! Have one?"

Kat offered him the bag. He shook his head and mimicked her actions, gagging as she had done with the rancid pemmican. Katherine threw back her head and laughed at his joke. She was almost having a good time.

Great Eagle laughed openly for the first time, showing teeth as white as Annie's milk and emitting a deep, resonant sound that sent shivers down her spine. Immediately motivated, Kat placed her hand on her own chest and said, "I am Katherine. Most everybody calls me Kat, but I would like you to call me Katherine."

She flushed under his scrutiny and felt less daring when his hand began to caress her cheek. Barely breathing she said, "Let's start again." Kat spread her hand across her chest. "Katherine." Then she touched his shoulder. "Indian."

Great Eagle pursed his lips, cocked a brow as if in thought, then splayed his hand across his chest. "Katherine." He lightly touched her shoulder and said, "Indian."

Wild Kat

Kat broke into gales of laughter. When he began to stroke her face again, she ceased to giggle, conscious of the sensual gesture. She reluctantly removed his hand.

Their eyes met and held for some moments before he spoke. "Tanguadal."

"Tanguadal? God only knows what that means…I sure as hell don't. It sounds enticing though."

Her heart leaped as he moved closer and ran his fingers through her hair, then slowly circled the hollow of her throat. He stopped short at the rise of her breasts. "Tanguadal," he whispered again.

Her fear was gone.

Kat composed herself with great effort. "That's about all the teaching I'd better do for now, Indian."

Great Eagle lifted her hands and kissed each palm. She was overwhelmed and fell backward into a lying position. He followed, harnessing a groan of desire which suggested pain. Although she had never heard the sound of passion, she recognized his.

Kat wanted to soothe him. Touch his hand. Graze his cheek. No, she was safe for now and decided against doing anything. Great Eagle folded his arms in the usual fashion and closed his eyes.

"You want me," she murmured. "But something is holding you back. I guess I ought to be grateful you didn't try to take me. Goodnight, Indian."

"Goodnight, Katherine," he answered fluently, his smile hidden under the cover of darkness.

Chapter Five

Sheets of rain slapped Deke's black slicker as he hoisted himself onto the tail-gate of the Forsythe's wagon. He smiled at Callie as she held the flap open for him, grateful for the blackberry cordial she offered. He sank to the floor, wet and defeated. Without a word he raised the tin cup to his lips and drank deeply.

"Just checking to make sure everybody's all right before I turn in."

"That's good of ye, but don't go blamin' yerself fer somethin' that couldn't be helped."

"I know, Miz Forsythe, I know."

"Yer wagon bein' gone and all, Mr. Stiles, we'd be more'n glad to put ye up."

"Thank you, ma'am, but I'll just bunk in the Stone's other wagon. I've been keeping an eye out for Linc and Todd so I won't be sleeping much anyway."

"So, ye think the Indians might have captured them?"

"Can't say. I hope they saw what was happening and found a place to hide."

James shook his head slowly. "I don't mind tellin' ye that I'm hopin' ye're right, Deke. But there's a lot o' room fer doubtin'."

Deke drained his cup and bid them goodnight. He could barely see as he pulled his hat down low to protect his face from the driving rain. The wind had blown up a storm and, as big as he was, Deke had to push his

Wild Kat

way through the irascible gusts. A nagging feeling prompted him to stop at Bess's wagon.

"Everything all right, Miz Stone?" he called.

Bess unfastened the flap and held it back for him to enter. The tail-gate groaned as he heaved himself up with one leg. Once inside, the lantern light shining on her stricken face told him all he needed to know.

"Sam's passed on, Mr. Stiles."

Deke dropped to his knees beside Sam's lifeless form and felt for a pulse at his throat. Sam still looked as though he was sleeping, but his skin had taken on the sickly pallor of death. It took all of Deke's willpower to meet Bess's gaze without taking her in his arms. He abstained and waited, realizing that she was receiving comfort from holding Bobby while he sobbed out his own grief.

"How long has he been gone?"

"Maybe an hour. At first I thought his fever had broken; he looked so peaceful. When his color changed, I knew."

Bitterness clutched Deke's heart as he fought off an array of emotions. "I'd best get him out of here."

"No, not tonight."

"But, Miz Stone, I can't…"

"I said **no**, Mr. Stiles. Goodnight."

Mud splattered Deke's boots and buckskins as he jumped down from the wagon. He understood how Bess felt. It brought to mind the stormy afternoon ten years before that he had buried his wife. It seemed like a lifetime ago.

* * *

Calm returned in the early morning hours. As the sun rose, Deke summoned James and the Swede to help him transport Sam Stone's body to the makeshift graveyard.

Lydia Joe Cates

Bess sewed fresh ducking around her husband after she dressed him in his favorite shirt and blue serge trousers. Bobby hovered nearby while his mother tenderly prepared his father for burial.

"There now, Bobby, your Papa looks real nice."

"You didn't put socks on him, Mama. I know he don't need his boots, but he oughta have his socks on."

"You're right, Bobby, and I know just the ones."

Bess rummaged in her trunk until she found the dark blue pair that she had knitted for Sam the previous Christmas. Underneath them she found the family bible. She had taken both articles out and closed the lid when she noticed that her son had already opened the end of the burial sack.

Bobby held out his small hand for the socks. "I'll put 'em on him, Mama."

Bess forced a smile as she gave them to him and opened the back wagon flap for Deke. "You can take him now, Mr. Stiles."

He nodded gravely and motioned Larsen and Forsythe to the tailgate. As Bobby jumped down beside him, Deke held up his arms to Bess. "Let me help you, Miz Stone." His heart knotted as he gripped her under the arms and set her on the soggy ground.

"Thank you for being so kind, Mr. Stiles. I hope you'll forgive my rudeness last night."

Admiring her boundless courage, he choked, "No call for an apology."

After the dismal task and final prayers were complete, the mourners gathered around the campfire for a meeting. Studying the familiar faces, Deke held little hope for the future and made a startling announcement.

"It's my decision that we turn back. We're just stragglers now. The ground ought to be dry enough for us to pull out in the morning."

Wild Kat

Bess stepped in front of him as he started to walk away. "Bobby and I won't be going back with you, Mr. Stiles. Todd and Katherine are out there somewhere and I'm holding on to the hope of finding my children."

Deke was astounded. "Why, you can't mean that! A woman and a boy alone in this country?"

"My mind is set." Unsmiling, back as straight as a rod, Bess stared the big man down.

"I'm responsible for you and your family, Miz Stone. You know as well as I do that I can't allow you to go it alone."

"I've said my piece, Mr. Stiles. That's that."

James spoke up. "We're goin' ahead, Deke. Callie and I've spent a good part of our lives stintin' and savin' fer this chance. We'll not be turnin' back. Bess and Bobby are welcome to be trailin' us."

Exasperated, Deke tried again. "It's foolhardy, James. If the Injuns don't get you, the weather and sickness will."

Larsen chimed in. "Me and the family'll be going back with you, Deke."

Lissie Larsen smoldered with bitterness as she lashed out at her husband. "What'd you expect, Borgas Larsen, a fancy tea party with crumpets and lace doilies?"

Borg's embarrassment ripened to anger. "You heard me, Lissie. We've had it out in private and I say we're going home. Don't want to hear nothing else about it."

Deke threw up his hands in a hopeless gesture. "Bess, if you change your mind I'll be thankful. If you don't, we'll be gone come morning."

*   *   *

The sun was rising when Deke ascended to the driver's bench and took his place beside Bess. "I'll get you on firm ground, Miz Stone, then you're on your own. She handed him the reins.

Lydia Joe Cates

At first slap the team lunged forward and pulled out of the muddied grass depression. Deke drove a few yards, then stopped and faced her. "I shouldn't be letting you go," he gruffly said, "It'll be hard living with my conscience from now on."

Bess broke his heart in one timeless moment when she smiled. "Whatever happens, you're not to blame. I'm a headstrong woman, Deke Stiles, and it's going to take a lot more hardship than what I've had to get me down."

He shifted his concern to Bobby for fear his eyes would reveal his feelings. "Well, son," Deke paused and ruffled the boy's cotton top, "You take care of your ma, you hear?"

Bobby smiled and shook the hand Deke offered. "Yessir."

The wagon master took one last look at the woman he had come to idolize, tipped his hat, and walked back to the forlorn wagon train.

Deke bought Bess's extra wagon to replace his that had been torched by the Indians. After hiring the Swede's oldest daughter to drive, Stiles mounted his bay and rode to the head of the train.

"Let 'em roooll!" he yelled in a far less triumphant roar than when they had started.

The stragglers…four wagons in all…began their journey of defeat. They were headed home.

*   *   *

After the Indian said goodnight, Kat's confusion turned to consternation. His English seemed better than the usual **go** and **sleep**. He was a contradiction, she deduced, and couldn't be trusted.

She listened to Great Eagle's even breathing. He had fallen into his usual peaceful slumber soon after saying goodnight. She would make doubly sure that he was asleep before she made her escape.

Wild Kat

There was just one problem. The wind seemed to be stirring up another storm. No use fretting about the weather. Her mind was set. It **had** been since the Kiowa braves left to go back to their village a few hours before. Although she had no idea which direction to take, she was not worried about the Indian catching up with her. She would be riding Guo-la-te.

Kat stole out of bed and stood quietly for a few moments, waiting to see if she had disturbed the Indian. Although Great Eagle rarely moved once he had fallen asleep, this night was an exception. As Katherine took a step back, he coughed loud enough to halt her progress and set her heart in rapid motion. When his breathing became normal again, she picked up the riding blanket.

After what seemed to be an eternity, she made it to the horse and spread the blanket over his back. "Good boy." She led him over to a large rock in order to mount him. "Please, please Guo-la-te, don't whinny now."

Holding tight to the reins, Kat crawled on top of the boulder, threw her right leg over the horse's back and paused once more. An owl hooted, harmonizing with the wind moaning through the trees.

"Giddyup!" she whispered, nudging him in the sides with her heels. Guo-la-te responded and, sooner than Kat had expected, they were cantering in high buffalo grass.

The young horsewoman felt nothing short of exhilaration. "Distance, boy! All we need is a few miles between us and the great Great Eagle." She laughed and wished that she could see the look on the Indian's face when he discovered her and his transportation missing.

Trotting along the moon's path of light, Kat stroked the enormous red horse's neck with affection. With a feeling of liberation, she relaxed and began to hum a melody from the fiddler's repertoire when a bolt of lightning struck. The clouds rolled in rapidly and broke in staggering force with blinding torrents of rain. Kat's shoulders began to sag and ache with the heaviness of her warm cloak, which no longer protected her against the elements.

Lydia Joe Cates

She skirted the woods in order to make better time, but it was not worth the effort. Yanking the reins, she headed toward the trees for sanctuary until the tempest subsided. Kat did not think to tether the horse. Exhausted, she crawled beneath the low hanging branches of a mammoth sycamore, rolled up in a ball and fell asleep.

Silence awakened Kat with a start. There was no more drip, drop, drip of rain invading the thick foliage where she lay. The howling wind had stilled.

The taste in her mouth was as thick as buttermilk. It reminded her of the pouch of grapes and deer plums that Great Eagle had given to her. She bit into a plum and her jaw tightened from the coppery, sour juice, but she needed the nourishment.

Faint and numb from the cold, Kat managed to get to her feet and weakly call, "Guo-la-te, I need your blanket." As if a bolt of lightning had struck again, the subconscious needling of the last few moments was verified. "Guo-la-te! Guo-la-te!" she screamed.

Katherine stumbled through the forest, reeling dizzily, calling for the horse that she knew was gone. No longer triumphant, she burned with fever as her body shivered with chills. Weeping, Kat fell to her knees and collapsed under the blurry image of a massive oak.

* * *

Great Eagle smiled, soothed by the fury of the raging storm. He was confident that he would have possession of Kat and his horse before morning. He waited. A cold, broad nose nuzzling the side of his face awakened him.

"I cannot let you rest now, my friend. Take me to Tanguadal before she becomes stiff from the frost."

The horse's tracks on the wet ground were easily retraced. When they reached the clearing he gave the animal free rein. Guo-la-te sensed the

Wild Kat

urgency of their mission and charged forward in a mad gallop. As the forest appeared, he reduced his speed and veered sharply into the woods again. The sorrel slowed to a walk and halted at the huge oak tree.

Great Eagle jumped to the ground and knelt beside Kat. As his hand touched her brow, dread grazed his heart and renewed hurtful memories. She burned with fever. He had not counted on **this** when he decided to allow her a fling at escape. In a moment of tenderness he caressed her cheek and whispered, "Tanguadal, can you hear me?"

"I'm not daydreaming, Father, if that's what you're thinking."

The fever. Great Eagle swept Kat into his arms as the painful recollection of his wife's death began to canker in his mind. He held her close and warmed her with his body on their way back to camp.

The fire was crackling in an instant. Great Eagle dug a small hole beside the fire pit and when the warmth began to seep through the earth, he placed a bark bowl of water in the cavity to heat.

Kat babbled incoherently as he carried her to the fire and positioned her beside the warmth. She was so limber that it was practically impossible to keep her upright as he labored with the buttons and loops on her bodice. When he reached her camisole it became difficult to keep his mind on his task. Staring at her naked beauty, he proceeded to remove her underpants.

"Such things are foolish and binding." He tossed them into the fire and draped the rest of her clothing over a rock to dry. His gaze strayed over her tenderly, almost reverently. The Indian felt the heat radiating from her feverish body and hurried to finish bathing her. Rigors seized her as he wrapped her in a blanket and held her in his arms.

Great Eagle groped in his belongings and pulled out a longshirt. He lifted Kat gently and wrestled the garment over her head. In the process his hand grazed a breast and, instantly aflame, he noticed the rosy bulb rigid with cold. Sparks arrowed through him with quickening force. Heat licked at his groin each time he looked at her. He wanted her. She had been right, but he knew it was impossible to think of such a thing. Not yet.

Two days passed and darkness prevailed when Kat finally rallied. Great Eagle stroked her hair. Was she dreaming? If so, she wanted to remain asleep. A cheerful fire popped and sparked nearby and her body was no longer cold or wet. She lay on the familiar fragrant bed of pine and the tangy, undeviating scent of finely tanned deer hide tickled her nose. Her eyes refused to open as her hands wandered curiously over her form. It was then that she knew why the leathery smell clung to her. She was wearing it. Soft against her flesh, it covered her far below the knees. A blanket hugged her feet and body.

Kat faded in and out of consciousness. Now she felt his presence. He was examining her for any sign of awareness when out of the fog came a whisper. "Tanguadal."

After a few moments Great Eagle arose and a rustle of twigs crunched under his footsteps as he moved away. She roused from the sound of a sizzling wet long chucked on the fire. He sensed her movement from the bed so he filled a sliver of bark with mush and sat down beside her again.

"Katherine…eat?" he asked softly.

She spoke haltingly as she gazed at him. "I'm weak. How long have I been sick?" He helped her into a sitting position. "I wish you could understand me. I wonder if you're angry with me for stealing your horse. I wonder so many things, Indian."

Great Eagle thought she was hallucinating again until she smiled. Kat made another attempt to rise, but her arm collapsed under her body. He lifted her and carried her to the fire.

He placed his hand on his chest and said, "Guo-la-te come back to Indian. Guo-la-te, Indian friend."

Wild Kat

"I know that now." Kat sighed. "I'm hungry." She took his finger and touched her lips. He seemed happy that she needed his help. Cradling her in his arms, he fed her.

*   *   *

Three days passed before Kat was strong enough to travel. The situation seemed different now; she felt protected as Great Eagle swung her up behind him on his horse. He had attended to her needs with profound gentleness. Yes, a bond had definitely developed between them.

Kat had no concept of what the future held for her, but the fear she had experienced in the beginning no longer existed.

"I'm ready," she chirped and placed her hands on his shoulders.

"We go," he declared. A few days ago it had been quite a different story. Stripping off her wet clothes while she bobbed against him had nearly done him in. He could not afford a mistake, now that his plans had been made. That first night in the forest he knew what his destiny would be. He would let nothing stand in his way.

*   *   *

Another morning had almost dawned. Great Eagle shook Kat. "Come, Katherine. We go."

She spread her arms and stretched. "It's as black as the bottom of a well. I'm sleepy, Indian."

Ignoring her complaint, he pulled her out of bed muttering with irritation. She hurriedly slipped into her shoes, cursing. "You make me so damn mad, Indian! I've been ill!"

Moonlight still sifted sporadically through the trees, giving the illusion of grotesque dancers as he pushed her ahead of him. He stifled his temper and allowed her to spout off her meager vocabulary of curses until they reached Guo-la-te.

Great Eagle clamped a hand over her mouth. "Enough!"

"I'm finished, Indian," she replied, somewhat subdued.

As the morning brightened, Kat guessed from the position of the sun that it was about midday. Her stomach growled and she ached from bumping over uneven ground. She was bored from the never-ending trouncing.

Mischief lit up her eyes as she removed her hands from his shoulders and wound her arms around his waist. When Great Eagle stiffened, she felt a tinge of delight. Leaving a hand on his waist and placing the other on his thigh, she shifted her weight as if she were trying to get comfortable. He tensed more and turned to face her.

"No! Katherine."

"I'm sorry."

"Katherine is sorry?"

"Yes, I'm afraid I've been too bold."

He pulled her arms tighter around him.

She could not help laughing. "So you like my arms around you?"

As they loomed out of the woods, Kat took in a long breath and let it out slowly. The sight before her eyes was astonishing. Fifty or more teepees were nestled in a shallow valley below.

The village appeared peaceful. The setting was neat and uncluttered, resting at least a hundred yards from a placid sky blue lake. Myriad colors of green spruce and pine bordered the water. Wildflowers splashed the hillside with the abandon of an artist's palette. Kat was sure that the scene was far more beautiful than any brush could capture when put to canvas by an old master. Not at all the way she had pictured an Indian village.

Great Eagle observed her interest in the scene as he dismounted. He shed his buckskins and rolled them into his blanket, then tied the bundle with only one leather thong. He wrapped the other around his wrist.

Wild Kat

Kat remarked pertly, "I'd like to know why you chose now to strip down, but I'm sure that would be impossible for you to explain. Anyway, I'll just admire your beautiful body."

A somber expression clouded his face and Kat was taken by surprise when he lifted her up and carried her back to the privacy of the trees.

He touched her cheek when he set her down. "Katherine." His hand then splayed across his chest as he said, "Indian..."

A dismal feeling engulfed her. It was as though he were saying goodbye. Tears welled up, changing her eyes into pools of liquid copper. Through the blur, a gray vision of emptiness appeared before her for a fleeting moment.

Unable to grasp any meaning from his actions, she asked, "Are you going to kill me?"

"Kill? No Tanguadal," he replied softly.

A look of wonder replaced her scowl as their gazes locked in the cool afternoon shade. His sooty eyes radiated a tenderness that made her tremble with awareness as he drew her into the intimacy of his embrace. Sheltered in his arms, an insistent stirring deep inside her began, magnifying as her passion surfaced.

Great Eagle's pulsing throat pounded visibly and sweat glistened on his muscled shoulders. His arms closed around her and she yielded. He moved his mouth slowly, relishing the lips he had yearned to kiss so many times. A kiss of exquisite passion. Wildly tender. Primitive in desire.

Kat's arms tightened around his neck to steady herself. Then, as if she was a flower in bloom, her body opened up and gave way to a deep, mysterious feeling that she had never known before.

"Indian," she whispered against his lips, "You've shown me a part of my soul that has been sleeping until now."

A snarl of pain escaped his lips as he clasped her face in his hands and kissed her once more. When he spoke, it was in a voice surging with emotion. "Great Eagle is sorry, Tanguadal."

Her look of astonishment grew as she digested his apology. "Sorry? Why should you be? I'm not."

Without a word he unwrapped the leather thong from around his wrist and bound her hands together. It happened so quickly that Kat could only stare at her bonds in puzzlement.

"Why?" she implored as she recognized the pain and anguish in his face. "Why?"

Great Eagle's hand covered Kat's mouth to stifle a scream. He endured the agony in her blazing eyes and allowed her to hammer away at him with her tethered wrists until her strength deserted her. Exhausted, she fell to her knees and lanced his heart with words.

"I thought that you were different! You kissed me with such longing."

Great Eagle picked her up, struggling to hold on to her as her strength renewed. His steps became labored as she thrashed about in his arms. A wild animal caught in a snare. Kat kicked him in the chest hard enough to push him off balance. He staggered backward several steps. When he looked up and saw the hatred in her eyes, his heart shattered.

"Enough, Katherine!"

"Enough? You savage sonofabitch!"

The emotional pain he had suffered in the last few moments far outweighed any physical wound he had ever received in battle. Resigned, he pulled the reins forward over the horse's head and proceeded to do what was expected of him. Chief Great Eagle led Katherine Stone into camp as his captive white prize to be counted among his coup.

Drums rolled in the distance welcoming the chief's return. Dogs barked, children giggled and old and young alike walked to greet him. Sadness lay heavy on their hearts, knowing what desolate news awaited their leader.

As the chief and his captive entered the meadow, Kat noticed an elderly woman walking ahead of the others. She knew beyond a doubt that the graceful figure striding toward them was Great Eagle's mother. An uncanny resemblance.

Deeper fears replaced Kat's old ones. She was among strangers of a different race. Heathens. How would they receive her? Bravely, she held her head high. Not once did she glance in Great Eagle's direction as he exhibited her to his village.

As Kat and the chief approached the circle of teepees the crowd slowed, but the lone woman kept up a steady pace until she was face to face with her son. Kat listened with fascination to their conversation in the Kiowa dialect. She could tell from their tone that whatever they were discussing was of a serious nature.

"Welcome, my son, you have been away too long."

"I have been lonely for my home and family."

The mother clasped his shoulders. "Prepare yourself, Great Eagle, I have distressing news." Her anxiety was apparent as she told him, "Your son is missing and cannot be found. He went hunting with Young Squirrel. They were lost from each other and only Sleeping Rabbit's friend found his way back to the village."

Alarm hardened the chief's eyes as he digested the dreadful news. Words came hard. "What…is being done to find my son?"

"When Howling Wolf and your warriors returned from the hunting expedition they organized a search party." She sighed deeply. "They are still gone."

Without hesitation he declared, "I will join them."

The slender woman, though middle-aged, had hair the color of black satin. No trace of silver. One long braid rested at the center of her back. Her visage seemed softly chiseled into an oval. The Indian woman's wide-set, kind eyes sparkled with the luster of polished ebony, reminiscent of her son.

She smiled compassionately at Great Eagle, then switched her attention to Katherine. A sudden flash of incredulity crossed her face before her expression returned to its natural serenity. She dare not question her son's obvious decision.

Kat clenched her teeth under such scrutiny. She labored to hide her humiliation and gallantly kept her facade of confidence. As they entered the main trail amidst curious onlookers, Great Eagle ignored her and led Guo-la-te to the end of the path.

A framework of tree limbs supporting a stretched buffalo skin stood beside the entrance of a large, gaily painted teepee. Colorful figures and ungainly animals gyrated across the hide. They depicted the chief's many accomplishments. His coups.

Great Eagle spoke to his mother, Ay-tah, in undertones and pointed to Kat. Ay-tah agreed with his decision. "Yes, I will return to stay with the girl when you are ready to leave," she responded.

The Indian woman nodded to Kat in a courteous manner and walked up the hill to her own lodge. The crowd dispersed, their curiosity satisfied. Others went about their daily routine, making preparations for the evening meal and fetching water in wooden buckets and containers made of buffalo skin.

Great Eagle heaved Kat to the ground and took her inside his lodge. The room was clean and neat. A deep fire pit lay cold and unused in the center. Kat appreciated the cool, dim atmosphere, noting that the only light other than the open doorway came from the smoke hole in the coned top.

The chief stood beside the entrance and watched Kat while she inspected his home. "Katherine like?"

She did not speak. She was amazed that, although her wrists were bound as if she were a common slave, she felt strangely free. The Indian released the leather thong and gave it to her. He pointed to a framework of birch with a thick pad much like an ordinary bed. It was covered with a velvety cream colored deer skin and a pillow delicately woven in a unique design. Another bed, larger than the first, lined the curved wall at the head of the feminine one.

Kat's voice dripped with sarcasm as she lay down. "Better not let your brothers see this fancy bed or they might start calling you a squaw chief."

Great Eagle's look sharpened. He controlled his tongue and finished gnawing on a hunk of venison. As he lay down on the other couch, he positioned himself so that his head was inches from hers. "Sleep."

She grimaced and flipped over on her stomach as he rested in preparation for his journey. Kat examined his noble, hawk-like countenance and noticed a boyish aspect in slumber. It made him even more appealing. She focused her attention on the comfortable surroundings since sleep was out of the question.

Another narrow bed lined the wall opposite the chief's and hers. A low cooking table made from small logs had been placed next to the fire pit. Four low stools rested nearby. Food and water pouches hung on wooden pegs attached to one of the many support poles.

Very organized, she mused. Fine handiwork too. The bed covers and clothes were expertly made. Even the water bags sewn from buffalo hide were of fine quality and workmanship.

An hour or more passed before Great Eagle awakened. He turned on his stomach and faced her with determination. "Come, Katherine," he said motioning her to his bed.

Katherine sighed with resignation. "I guess you've decided to have your way with me, Indian. Well, go ahead and get it over with."

She stood beside his bed, not entirely sure of what he wanted from her. "Come, Tanguadal," he assured gently as he patted the mattress and held out his hand.

Kat did as he asked. As she lay down, the Indian turned on his side and wrapped his arms around her. He cuddled her close. "Katherine like?"

"I know you want me to say, Katherine like. Well, I won't!"

Lydia Joe Cates

"No, Katherine, I expect much more from you," he articulated in English.

"I've…" she paused and stared at him, trying to digest what she had just heard. "What did you say?"

He chuckled. "I envision much more than you have given, Katherine. I do not expect it today…or even tomorrow…but soon, Tanguadal, soon."

"Your speech! You lying bastard! You've made a fool of me for the last time." Her eyes simmered with rage. Why had he hidden the fact that he could speak such perfect English?

"It was not my intention to make a fool of you. Fewer words worked to my advantage while transporting a captive of such spirit." He lifted her hand and placed it over his racing heart. "This is what I feel for you, Katherine. I felt it the first time I saw you. I followed the wagon train hoping for another glimpse of you when I decided that I must have you. I hope I have gained your trust."

Acid spewed from her mouth. "Well, well, we're certainly full of the English language now, aren't we?" She paused. "Yes, I **trusted** you. And what was my reward? You bound me like a common slave and paraded me in front of your whole village. And all the while you refused to speak my tongue. I am humiliated!"

"It was expected of me." Then his hand went to her breast and lingered there. "Your heart speaks also. Tell me, Tanguadal, what does it say?"

"It says nothing. My heart is dead."

An urgency invaded his voice. "Look at me, my Wild Kat."

With keen attention, her eyes locked with his. "Only my family calls me by that name."

He cocked his head to the side as recollection glimmered in his obsidian eyes. "The nomen, Wild Kat, holds great meaning for me as I recall my visions."

They had changed positions and were sitting on the side of the couch. When she turned to him, an expression of recognition through tangled memories lurked in the shadow of her gaze. "I can't help but think of the days and nights of our journey. All that time you laughed behind my back."

"Never, Tanguadal. Never."

Great Eagle needed to show her the extent of his affection. He moved behind Kat and gently positioned her between his thighs.

She fought to compose herself. "I'm tired of playing games, Indian."

"Be still, Katherine. This is no game."

She felt his heart battering her shoulder blade as he began to caress her breast. She arched to his touch and urged him on, moaning softly as his lips idled behind her ear before kissing the nape of her neck.

"I am not free to give myself to you now, Katherine."

The throbbing of his hunger against her buttocks was driving her mad. Shivers of pure desire spread throughout her trembling body, entering secret places never touched before. Her breath shallow, she gasped as his finger feathered over her stomach and buried itself in the nest of her womanhood.

Her speech wavered as his sensual motions led her closer to the edge. "What do you mean you're not free to give yourself to me?"

"The time is not right, my dearest one. Although I yearn to shelter myself within you, we must wait for a while longer."

She wished to prolong the erotic moment. "I only know that I want to please you, but I've never been with a man before and I'm unsure of myself."

"You need not be uncertain, Tanguadal. You will know what to do when the time is right. Always be aware that I want you."

Kat twisted her head and saw his expression of painful restraint. "Then take me," she wailed. His fingers stilled. She was so beautiful. He craved to give them both more pleasure than what he could offer her now. Again his gentle fingers slid between the delicate folds of flesh and tempted the pulsing bud…the center of her…until she whimpered with the first strains of rapture to the last.

Afterward she lay in his arms, assuaged temporarily. Although his torment had not lessened, Great Eagle held her close. The Kiowa customs had been instilled in him at an early age. The chief respected their law and was reconciled to wait for the great Sun Ceremony, when it would be fitting and proper to make Katherine his bride. Then he would take her with honor.

Unaware of this tradition, Kat became more confused. She remained so when Great Eagle rudely jolted her aside. The unfettered heat in his groins had become overpowering. He got up without a word and bolted from the lodge.

He reappeared moments later, composed, and set about getting ready to join the search for Sleeping Rabbit. After slipping into his buckskins, he filled a pouch with pemmican and a canteen with water. Kat watched him in bewilderment.

Sullen. "What are you doing, Indian?"

"I am gathering provisions. I must join the search to find my son."

"Does it give you satisfaction to turn away from me after you've ravaged my soul?"

Exasperated, he replied, "No, Katherine. I only wanted to satisfy you."

Her anger rose to new heights. "I'd say there was something wrong with your manhood if I hadn't felt its strength. But I guess it excites a savage to arouse the demons hidden within the depths of a white woman." She took a breath and blistered him with a fiery oration. "I'm not a squaw to submit to your every whim with lowered head and yielding body."

Whirling around he roared, "I do not look upon you as a squaw! You are my woman. You have been since the day you were born."

"Your woman?"

"Yes. Know, first, that I am a Kiowa. You will learn our ways."

Wild Kat

"You talk as if you think I'm willing."

"I am leaving you in my mother's care. She is a fine teacher. Learn your lessons well, my wild one. My son and I will return to you soon."

Great Eagle turned in the doorway. "Never call me savage again."

Fear's cold hand squeezed her heart as he moved swiftly through the opening of the lodge. She watched him mount a black stallion. Guo-la-te was given a well-earned rest after the arduous hunting excursion.

As he reined the stallion away from his teepee, an older brave caught up with him. Great Eagle's surprise and joy was obvious when he caught sight of his old friend. "Ansote! Much time has passed since our last meeting."

"Too long, my son. I have come to take you to Howling Wolf's search party."

The young chief beamed and clasped Ansote's arm. The older man had been a second father to him since his birth twenty-eight years before. Despite his age, Ansote was still a handsome, dignified figure. Tall and thin, with glittering eyes the color of a raven's wing, the wise one never seemed to change. Steel gray hair fell in two long braids over his chest. His nose was broad, centering an angular face and high cheek bones, but a very square chin remained a contradiction to his ancestors.

Ansote smiled, the creases around his mouth deepening as he spoke. "I know you are anxious to go, my son. Let us ride."

A roaring cry split the atmosphere as the two galloped toward the river. "Whoooeeeyah! Eeeyah! Eeeyah!"

The clattering of horse's hooves thundered in the distance and Kat listened with sadness as they diminished.

Chapter Six

Bess clucked her tongue, raised the reins and slapped the horses into action. After they began to move she handed the leather straps to Bobby. "Here, son. It's fitting you drive. You're the man of the family now."

Bobby took the reins proudly and grinned as he pulled in behind the Forsythe wagon. Bess leaned out to wave to Deke. The kind gentleman sat on his bay and waved his ragged bandanna in a perfunctory farewell. Pangs of melancholy sucked the life out of him at the thought of never seeing Bess Stone again.

* * *

Bess tugged stray wisps of hair from the corners of her eyes, grateful for the slight breeze even though it was a hot one. The crude, rutted trail they had been following for nearly two weeks was obscured by white sage grass, waist-high during the summer months.

Near noon she drew a thankful sigh when James signaled to her and turned toward the shade of a few cottonwood trees bordering the Missouri River.

"We'll be safe enough here," James assured. "It's time to be restin' a spell and we're needin' water too."

They tethered Annie and inched out the rope enough to enable the goats to graze along with the cow. Bess filled a basket with a crock of molasses, leftover corn fritters and a handful of wild plums gathered the day before.

Wild Kat

"Come on Callie, bring a blanket with you. We can sit by the water while Matthew and Bobby wade."

Bess watched the boys skip rocks over the water for a moment, then turned to Callie. "Just look at you and Matthew, a stranger would think you bore him. Your black hair and all."

Callie smiled wistfully. In a state of denial she said, "Sure'n they would except fer our skin. But me hubby is a wee bit dark and that'll be makin' up fer it."

James filled two buckets from the river and busied himself watering the animals. When the women caught sight of him again, he was racing through the tall grass, trying to catch his breath and talk at the same time.

"Stay with the boys, Callie. Bess, come with me, we'll be hidin' the wagons in that thick oak grove near the woodlands."

Running. "What's wrong, James?"

"When I was waterin' the blasted goats I could barely be seein' somethin' black movin' from the southeast. The grass bein' so high and all, I couldn't be makin' out what."

As they rattled and curved around a thick cluster of tree trunks, Bess prayed that the wagons would hold together. While struggling to keep the horses in line she wedged the wagon between two trees. Summoning all her strength, she yanked the reins until the team backed up enough to set it free.

"Thank the Lord I didn't tear up the wagon. There were a few times when I didn't think we'd make it."

"Be thankin' Him again if He'll be allowin' us to get out o' this place." He turned in all directions beaming.

Eyes sparkling, Bess raised her hands to her mouth and looked around. "It's a fine hiding place, James."

"Aye, sure'n 'tis that."

Lydia Joe Cates

The grove, nestled at the foot of a small hill, sheltered the wagons as if the terrain had been arranged for just that purpose. More secure now, James said, "Stay here, Bess. I'll be fetchin' Callie and the boys."

Callie was hiding in the tall grass with the children when James yelled, "Everybody run!"

She looped her pink gingham dress over her free arm and shoved the boys ahead of her. James waited. When they caught up with him, his voice grew stern. "Be runnin' like the devil's chasin' ye!"

The five of them crowded into Bess's wagon.

Silence.

James watched through a gap in the canvas. Minutes passed like hours and still no sign of the dark object he had spotted earlier. Random gusts of wind made fluting sounds in the high grass. One more tacit, hot day.

More silence. Matthew and Bobby grew restless and began to squirm. The games they knew were too noisy to play and sitting for any longer was out of the question in their minds.

"Ye've been hobbled long enough," groaned James.

"Can we get out, Father James?" Matthew's proclamation surprised and pleased James.

"Aye, that ye can, Matthew. Ye and Bobby need to be gettin' rid o' the vinegar and vigor ye've both been storin' up. We'll not be seen."

The children cleared a smooth place on the ground to play marbles. Bess and Callie sat on the tail-gate of the wagon, legs dangling. Still agitated, James leaned against the back of the wagon with a shotgun resting in the crook of his arm and a rifle at his elbow. It was moderately cool in the thickness of the grove. Not at all unpleasant.

The longer they waited, the more ridiculous James felt. "I'm guessin' I'm a mite jumpy, what with two women and two younguns to be lookin' out fer." His chagrin was apparent as he hoisted himself up on the tail-gate, his legs swinging free along with the ladies.

Wild Kat

"Ye're takin' good care o' us, me darlin'."

Bess nodded in agreement. "Yes, you are, James. You're just being cautious, that's all."

"I'm thankin' ye, ladies, fer understandin'." He continued to peer through the lacework of trees when his eyes suddenly widened. "Look!" he pointed toward an opening in the maze of leaves. "There's a man on horseback comin'. All of ye be stayin' out of sight."

James idled behind a large umbrella oak, his nerves on tenterhooks, as the rider trotted in the direction of the river. When the stranger slowed his sprightly bay mare to a walk and swabbed his face with a red neckerchief, James broke into a run. His stout legs plowed through the high grass as though his boots had wings. Waving his hat in the air, he shouted jubilantly as he reached the clearing.

"A prettier sight I've never seen!"

Deke Stiles shook with laughter as James bounded clumsily through the sea of grass. "Slow down, James boy, I'll wait for you," came the familiar gravelly voice.

"Ye old hound dog! I never thought I'd be wantin' to kiss that ugly face of yers," he bellowed, vigorously pumping Deke's hand.

A warm feeling came over the wagon master. Pursuing his friends had been the right thing to do. "I'm glad to see you, James. Mighty glad."

"Whatever could be bringin' ye here? And where might the rest o' the wagon train be?"

"One question at a time," Deke proffered, still laughing. "I've been worrying about you from the day we said our good-byes. As for the others, that bunch can take care of themselves. I had a talk with the Swede and he encouraged me to follow you. He knows this country like the back of his hand." Deke snickered. "Besides, the three Larsen girls are so ugly they'd scare any redskins away for sure."

"Aye. I'm agreein' to that," James added with a grimace. "I won't be lyin' to ye, Deke. I've been havin' me doubts and I'm thinkin' it's a blessin' ye're here."

"Where is everybody?"

"Come along, I'll show ye where we are."

Deke shook his head in wonder when they slipped into the oak grove. "I swear! I've roamed these parts for years, but never run across anything like this."

"Callie! Bess! We'll be havin' company fer supper," clamored James.

Deke's heart lodged in his throat as each familiar friend scampered out of the wagon to welcome him. "Sure'n ye're a bloomin' handsome sight, Deke Stiles," Callie squealed and hugged him around his broad neck as Bobby and Matthew each grabbed an arm.

The modest man's color reddened from the display of affection. Looking down, he cleared his throat and began mopping his sweaty face. His hand stopped in midair as Bess stepped onto the tail-gate.

"Mr. Stiles!" Her smile sent a ray of sunshine to his watery gray eyes and warmed his soul. "It's a downright joy to see you! What made you come all this way?" She shook his hand with enthusiasm after he had helped her down.

"I couldn't stop worrying; it pretty near drove me crazy thinking about you…and the rest, of course." He blushed again. "So I talked it over with Larsen and the others and here I am."

Deke gazed wistfully at Bess. He did not say what had been on his mind since he left. **I'm here because I'm in love with you, Bess.**

James interrupted. "I'm thinkin' it's time we're celebratin'. Callie, be gettin' out a bottle of yer blackberry cordial. We'll be takin' a swig er two." He noticed that his wife's fragile face was rosy, almost feverish in color, when she set the wine and hardtack on the water barrel. "Are ye feelin' up to snuff, sweet Callie?"

"O' course, me dear. I'm just overcome with pure delight."

Wild Kat

The women chattered and watched the children play while the men made plans. "It'll be sundown in a couple of hours. Even if we left now, we wouldn't get far before dark," Deke offered. "Let's stay the night here and get a fresh start in the morning."

"Then that's what we'll be doin'. I'll be feedin' the stock while you go to the river fer water, Deke."

Bess and Callie made preparations for the evening meal. As usual, Bobby and Matthew dug the fire pit and gathered kindling to start a fire. Bess set a pot for the potato stew over the heat and turned to the boys. "That's a mighty fine blaze you and Bobby made, Matthew. Your papa taught you well."

The small Indian's eyes filled. "Your people have been good to me, but I miss my father and grandmother very much."

Callie's eyes glistened sadly. For better or worse, she was not sure which, she and James had come to love Matthew as if he were their own son. "Don't ye be worryin', me dear. When we get to Fort Riley we'll be inquirin' if there's been a party lookin' fer ye."

The group sat away from the heat of the fire while Bess ladled up the stew. She handed Deke a steaming bowl and smiled. "Here you be, Mr. Stiles."

"Thank you, ma'am. Isn't it about time you called me by my given name, Miz Stone?"

"I reckon so, Deke, if you'll call me Bess."

Deke's weathered face brightened as he lowered his eyes to the bowl of soup. "I will for sure, Bess."

After dinner James covered the fire pit with dirt and said goodnight. Deke unsaddled his bay and was untying his bed roll when Bess approached him. "You might as well put that thing away, Deke. You're sharing the wagon with Bobby and me."

Lydia Joe Cates

Every pulse in his body resonated at the thought of sleeping anywhere near Bess Stone. "Why, I can't do that, Miz, uh, Bess. It wouldn't be proper."

"Pish-posh! Why not? We're grown-ups and we sure know right from wrong. Before you start an infernal argument, come and see what I've been fixing."

Bess had strung rope down the center of the wagon and draped quilts over it for a privacy curtain. "Does that suit your fancy, Deke?"

He looked down at his comfortable pallet and said, "Well, now, that's mighty inviting, but…"

"No buts about it. If you've a mind to drive my wagon and take care of us, the least we can do is try to make you comfortable."

"You're a fine woman, Bess. I knew it from the first day I set eyes on you." He could not look at her. His feelings flashed like a beacon in a storm.

Bess grinned. "There's nothing to be embarrassed about, Deke. Bobby and I are proud to have your company."

"Mighty kind of you," he said as he squatted down on his mattress and removed his boots with clammy hands. Sleeping next to Bess with only a quilt separating them would not be easy. He groaned softly and turned on his side, sniffing a pleasant scent. "Is there some mint stored in here, Bess?"

"You bet your Sunday boots there is. It's mixed in with our clothes and bedding."

"It's right refreshing." He knew that he would never smell the fragrance of mint again without thinking of her.

Bess had just blown out the lantern and set it aside when James scratched on the canvas. In a cautious tone. "Deke, get out here. Quick!"

Bess followed Deke to the tail-gate and stopped when James held his hand up. "Listen! Ye hearin' anythin'?"

"Horses. Heading this way. No doubt about it," said Deke.

Wild Kat

The men wasted no time. Leaving Bess and Callie sitting atop a grain sack with a shotgun across their laps, Deke and James hurried to investigate.

Apprehensive, Bess remarked, "I don't favor using these things, Callie, but if need be, I will."

"I'd be grateful to ye. I'm a fair shooter, only much better by the light o' day."

The two men darted through the trees to the center of the woods and stopped short when Deke whispered a shout to the Irishman. "Take cover!"

They hit the ground behind a thick growth of blackberry bushes not a minute too soon. A band of riders reined in their horses beside the river. Their voices echoed in the hot, still night and Deke recognized enough words to know who they were.

"Kiowas," he croaked.

"Aye. One o' the more gentle breeds, if ye can be callin' an Indian anythin' close to bein' civilized."

The Kiowas' campfire shed light on a half dozen men. Shortly, two more braves came from the river toting a seine full of fish.

Deke scowled. "Looks like they're planning to stay for a while."

"Sure'n it does. What now?"

"We'd best keep an eye on them for a spell. If they wander in the direction of our camp, we'll be ready."

"You stay, Deke. I'll be checkin' on the brood and the womenfolk."

*   *   *

Bess and Callie were crouching between the wagons, listening for the slightest sound. Callie poked Bess with her elbow after a tree branch snapped with a loud thwack. "Did ye hear that?"

"I did. And I see something moving toward us." Bess raised the firearm and pulled back the hammer with a sharp metallic click.

James muttered a curse. "It's me fer godsake! Be uncockin' the gun."

Bess audibly sighed. "Thank goodness! Where's Deke?"

"Standin' watch. I'll be checkin' on ye from time to time."

"James, me dear, from the way ye're talkin' it sounds like ye're intendin' to be gone fer a spell. What's happenin'?"

He explained their predicament. "We'll be keepin' a lookout 'til the redskins leave. Where're the boys?"

"Bess was seein' to 'em a few minutes ago, me dear. They're sleepin' like babes in a buntin'."

"Be gettin' in the wagon with them and be stayin'. We're safe fer now."

✶   ✶   ✶

Firelight splintered the bushes and splashed across their faces as James and Deke observed the Indians' preparations for the night.

"Look, Deke, two more just came ridin' in."

They watched as Great Eagle and Ansote greeted their comrades. "Have you found any evidence of my son's whereabouts, Howling Wolf?"

"Only yesterday we found Sleeping Rabbit's pony wandering in the meadow near Rattlesnake Canyon. There was no sign of the boy."

Great Eagle shifted his gaze to the blackberry bushes where James and Deke were watching. Ansote walked to his side. "What is it, my son?"

"Over there, in the bushes." Joined by Ansote and two braves, the chief moved toward the men's hiding place.

Sweat beaded Deke's forehead and drenched his shirt, but he did not move a hair, nor did James. They were well camouflaged in the thorny lair and Deke hoped that the Indians would not detect their scent. Breathing as shallow as death, Deke silently thanked God that there was no wind.

"Blackberries," said Great Eagle as he reached for a thick vine and plucked a handful of the fruit.

Deke's eyes burned from the salty sweat. He swallowed hard and glanced sideways at his friend doubled up into a ball. James flinched as a harmless snake slithered over Deke's arm and coiled around a braided vine.

Great Eagle tasted a berry and tossed it on the ground. The rest sauntered back to the campfire. The chief and Ansote lingered a while longer. Deke's head was bent over, eyes level with the toes of Great Eagle's moccasins. If he had moved his hand mere inches he could have touched one.

Howling Wolf raised his voice. "Come back to the fire, my brothers. We must talk."

As they strolled away, the hair on the back of James's neck stilted. His heart hammered steadily, but he denied himself the luxury of movement until the Indians had settled down.

Whispering close to Deke's ear. "I don't mind tellin' ye, that was just a wee bit too close. The snake came near to pettrifyin' me! What're they sayin', Deke?"

"We're too far away now, but I understood enough to know that they're searching for Sleeping Rabbit. They're just the ones we've been trying to dodge."

"Heavenly saints. That's Great Eagle standin' there."

"Yeah, that's him all right. Now's a good time to move farther back, while they're having their pow-wow."

One at a time, they inched out of their hiding spot on their bellies, slowly elbowing their way to safer ground. The Indians were unknowingly providing them with a cover of loud talk and boisterous laughter. Deke still cringed each time he snapped a twig or crunched leaves under their prostrate forms.

Lydia Joe Cates

"We're sitting on a powder keg," Deke whispered. "If those redskins get wind of us, be ready to meet your maker."

"Yer right," James declared. "We'd be havin' a helluva time gettin' those wagons out of the grove in a hurry, wouldn't ye say?"

"Be damn near impossible."

All was quiet around midnight. James carefully got up and moved steadily away to see about the women. Callie and Bess were wide awake, but the children continued to sleep. Callie sat on the tail-gate with James while he rested.

"Ye're smellin' mighty nice, sweet Callie."

"I'd like to be sayin' the same about ye, James Forsythe, but not 'til ye've had a dunkin' in the river." She laughed softly, smoothing back a lock of his unruly brown hair. "Ye're as quiet as a mouse, just like ye always are when yo've a burden on yer mind. Spill it, me dear."

"'Tis a waste of time to be tryin' to fool ye, darlin'. Great Eagle joined his braves tonight."

"How're ye knowin' that?"

"I saw 'im. It's the searchin' party fer Matthew."

A half-moon hung low in the sky and touched Callie's pale, frightened face. Oh, James, if that devil knew how close his son was to 'im this minute, I hate to be thinkin' what'd be happenin' to us all."

"I'll let nothin' happen to ye, Callie."

"It's not me I'm thinkin' about."

"Be rememberin' that Matthew belongs to another. We've only been borrowin' him fer a time."

"I'll never be forgettin', me dear."

     *   *   *

James clawed his way back through the high grass to their lookout. As he stretched out on his stomach, Deke elbowed him in the ribs.

Wild Kat

"Take a gander. All of 'em are asleep except for Great Eagle. It's making me skittish."

The chief lounged against the trunk of a tree, alert with inquisitive eyes. He straightened at the least sound, always focusing his attention on or near their hiding place.

"Stay put," said Deke. "That bastard hears everything."

A skirmish in the underbrush brought Deke close to panic. James yanked hard on his shirt and nodded his head in the direction of two playful raccoons tumbling over each other.

"Gawdamighty!" he mouthed.

Great Eagle squinted to penetrate the inky curtain of darkness. When he discovered what was causing the bushes to shudder, he laughed softly.

"So. You want to play, do you?" The two beady-eyed coons toppled over a tree limb and romped to the water's edge.

It was dawn when Great Eagle raised his deep, resonant voice. "My son is waiting. It is times to ride!"

James was dozing when they heard the Indian's thunderous tone. Deke grinned with relief. "Looks like they're leaving."

The chief and his braves mounted and cantered away. Deke and James hustled out of their cramped positions. "Hellfire and damnation! I've been doubled up so long I feel as stiff as a buffalo's cock."

"Aye, well, I'm thinkin' that's mighty rigid. I'm also thinkin' that we'd better be gettin' our crooked rumps back to camp."

*   *   *

A delicate color of pink splashed the eastern horizon as the Kiowa chief signaled for his men to halt. The search party had reached a fork in the trail that spiraled off toward Rattlesnake Canyon. He spoke in an authoritative manner.

"Last night I felt a presence near our camp. I must see the site by day. Ansote, come with me. The rest of you wait at the mouth of the canyon."

Great Eagle led Ansote to the exact spot where Deke and James had hidden. The chief scoured the ground inch by inch. He found broken branches, crushed leaves and weeds flattened by more than one. "Two white men. They are ignorant and careless."

"I see the signs, my son."

Great Eagle stooped low to the ground, eyeing a shiny object. It was half-covered with dirt and leaves. He picked up a jackknife and carefully examined the engraving on the side. Initials **D.S.** The chief slipped the knife into the waist pocket of his breechcloth and motioned to his friend.

"Come, Ansote, there is a meadow on the other side of the woods. I am curious."

They reached the clearing. "Whoooeeeyah! Eeeyah! Eeeyah!" The cry whirred from Great Eagle's diaphragm with the vibration of a gale. A signal to his son if he was near.

Chapter Seven

Great Eagle's mother attempted to console Katherine. "Do not be sorrowful, my child. Our chief will soon return." Ay-tah was torn between amusement and compassion for her son's chosen one.

"I hope he never comes back." Kat snapped.

"You will feel different after a little time has passed."

Eyes sparkling with belligerence. "No, I won't. He lied to me by pretending to be uneducated in the white man's way. Besides that, he kissed me as if he were my lover."

"It is not my son's intention to ridicule. He does not wear a false face…or a false heart. In time you will understand his actions." Ay-tah suppressed a smile. She noticed the way Kat's skin pinkened when she was angry, plainly enhancing her beauty. The Indian woman liked the girl. It was quite clear why the chief had chosen this spirited one.

"I am tired, and I am sure that you are too, Tanguadal."

"Your son calls me by that name. What does it mean?"

"It means Redbird."

"What does your name stand for, Ay-tah?"

Serenity haloed her lovely face. "I am Autumn Woman."

"It suits you." Kat was beginning to feel comfortable with Ay-tah. "Does Guo-la-te stand for anything?"

"Yes. Big Red."

Kat murmured, "Redbird, Big Red. Great Eagle must like the color red."

Ay-tah's downy laugh rippled across the room. "He does. Rest now, Redbird."

* * *

Many days passed, all with the same routine. Ay-tah, in her helpful manner, continued to subtly teach her student the way of the Kiowa. The knowledge acquired each day crept up and surprised Kat.

As usual, Ay-tah silently planned the day for Katherine. Her nimble fingers sewed with sinew and a needle carved from animal bone. She looked up from the garment and smiled as Kat stirred and awakened.

"Did you sleep well?"

Sulky. "No, I didn't. I had a dream about wild heathens."

A stab of pain passed over Ay-tah's placid countenance. Katherine was contrite as soon as the hateful words had escaped her lips, but pride prohibited the offer of an apology.

"Our way of life is different from yours. You will come to understand and appreciate it."

"I don't plan to stay that long."

Ay-tah maintained her friendly attitude and overlooked Kat's arrogance. She held up a long skirt fashioned from doeskin the color of cream. "I have remade this for you. Do you like it?"

"No, I don't like it. You may as well put it away. I won't dress like a savage."

Masking her feelings, Ay-tah laid the skirt on the table alongside an exquisitely beaded blouse and a pair of fringed leggings. Moccasins of the same supple skin lay on the floor beside Kat's shabby, high-button shoes.

Ay-tah turned away. "I will respect your privacy while you dress in your new clothes."

Kat sighed in defeat and examined the beautiful apparel, secretly admiring Ay-tah's skill as a seamstress. Brushing away ashes from embers in the firehole, the Indian woman still observed the girl. When Kat made no attempt to undress, Ay-tah set aside the bowl of potatoes she had begun to peel. Trader Charley Bone occasionally brought their favorite vegetables to the village to exchange for corn and buffalo hides.

Wild Kat

"Maybe you prefer to be alone." Ay-tah lifted an ungainly pouch from a peg by the door. "I will go to the pond for water." A double purpose, she mused. Not only for water, but for Katherine to realize that she now trusted her completely.

Not once did the Indian woman glance toward the chief's lodge while filling the water bag. She knew in her heart that Kat would not try to escape. When she returned, Katherine remained slouched on the bed in her filthy clothes.

Ay-tah offered an alternative. "I will find you something else to wear." She left the teepee again and returned with a plain doeskin shift which had been dyed dark red. "Try this," she said with a smile.

"I won't wear animal clothes!"

Ay-tah sat down beside Kat on the bed. Taking her hand, she explained softly, "You are too beautiful to wear soiled clothes. I will take you to the lake where the women bathe. You will feel better after you have washed yourself.

*   *   *

Weeks passed before Kat found herself looking forward to each day's chores. One morning, while Ay-tah was busy tying a fresh deer skin to the stretching frame, Katherine decided to try on her new clothes. She removed her tattered dress and one remaining petticoat, keeping on her camisole and the ridiculous underpants she had secretly made from remnants of the other ruffled chemise.

Kat slipped the delicate blouse over her head and loosened the lacings across her full bosom until it felt comfortable. The skirt was a perfect fit, as were the moccasins. She was delighted with the sensation of the smooth animal skin caressing her body with satiny fingers.

The Indian woman stood in the doorway. "You are pleased?"

"Oh, yes! I've never worn such softness. The feel of it is, uh, divine." A word she had learned from a great aunt who thrived on impressing others. "Thank you, Ay-tah. How did you fit me so well?"

"You are near the size of White Doe, my son's wife who died of the fever."

"I'm sorry. What was she like?"

"She was fair. You remind me of her, except for the color of your hair. Hers shown like spun gold in the sun."

"I've heard that your people favor fair hair. Is that true?"

"Some do. Ah, but yours becomes the sun and the moon."

"Did White Doe have blue eyes?"

Sensing a slight jealousy. "No, Redbird, hers were the color of an acorn." Ay-tah added, "She came to us seeking shelter in the night. She and her father had come from England and were traveling by rail to Bolton, Colorado when a gang of white renegades attacked them."

"I doubt that they were white," Kat enunciated in a condescending tone. "Go ahead, I'd like to hear the rest of the story."

Ay-tah nodded, patience intact. "Margaret told us that the bandits were white. She had no reason to lie. The marauders killed everyone on the train, including her father. Margaret managed to escape by pretending to be dead. The poor girl wandered for days, finally stumbling upon our village."

"You called her Margaret?"

"Yes. She accepted the name of White Doe when my son chose her for his bride."

Kat had heard enough. She was not interested in discussing Great Eagle's wife anymore.

Ay-tah lifted the cooking pot from the hot coals and said, "A treat for your palate, Redbird. Come."

"What is it?"

"Eat first. I will tell you later."

Wild Kat

They ate in friendly silence, relishing the savory bowl of thick, steaming stew crammed full of tender chunks of white meat.

"This is delicious! The taste is different from anything I've ever eaten."

Ay-tah agreed and began to clear away the mess. She took a thin willow stick from the work table and stuck it in the fire. "It is time for your lesson, daughter," she remarked as she lit a candle made from buffalo tallow.

It was the first time she had referred to the girl as *daughter*. Kat thought of her own mother and how worried she and the rest of the family must be over her abduction. Why wasn't she, Katherine, lonely for them?

"Now we must study so that you will be able to speak our tongue with fluency by the time Great Eagle returns."

"I'm not learning the Kiowa dialect for him. I'm doing it for myself. It's entertaining."

Ay-tah laughed. "You have brought joy again to this lodge with your presence. I am grateful."

The Indian woman's laughter gave Kat goose bumps and a wave of nostalgia permeated her soul. Ay-tah had given Great Eagle her laugh, differentiated only by his deep resonance.

Kat's eyelids began to droop. She emitted a loud yawn and fell back onto the bed. "I think I can sleep now, Indian Mother. Thank you for teaching me," she articulated in dialect.

"Goodnight, Redbird." Ay-tah blew out the candle and lay down thinking, her son had chosen well.

Kat sleepily remembered, "You promised to tell me what kind of meat was in the stew."

"So I did. One of our braves went hunting early this morning and brought a fat rattlesnake to my lodge as a gift. When we are fortunate enough to receive another, I will teach you how to prepare it."

"Rattlesnake!" Kat swallowed hard. "It was good."

Ay-tah laughed softly, happy with Kat's gradual acceptance of the Kiowa way of life.

Chapter Eight

"I'd best fill these last two canteens. We don't want to have to stop and dip into the water barrel every time we get thirsty," Deke told James as he tied the goats to the wagon.

"Aye, but get movin'. I don't mind tellin' ye I'm gettin' a mite jittery."

At the river's edge Deke slid down from his saddle and stooped to fill a canteen. By the time he had filled the second one he was feeling threatened, imagining a wide array of problems. Then came the familiar thunderous sound in the distance. He hurried back to the shady confines of the grove.

"Ye're lookin' like the devil himself is ridin' yer tail, Deke."

"He may be."

No sooner had he spoken, a roaring yell besieged the grove. Fine hair on the back of Deke's neck prickled. They swept the women and children into the back of Bess's wagon and told them to stay out of sight. Both men climbed a tree half way to the top and balanced themselves on thick branches. There, they could observe without being seen.

From his peripheral vision, Deke saw movement and glanced down to the ground. Matthew whizzed past them, running toward the clearing with Callie in hot pursuit.

"James!" Callie squealed.

The Irishman scrambled down the tree within arm's reach of the child and tackled him before he could dash into the open. Matthew fought and kicked as James dragged him back to the wagon and heaved him over the tail-gate. The boy became rigid when a strong, familiar sound reached his ears.

"That is my father's voice, please let me go to him."

"We've no way of knowin' if he's yer pa, son," he lied.

Matthew read the message in James's expression and decided that he had no alternative but to signal his father in the way he had been taught. He opened his mouth wide, but James was quick enough to cut off the child's scream with his kerchief. Amazed at the small Indian's strength, James managed to wrestle him to the floor of the wagon and hold him there.

He looked up at Callie. "Be doin' what ye have to do to be keepin' the boy quiet."

The women struggled along with Matthew. When he finally ceased to fight, Callie moaned at the hatred she saw in his eyes.

Bess patted her shoulder. "We can't take any chances, Callie, and you know it."

"I know," Callie sobbed. "Oh, Matthew, will ye ever find it in yer heart to be fergivin' us?"

* * *

Great Eagle and Ansote burst into the clearing, slowed their horses to a walk and scanned the horizon. The chief glanced toward the grove of trees, then switched his attention to the ground.

"There are wagon tracks here. Let us follow the white man's path."

The two Kiowas rode in the direction opposite the grove. James and Deke watched them fade out of sight. They were careful not to attract attention to their roosts and, after the Indians were beyond the range of sound, they shimmied down from their perch.

Wild Kat

Deke's heart still whacked at his rib cage when he breathlessly said, "Gawdamighty, it's hot! And speaking of warm places, let's get the hell out of here."

"Ye're right. I'm thinkin' it'd be wise to be partin' company with the cow and the goats. What do ye think?"

"Good idea. We'd best be saying our prayers. My gut's telling me we'll be calling on the good Lord more than ever now."

The exodus began before noon with Bess driving her own wagon. For safety's sake, Deke rode his mare the first few miles to scout the countryside ahead of them.

Matthew refused to have anything to do with Callie or James, no matter how hard they tried to make the situation better. The boy declared that he would ride with Bess and Bobby. Bess agreed, gladdened that a bond had developed between the youngsters in the short time they had known each other.

Bess studied the child for a moment. "Matthew, you shouldn't be sulking at the Forsythes. They were only trying to protect all of us. We had no way of knowing whether your papa was here or not."

The Indian boy stared straight ahead. "I know my father's voice as I know the wind."

She knew that his pain from hearing his father's cry was still an open wound. Bess also understood how both son and father must feel. She tried another tactic.

"I sympathize with you, Matthew, and with your papa as well." It was ironic, she ruminated, that she would be able to commiserate with the one who had stolen her own daughter and left her desolate. "I promise, with God as my witness, we'll see that you get back to your papa." Bess smiled and put her arm around the child. He made no further comment and seemed to take comfort from her display of affection.

The heat of the July afternoon was so oppressive that Bess donned her sunbonnet. She suggested that the children ride inside of the wagon for a while. The boys settled down on a mattress to play a stick game that Matthew's grandmother, Ay-tah, had taught him.

Bobby grappled under his belongings and came up with a small box containing an uneven number of thin willow sticks about three inches long and handed them to his friend. After Matthew had divided them into two handfuls, he held them up. "Now guess which hand holds the most."

Bobby guessed the right amount and won a point. "I got it! It's my turn."

The children grew tired many games later. Bobby suggested, "These twigs are old, let's throw 'em away. We can git some more when we find a place to camp tonight."

Matthew's eyes took on a curious gleam. "You are right. I know! Let us make a trail of sticks. I will throw one out, then you, until they are all gone." He was enthusiastic about Bobby's suggestion for one reason…he wanted to leave a sign for his father.

They crawled to the back of the wagon and tossed out the fagots, two and three at a time. Matthew dropped the last ones in a bunch so that they would land in the top of a huge clump of grass.

Deke rode ahead to scout for a place to camp. He returned within the hour wearing a craggy-faced grin. "I found a dandy one."

He led the wagons off the trace less than a quarter of a mile to twin knolls. Disappointed, James shook his head. "I'm not meanin' to be critisizin' ye, Deke, but I hardly see a place to be hidin' two big wagons."

"You don't, huh? Follow me around to the other side of those hills." Deke laughed and trotted ahead, leading them to a copse of sycamores growing opposite the headlands. Combined, the knolls and trees made a pathway of reasonable protection.

"I oughta be knowin' better," James conceded.

"Stiles turned to the women. "Now, ladies, looks to me like you've got a hankering for a swig of real cool water. Get your buckets."

Wild Kat

He led them midway into the trees to a natural spring. "If I didn't know better, Deke Stiles, I'd swear you were a magician." Bess laughed and dipped her bucket in the clear water.

"I'm sure not one of those fellows." He smiled with a twinkle in his watery gray eyes. "Springs are plentiful in this part of the country. But more than anything, it's the good Lord looking out for us."

Although exhausted, each worked diligently to set up camp. James watered the horses and tethered them to graze. Callie put a large pot of water on the fire to heat. With the spring so near, it was a good time to wash clothes. Deke discovered a hole in one of the water barrels and plugged it with tree gum while the boys gathered kindling.

"I'll fetch an extra pail of water for cooking."

"I'll get it, Bess."

"No bother, Deke, I need to stretch my legs anyway."

He watched her go, swaying like a graceful willow in a summer breeze. Night after night he had pretended to sleep, wanting her more and more. Damn! At least he was with her. He admitted that just being near her would have to do for now.

Bess strolled into the shade and knelt at the spring. An eerie feeling swept over her as she dunked the bucket into the water. When the ripples cleared she saw her reflection and that of a tall Indian standing behind her. He was naked, except for his breechcloth and moccasins.

* * *

"Where's Mama, Mr. Stiles?"

"At the water hole, son. We'd best go help her."

Claps of thunder resonated overhead as man and boy sauntered into the cool sanctuary. "Sounds bad, don't it, Mr. Stiles?"

"Yeah, it does, Bobby. I sure hope the rain holds off 'til we cross the river."

Before they reached the spring, Bobby could see Bess crumpled beside the pond. Her hand still clutched the handle of the overturned pail. "Mama!" The boy fell to his knees and began to pat his mother's face. "Mama, what's the matter?"

"Get back, Bobby." Deke's red face paled with concern as he soaked his kerchief in water and began to bathe Bess's forehead. "Bess girl, talk to me," he pleaded.

Her complexion had taken on a waxen glow. Eyelids fluttered open. She stared into space for a moment, then bolted upright. "Where's the Indian?"

Deke jumped to his feet, his eyes nervously darting in all directions. "Injun? You're not imagining things, are you?"

"I know what I saw!"

"I'm not calling you a prevaricator, Bess, but you've been more than a bit shaky since the Injun raid."

"I guess you're saying I'm just plain crazy." Pouting, she took Bobby by the hand. "We'd better make tracks out of these woods right now!"

"Gawdamighty! Don't be so touchy, Bess, I only asked a simple question." Deke followed on her heels, grumbling and wishing he had kept his mouth shut.

James and Deke scoured the woods and found nothing. Satisfied, they went back to camp to hear the rest of Bess's story.

"I got down on my knees and dunked the bucket in the water. When the rings cleared I saw my reflection and that Indian was standing right behind me. He was stark naked except for that funny little skirt he wore. He spoke English, told me to be quiet, said he wouldn't hurt me."

"If it'd been me, sure'n I woulda died of fright," Callie chimed in, "But don't be keepin' us danglin', me dear, get on with it."

"Well, I was quaking all over and just plain tongue-tied. The Indian stared at me real hard and moved closer. By that time, my heart was running away with itself. He reached out and said, 'I've seen your eyes before.' That's when I fell faint."

*   *   *

Wild Kat

Katherine sat cross-legged on the couch while braiding her hair. Occasionally she glanced at a small girl poised outside the lodge door. Kat grinned and spoke in Kiowa. "Come in, little one, and tell me your name."

The child shuffled into the teepee. "I am Bright Morning." Shyly, she dropped her head and rocked back and forth on her bare feet.

"What a pretty name. I am Katherine. Ay-tah calls me Redbird." Pause. "Are your people getting ready for some sort of celebration?"

"Skaw-Tow." The girl, no more than six, giggled. Her dark eyes kindled radiantly as she pronounced the two words. "It is the biggest gathering."

Listening from inside of the doorway, Ay-tah was warmed by the benevolence in Kat's tone. "It is already so hot, and the sun has not been with us even an hour. I overheard Bright Morning telling you about our Skaw-Tow."

Kat nodded with interest. "Tell me more about it, Ay-tah."

"It is nearing time for our yearly thanks to the Sun God, a momentous occasion, Redbird. Our people from the other villages will begin arriving in less than ten days."

"White people celebrate their God, too. It's called Christmas." Kat's expression turned wistful for a moment. "How many are coming?"

"Hundreds. All bands of our tribe will gather and pitch their teepees in a huge circle by the lake. We will have mounds of food, many games of competition and dancing. Old friends and relatives, some we have not seen for many moons, will come. It will last three days and three nights. One of the most important events of the Sun Ceremony will take place on the last day."

"It sounds thrilling, but a bit bigger than my family gatherings ever were." Kat glowed with enthusiasm.

"It gladdens our hearts. There are solemn rituals that must be performed too." Ay-tah motioned to them from the doorway. "Now we must go to the lake."

"Go ahead, Indian Mother, I want to change my clothes first."

Ay-tah took the small girl's hand. "I will take Bright Morning with me."

Katherine shed her undergarments and rolled them up in her dress and petticoat. Chills of delight spread over her skin as she slipped on the dress that Ay-tah had remade for her. She wondered if it would please Great Eagle. Now that her anger had diminished, Kat realized how lonely she had been without his presence.

*   *   *

Dipping a garment in the lake, satisfaction encircled the Indian woman's tranquil face as she and Kat washed clothing under the close scrutiny of Bright Morning. Kat had been an apt pupil. She tackled every task with equal enthusiasm and had successfully transformed herself into a responsible Kiowa maiden. Although she remained strong-willed and stubborn, Kat had achieved measurable wisdom to soften these traits. Great Eagle would be in awe of her quick mind.

As Bright Morning tired of watching the two women wash, she left to play a game with the other children. Kat waved to her and focused her attention on Ay-tah. "Am I the only white woman here, Indian Mother?"

"Why do you ask, Redbird?"

"A friend of mine was taken from the wagon train along with her little girl. I saw them once after the raid. I thought you might know something."

"No, my child, I am sorry." Ay-tah's gaze shifted to the main path that led into camp. "Look! There is a gathering at the river. Shall we go and see what is causing the commotion?"

"Oh, yes! I'll leave our wash on these rocks."

Knowing that the excitement was for her son's return and wishing to surprise Katherine, Ay-tah said, "Hurry! Maybe we have company." Animation charged the air as a crowd of young people began waving their arms in welcome.

Wild Kat

Great Eagle rode slowly up the path leading his son's pony. Ansote followed with six goats and a cow. The chief's expression was sober as he raised his hand to acknowledge his reception. Kat's heart sank as he passed her without so much as a nod and went directly to his lodge.

Ay-tah left Kat in the crowd and rushed ahead to wait for her son. She somberly greeted him as he entered his home alone. "Did you see Katherine?"

"I saw her, but I felt no desire to speak."

His indifference ruffled Ay-tah's usual placid nature. "A disappointment is no excuse for insolence."

"You are right, as always. I will make amends to Katherine."

"My dearest one, you mourn because you think that your son is dead. He is not. I feel it in my soul."

"I hope your soul speaks the truth, Mother. The path Sleeping Rabbit followed is cold and I fear animals may have…" Brimming with emotion, he stopped speaking and held up a bundle of willow sticks in his hand. "I found these scattered along the white man's trail."

"The sticks resemble those of Sleeping Rabbit's game."

He nodded slowly, anguish dwelling in his eyes. "Am I being punished for ill deeds that have faded from my memory?"

"The Sun Spirit does not punish in that respect. It is folly to voice such foolish words. I lost your father two moons before White Doe left us." Ay-tah spoke haltingly as her composure switched to impatience and gained volume. "Since that time, you have led our people with honor."

"You are a wise woman, my Mother. It is no wonder that my father chose only you."

A distant look clouded her eyes before she asked, "Where did you find the cow and the goats?"

"They were grazing along the white man's path, where I found the willow sticks. It was a mistake to leave the animals for us to find, and stupid not to have killed them for food. I feel the need to return to the same place after the Sun Dance Ceremony."

"Why must you wait, my son?"

"I do not wish to leave again without Tanguadal."

Ay-tah smiled and left her son to rest. Great Eagle stretched out on his bed, but was too spent to sleep. Closing his eyes, he listened to the threats of an approaching storm. The growing magnitude soothed his jangled nerves and he relaxed. An occasional rain drop tapped at the curved walls like a pat on soft flesh.

His mind strayed to the lovely, flame-haired Kat who would become his bride on the last day of the Sun Celebration. While dozing, he decided to greet her after his nap. He would be fresh and receptive. Besides, Katherine's patience was too short. He would join his mother in teaching a lesson.

*　　　　　*　　　　　*

Kat walked along the path griping about Great Eagle insulting her. No matter. She would delay her return to the lodge and show him that she was in no hurry to see him. She stopped at the teepee of Bright Morning.

"Come, my little friend, I will take you to the foothills to pick wildflowers."

The child was delighted and soon filled her basket with treasures. Kat smiled down at the Indian girl whose fat little arms were ladened with colorful paintbrush, daisies and columbine.

"I'll take you home now, Bright Morning. Your flowers are beginning to look thirsty."

Bright Morning laughed. "I will give my blossoms water so that they will not wilt in death."

They strolled hand in hand among the yellows, reds and blues of God's natural tapestry, a delicate sight in the fading afternoon sun. Kat

Wild Kat

left the little girl at her door with a promise that they would gather more flowers soon.

As she neared the lodge, Kat's heart began to thump when she saw Great Eagle's black stallion tethered beside Guo-la-te. She stopped to pet the horses and felt a pang of remorse when she caught sight of the dappled pony that the chief had led into camp. It was one that only a child could ride.

Beyond the horses, a cow and six goats nuzzled in thick bunches of buffalo grass. Her eyes widened with curiosity; she had never thought of cows as having their own identities. For a fleeting moment she could have sworn that the Stone family cow, Annie, was grazing with the small herd.

Licking her fingertips, Kat plastered down the unruly auburn wisps that drooped around her face. Upon entering the teepee, she immediately sensed his presence. A familiar ache in the pit of her stomach began to pulse, a reminder of her ravenous hunger for the man.

"You have gathered all the blossoms on the hillside?" he asked with his eyes still closed.

"How did you know?"

"I saw you in my dreams." He opened his eyes and sparkled with pleasure at the sight of her.

"I had many visions while you were away, Great Eagle. I hope yours were as delightful as mine," she said in perfect dialect.

"Well, well. You have been busy in my absence. I told you that my mother was an excellent teacher, and now you have proven it." He patted the bed. "Come sit with me, Tanguadal."

His sensual voice washed over her as a thrashing wave ravages the shore. "It is time to talk, Wild Kat." She sat with a thud.

"What is there to say?"

"Forgive me for passing you without a word. I am despondent because I found no trace of my son, only his pony. It was no excuse to treat you badly."

Overwhelmed by his apology she offered, "I understand why your heart is sad."

He kissed her lightly on the lips. "Your wisdom has grown, Katherine. You speak with a woman's tongue."

She blushed. "I am a woman."

"Night upon night I have wanted you with me. You must know the strength and depth of my feeling by now."

At the touch of his hand she thought her heart would leap from her chest. Beads of perspiration mottled her forehead as his caresses became bolder. "There are times when I know your feelings," she murmured breathlessly.

"Katherine, I love you; I have never wanted a woman like this before. But once I touch, I find it hard to restrain."

Unashamed. "I want you too."

Their eyes locked. Two hearts pounded as one. Great Eagle gathered her into his arms, kissing her with the fervor she had experienced that afternoon in the forest. Cradled within the safe confines of his embrace, she wept with desire.

"Tanguadal," he soothed as he unbraided her hair and ran his fingers through the tangles. "My little Wild Kat. Our wait is almost over. You have my word."

When her tears began to subside, so did her feelings of rejection. He was a chief, and he lived by the rules he had been taught. Whatever they were, she would accept them. Kat disentangled herself from his arms and said, "I can't help but feel used, Indian, as only a white woman can feel."

Scowling. "Used? I thought that I had pleased you, Katherine. According to our law, our union has a time."

"Time?" she scoffed. "I only know when it is time to eat, or sleep, or tend to my body's needs. I did not know that making love required a special time."

"Patience, Katherine. You know the reason for my discipline."

Wild Kat

He stood, ambled to the bucket of drinking water on the cooking table and sipped slowly from a wooden dipper. Over the rim, he scrupulously inspected her attire. With no forewarning, he threw down the ladle. Curse after curse exploded from his lips in a surprising frenzy.

A tearful voice. "Each time I allow you to touch me, I fall in love with you again. You then shame me in some manner, but never before like this." She was speaking in dialect and, even at that shocking moment, she wanted it to be perfect.

"Tanguadal, the clothes you wear belong to someone else."

"Who, Great Eagle? Your wife?"

"Yes, Katherine. They belong to White Doe."

"No, Chief Great Eagle, they belong to me. Ay-tah sewed them to fit me. Your wife is dead…let her rest in peace. I have no objection to wearing them. Surely you should not."

He stared into her muddy eyes and thought of the Red River he had seen as a child. They gave him the illusion of a thousand stars floating on the water's surface. She made sense. What was wrong with him?

Kat turned her back and undressed. Her clothes slipped to the floor. Great Eagle knew that she was lashing out at him the only way she knew how. It was working. He was hot and hard and she was aware of it as she let the shift slither down her nakedness.

Hurt finally eclipsed anger. She hunched down by the fire pit and softly said, "I cannot share you with another woman."

Great Eagle felt a pang of sorrow and a degree of puzzlement. Did she not understand that she was his only one? He retrieved a blanket and draped it around her trembling body, still trying to explain. "I do not like to be reminded of those last days, Katherine. They have faded from my memory and are best forgotten. Look at me."

Kat continued to stare into the fire. When she made no effort to respond, he left. Once alone, she was reminded of Ay-tah and the security she offered. Tomorrow she would find her Indian Mother and talk. Drained mentally and physically, Kat dropped off to sleep.

Late in the night she felt herself being lifted and carried to her bed. Great Eagle made no sound except to whisper in her ear. "There is no other woman, Tanguadal, I love only you. Only you."

As morning dawned, Kat gazed at the dim light through the smoke hole and watched a ribbon of gray vapor wind its way to freedom. A piquant odor tickled her nose. Ay-tah squatted by the fire, vigorously stirring something with a delectable aroma.

"You must be starving. Come and eat, daughter."

"I am hungry. I have not eaten since noon yesterday." She arose, but the ache from her quarrel with Great Eagle remained. She had no choice but to wear the dress which she had forsaken some time ago for Kiowa trappings. The Moccasins were still on her feet. She left them there.

"I am glad that you are here, Indian Mother." Her soft Kiowa dialect lilted over her quivering lips as though she was on the verge of tears.

Ay-tah took Kat into the circle of her arms. She was certain of what had happened between Great Eagle and Kat. "My son is not a cruel man, but he has suffered more than most. He accepts the blame for being unable to save White Doe from the fever. Forgive me, Redbird, I did not think that he would remember so simple a thing as a dress."

"There is nothing to forgive. You are the dearest, kindest woman I have ever known." She smiled. "I love you."

A genuine look of amazement passed across the woman's face. "I love you," she softly said.

"What will Great Eagle do with me, Ay-tah?"

"Surely you know that my son plans to make you his wife."

Katherine's eyes flashed. "He could have at least asked me; I'm not deaf!"

Ay-tah smiled as Great Eagle entered the lodge. "Please leave us," he kindly asked his mother. She nodded and left promptly.

Wild Kat

The chief examined Kat's eyes for some moments before saying, "Yes. Your eyes belong to another."

She cocked her head. "What do you mean?"

"When I sent my braves home, Ansote and I searched another day for Sleeping Rabbit. We came upon a timberland with a natural spring hidden in its depths. I recognized it as a place where I often hunted as a boy."

Confused, Kat disregarded what she surmised was his approach to a reconciliation and sauntered to the fire pit. She sat on her haunches the way she had seen the older squaws do, picked up a pointed stick and speared a hunk of meat. She held the stick high and let the morsel drop into her mouth.

"You are rude, Katherine. Hear what I have to say and your interest will grow with my words."

"Nothing you can say will hold my attention," she snapped.

"We shall see. I encountered a white woman two days ago." He smiled broadly when she settled down.

"A white woman? Where?"

"Ansote kept watch while I went to fill our water pouches. There was a woman at the spring."

Kat sat straight with growing curiosity. "Did you hurt her?"

"You are a child, Katherine."

"If I am such a child, why do you want to marry me?"

He chuckled. "You will become a woman before you become my bride."

Kat glanced down at her ragged dress. "Why didn't you tell me that you wanted me to be your wife?"

"I have told you in many ways, but more importantly, I have not stolen your virginity."

She sighed. "I'm well aware of that. Please go on with your story."

"The woman I speak of was arrogant and straight of back, as you are at this moment. When I saw the color of her eyes, I saw you."

Katherine paled. "My mother. You talked to her?"

Chapter Nine

Bess ended her story with reluctance. She was enjoying the undivided attention of her friends, but there was little left to tell. "As the Indian studied my eyes, I passed out."

Deke grinned; Bess was strong one minute and soft as duck down the next. He loved her with a passion so strong that it almost scared him. He shook his head to clear his mind and stooped to pick up some twigs. "We'll draw straws. The short one stands watch 'til midnight, the long one 'til daybreak."

James drew first watch. "I'll be gettin' my gun and I'll be sittin' on that grassy slope above us."

The evening quietly slipped by. Around midnight Deke stretched and sat up. He knew Bess was awake. Her russet eyes penetrated the privacy curtain.

"Deke," she spoke softly, "Are you awake?"

"Yeah, Bess girl."

I want to thank you again for coming after us. I trust James, but I just know we're going to make it to Fort Riley now."

Desire throbbed in his big body with the power of a prod as her sweet voice beckoned from the thin barrier separating them. "You don't owe me any thanks, Bess. I wouldn't have rested if I'd let you go it alone." Husky voice. "I'm the one who should be thanking you."

* * *

Wild Kat

At Sunup Deke tied his mare to the back of the wagon, climbed to the driver's bench and took the reins from Bess. "We've passed the bluffs for now and you can see for miles around. No sense in me tiring the horse with extra weight."

"Happy to have your company." Bess relaxed and sniffed the air. "The rain's a lot closer now, you smell it?"

"Yeah, it's in the air all right. It won't hit for an hour or two, but we'll be wet before the day's over."

By mid afternoon plump drops of rain began to splatter the dusty ground. Bobby piped up, "Mama, it's startin' to rain, can me and Matthew walk by the wagon for a while?"

"I don't see any harm in it. Go ahead, boys."

The youngsters hopped over the tail-gate while playfully jabbing at each other. Bess nearly fell off of her perch when she spied Bobby running alongside the wagon with Matthew. The boys had fashioned a breechcloth for Bobby by cutting off the legs of an old pair of Sam's pants, creating perfect flaps. Their small hands and the scissors had been busy. She recognized one of her blue apron strings tied around Bobby's waist to hold the flaps in place.

Dark clouds began to boil overhead. The sky was mushrooming into the storm that had been brewing for days. Deke shouted to James and pointed toward the river.

"It's now or never! Get in the wagon, boys!"

"What is it?" Bess asked.

"The river. We've got to get across before the rain comes; it'll be impossible to get through the water when it starts to rise. We can't wait."

The wind was uncommonly strong and Bess leaned close to his ear. "What if we sink?"

"Stop frettin', Bess, we won't!" Deke lashed out at the animals laying on leather to pick up speed. "I've been across this river before, it shallows down to almost nothing!" he shouted.

In an instant the wind died. Bess sighed with relief. "It was so windy I couldn't think."

"Hold on, Bess, we're in for a rough ride."

"I'll bet you kind of like this bit of excitement, Deke Stiles."

"I'll take care of you," he said, ignoring her statement and giving her a wink.

"You're grinning like a satisfied tomcat."

Chuckling now. "I've been called everything in the book, but that."

Deke reflected. His wife had called him a lovable old bear. He was a hollow of a man after she died. At the age of forty-five he had resigned himself to a lonely life. He never expected to find that special relationship again. Than along came Bess Stone.

Bess frowned at the shadowy clouds churning overhead. "It's going to be a real gully washer."

They jiggled along as their voices zinged and vibrated over intermittent thunder and the creak of the wagon. When they reached the river's edge, Deke jumped down and untied his mare. His mind was eased when he spotted the giant cottonwood tree with a crooked trunk, a trail sign that he had depended on in years past. It was a natural marker for one of the shallower parts of the Missouri River.

"This is it. Stay put while James and I ride upstream a piece."

As the women waited for the men to test the river's depths, Callie and Bess conversed on a more serious note. "What're ye plans when we get to Fort Riley, Bess?"

"I'll ask around about my kids and stay at the Fort until I get a clue about how to find them. After that, I aim to stake some farm land for me and my family."

"From what Deke was sayin', the Kiowas are on good terms with the Fort Riley troops."

Bess raised a brow. "I wonder if that includes passing along information about white captives?"

Wild Kat

"Sure'n it's a fact. Ye know that the treaty says that all white prisoners'll be returnin' to their families before the signin'. If the Indians in this territory are knowin' where our people are, the troops'll likely be knowin' about it."

"That's right. I'll tell you something else, Callie. The redskins are accommodating because some Indians just can't keep from bragging when they've managed to capture a white, especially a woman."

"Aye, true enough. I'm hopin' and prayin', just like I know you're doin', that somebody at the Fort'll be havin' some news about Todd and Katherine."

"I'm trying to keep from getting my hopes too high, Callie. What we find out just might not be tolerable."

They sniffed the sharp fragrance of rain and watched the children play a game of tag. Callie caught Matthew's attention and waved to him. He turned his back. "The boy'll never fergive us, Bess."

"Don't dwell on it, Callie, he'll come around one of these days." Then Bess laughed and asked, "How do you like Bobby's Indian skirt?"

"It's been ticklin' me funny bone ever since I saw it a wee bit ago. I'm thinkin' it'll save on clothes washin'."

Deke's mare whinnied and danced in water below her shanks as he called out, "Let's go! This is the best place to cross!"

The traversing was slow, and calm enough for Matthew and Bobby to ride Deke's horse across the river. The wagons were midstream when the sky opened up and belched forth its wrath. James made it across first, driving his team relentlessly. As the animals strained and heaved under their load, they lost their footing twice on the muddied slope.

Deke slapped the reins and yelled, "Giddyup, you sons of satan, giddyup!" Bess's washtub was swept away as the team struggled to reach level ground.

Both wagons moved along as fast as they could on the sodden earth, hitting rough stretches that rocked them fiercely. While trying to alter their course, James's wagon rolled over a loose pile of stones, disengaging a wheel.

"Heeey, hold up!" he shouted over the gale, whipping their thinly-clad bodies with a vengeance. This was no ordinary storm.

Sheets of rain pelted their faces with the wrath of a hurricane as the men fought to tie down the canvas sides of the wagons. James was already in his wagon when Deke secured the reins and crawled inside with Bess and the boys.

"We can't do anything 'til this lets up," he told Bess.

Matthew and Bobby huddled in a corner while Deke and Bess sat just inside the mouth of the wagon. When a lull came, Deke climbed out and saw James plodding toward him, carrying his wife in his arms.

Looking up at the sky, James offered, "There'll be another onslaught before ye're knowin' it. Sweet Callie and I'll be joinin' ye."

Deke chuckled. "You scared to be alone, James boy?"

"Aye." He grinned. "We'll just be enjoyin' the pleasure of yer company 'til the weather quiets."

Deke stared helplessly at the teaming river and glanced downstream. "Look down there. Can you see something bobbing in the water?"

James squinted. "I'm seein' it, but I'm not knowin' what 'tis."

"We'd best check it out when the rain slackens."

James set Callie on the tail-gate and crawled up behind her, followed by Deke. They crowded together, clustered in blankets and packed like sardines in a tin. The smell of sweat and dirty clothes became overpowering as they waited. Finally Deke threw aside his cover, eased a bandanna out of his hip pocket and wiped his grimy face. As he stuffed the dirty kerchief back in his pocket, Bess wrinkled her nose. The rank odor building in the small interior had become almost more than she could bear. Certain that Deke had used the same handkerchief for...no telling how long, she made a mental note to dig out some of Sam's for him.

Wild Kat

Deke picked up a gallon can of coal oil and filled two lanterns. Passing one to James he said, "Let's take a gander downstream." Turning to Bess, he explained, "Stay put. Nothing'll bother you in this downpour."

Water spilled over the earth in rushing streams as the river began to swell and top the banks. Deke's worries compounded when he thought about the river rising high enough to sweep their wagons away or bog them down for days.

He remembered James damaged wagon wheel and decided that as soon as they checked out whatever was bobbing in the water, they would have to fix it in the deluge. Muck sucked up their boots with each step, making a challenge out of setting one foot ahead of the other.

"I'm gettin' nowhere fast in this quagmire."

Deke gave him a sideways glance. "Step up your fancy pace, James boy, or I'll have to call you James girl."

"I'm thinkin' ye're inferin' that I'm a dandy wearin' lace on me bloomers. Well, ye're wrong. No lace, just ruffles."

Their laughing ended abruptly when they neared the spot. The remains of a wagon was partially submerged in the water. The object floated at the water's edge with only half of its canvas top intact. For seconds both men stared at the familiar battered frame. Deke skirted the front of the wreckage and saw that the reins had been slashed with a knife.

"Looks like the horses were stolen. Whoever it was must have been scrounging for booty. I'll take a look."

As the wind picked up, James yelled, "Deke, I'm swearin' I heard a human voice, and it wasn't comin' from the wagon!"

"I can't hear anything above this frazzling bluster!"

James cupped his ear to listen. "Ye hearin' that?"

Deke nodded. He also heard the weak, mournful cry drifting on the tumult of the riveting rain. "It's gotta be coming from the wagon." Thrusting a toe of his boot between the spokes of a wheel, he hoisted himself up to the driver's bench and peered inside. "Gawdamighty!

Lydia Joe Cates

It's the Swede's family," Deke cried out, gawking at the horror before his eyes.

*   *   *

Great Eagle studied Kat's eyes as if they were fine jewels while she pursued her interrogation. "You talked to my mother?"

"Briefly. She was frightened and fainted. I did nothing to summon the others on the wagon train. It would have been foolish to try anything since Ansote and I were alone. The white man's gun far outweighs the success of an Indian's arrow."

"Did she ask about me?"

"Why would she? She does not know that I was the one who took you," he proffered, evidently amused.

Sarcastic. "I keep forgetting that you took me without asking. Were there any children near?" she asked, thinking of Great Eagle's son and her brother, Bobby.

"As I told you, your mother was alone."

"How did she look?"

"Exactly like you, but older."

"I meant, was she well." A faraway look invaded her eyes. She took a step nearer, taking pains to control her voice. "Will you take me back to see my family before I become a part of your life?"

His tone was soft, but final. "No, Katherine. My plans are made."

She tossed her head defiantly and paced back and forth. She had never gone up against such a mighty fort. She guessed that the Indian came nearer to being one than any human she had ever encountered. As enraged as she was, she still yearned for his touch.

Before Great Eagle stalked out of the lodge he turned to her. "Remember, Katherine, I am Chief of the Kiowa. You will learn the meaning of my rank."

*   *   *

Wild Kat

Two days before the Sun Celebration, Ay-tah arrived to stay with Kat in Great Eagle's lodge. The Indian woman presented Kat with a bundle of soft doeskin, a ball of sinew and a needle crafted from bone.

Kat smiled weakly. "I was never taught to sew, Ay-tah."

"You must learn, Redbird. Everything we wear is made with these articles." She smiled. "I will teach you."

Kat nodded with a sigh of defeat. "I'll try."

"Good! The day after tomorrow our friends and kinsmen will be arriving for the festivities. It is important that you have something appropriate to wear."

"Great Eagle doesn't care what I wear. He probably won't let me come to the ceremonies anyway."

"He does care, Redbird. Great Eagle would be disgraced in the eyes of his friends if you were not dressed properly. The most portentous aspect of the ceremony, to him, will be his presentation of you on the final day."

Bewildered. "Presents me for what?"

Ay-tah smile radiantly. "As his bride, of course."

*   *   *

Later that evening Kat fingered her new attire in progress, proud of what she was accomplishing with Ay-tah's assistance. The idea of becoming Great Eagle's wife secretly thrilled her. She picked up the bone needle and began to sew again.

Approaching midnight, the tribal wedding dress was complete. Ay-tah and Katherine agreed that it was more impressive than they could have imagined. Each woman seemed to sense the others' feelings. The bond between them was growing stronger.

"You are an admirable teacher, Ay-tah."

"You are an adept pupil."

Kat stretched and rubbed her eyes. "Where is Great Eagle?"

"He and Ansote left for Fort Riley as the sun set."

"Fort Riley is a long way to go to stay away from me."

"You are wrong, my child. My son is as strong as his father was. Nothing can keep him from doing what is right." Ay-tah hid her amusement with a yawn. "Great Eagle went to the Fort to make inquiries about his son."

"Is the chief in any danger?"

"No, Redbird. He goes in peace. The soldiers are our friends."

Disappointed. "But he'll miss the celebration."

The concern in Kat's voice did not escape Ay-tah's empathetic ears. "They will return tomorrow evening." She knew that Katherine had fallen deeply in love with her son and was on her way to becoming the woman that Great Eagle had been in love with all along.

Though tired, Kat tossed about and finally scooted out of bed to slip outside for a breath of air. Her mind began to ramble as she sat by the entry. Living with the Kiowas and speaking their tongue seemed so natural now. She hummed softly as she reflected about the lessons she had learned.

She could stretch a deer skin as expertly as Ay-tah. Clothing she washed came out spotlessly clean, now that she used the rocks in the pond for a scrub board. One of her prouder accomplishments was the preparation of her specialty, rattlesnake stew.

She laughed softly, recalling the first time she had eaten the reptilian dish. Her stomach had mutinied and threatened to send it back a few times before she fell asleep that night.

For the first time in her young life she was content. She was a Kiowa. Great Eagle was her destiny. She had envisioned this long ago, when he first appeared to her as a reflection in her looking glass.

* * *

Wild Kat

A shaft of morning sunlight danced through the open doorway as Ay-tah knelt at the fire pit tending breakfast. A mouth-watering aroma wafted past Kat's nostrils and tightened her jaws with hunger.

"Ah, you look hungry." The Indian woman stabbed a hunk of meat and handed it to Kat. They ate in silence. As Ay-tah went about her morning chores Kat dressed. She was no longer shy about her body and had given up her undergarments altogether.

Ay-tah was sewing the finishing touches on Kat's wedding dress. Her graceful fingers worked swiftly as she stitched the remaining beads on the long blouse. Smiling, she held it up for Kat's approval.

"It is done, Redbird. Do you like it?"

"It's lovely, Ay-tah." Kat kissed her cheek.

Pleased, but unaccustomed to an open display of affection, her eyes filled. "You touch my heart, daughter."

Taking two large buckskin pouches from the cooking table, Ay-tah said, "It is time for another kind of lesson. We will gather plums, berries, sunflower seeds and roots for cooking the feast."

Kat wore the dark red chemise that Ay-tah had given to her, but it was too long and got in her way when she walked. She gathered it around her knees and followed the Indian woman down the dusty street to the primitive path of crinkled buffalo grass.

"Wait!" Kat called out, "I am tripping on my dress."

"Do not fret, Redbird. Come here."

Ay-tah slipped the knife from its sheath at her girlish waist and squatted on her haunches. She carved away at the sack cloth until it was just below Kat's knees. She then split it and tied a knot on each side. The dress hung close to Katherine's calves allowing ample walking room.

Kat laughed. "You make me think of my mother."

Ay-tah paused for a moment, smiling before she spoke. "I am your mother."

As they entered the woods she began the first lesson by pointing out poisonous plants along the way, as well as those used for cooking and common ailments. They picked from an abundance of bushes and dug in the rich, moist earth for hours.

The two women had started back to the lodge when Kat remarked, "Our sacks are overflowing with nature…nuts and berries that I didn't even know existed, Indian Mother."

"That is only a small part of what you have yet to grasp. Before dusk becomes darkness, show me what you have learned. Find some sassafras; it is not only a good tonic, but it makes a fine tea as well."

Eager to please, Kat wandered along the edge of the woods where the grass was sparse. Soon she spied the young shrubs with bright green twigs. Unevenly numbered lobes on the burnished leaves and the pungent fragrance of the bark told her that she had, indeed, found sassafras.

"I found it! And more wintergreen too."

Ay-tah rested on a rock while observing Kat from a distance. Turning the earth with a crude stick, Kat dug up a large clump and waved it in the air, shaking tiny balls of dirt from the roots. The woman was pleased with her daughter's enthusiasm.

The Indian woman clapped her hands and said, "You are definitely a tosawi, Katherine. A good Indian."

Kat regally bowed to Ay-tah's applause and replied, "I plan to be the best."

"I have no doubt that you will be, my daughter. Come, we have more work to do before Great Eagle returns."

Kat walked proudly beside her new mother, looking forward to the festivities. She shivered with anticipation and wondered what it would be like to lie in the fluffy buffalo grass and make love to the chief.

"Katherine like," she spoke aloud in dialect.

"You like what, Redbird?"

"Everything, Indian Mother…everything!"

Chapter Ten

∞

"Ye say it's the Larsen's ye've found?" James shouted as he stumbled over a mound of slippery rocks.

"Yeah! It's a hell hole in there," Deke croaked. "Take a gander."

The big man held the lantern high, illuminating the grotesque bodies of Lissie Larsen and her three teenage daughters. Lissie's dress had been torn away to the waist. Her partially nude body floated atop the swelling water.

The three daughters lay entwined, a hideous stare from the youngest's bulging, terror-stricken eyes. It was as though she had seen the horror coming and had frozen. James gasped and looked away.

"Out o' me way!" His head lolled over the side of the wagon. He could not erase the image of Lissie Larsen from his mind as he heaved. His recollection of the night in Bonner Springs when they had danced to the cadence of the fiddler's lively tunes grew intense. Lissie's long blonde hair had been braided and wound around the top of her head, reminding James of a fat cow patty.

Except for a few short strands, there was no trace of the yellow hair left on her head. The girls were scalped so sloppily that hanks of thin wisps waved in the water, resembling the tentacles of a jelly fish.

One daughter who had suffered through her youth with two buckteeth, no longer had them. Her mouth gaped open in what appeared to be a silent scream.

Lydia Joe Cates

Weak and pale, James leaned over the side of the wagon and wet his handkerchief in the water to bathe his face. He looked up at Deke with a puzzled expression. "I'm wonderin' where Borg is."

"I can't figure it."

A flash of lighting guided them to the Swede. He was bound and smothered in the shadow of the trees only a few yards from the wagon. Deke concluded that Larsen was obviously positioned to watch the wretched act of his family being slaughtered.

"That must o' been the cry I was hearin'," James said in a high-pitched, hysterical tone.

"Had to be, James. We'd best see to him." Deke had kept his emotions in check, but hearing his friend break under the strain, he allowed the tears to spew down his craggy cheeks like rain puddling through ruts in a sunbaked trail. "Gawdamighty! Borg's dead too. Every damn one of them. What I can't understand is how they ended up here."

"I'm guessin' that Lissie changed the big hulk's mind."

Deke covered his face with the old bandanna. "I shouldn't have left them."

"Damn it all! Now don't be takin' the blame fer somethin' ye had nothin' to do with."

"Let's get them onto the bank." Deke eased back into the waist high water and grasped Lissie's corpse. Head turned, he gently pulled her out. "Can you get her down by yourself, James?"

James nodded, sliding his arms under Lissie's. His stomach churned as he touched her flaccid, chilled flesh. Clenching his jaws, he closed his eyes to the repugnant sight and worried her over the drivers bench.

Deke was edging the last cadaver out when the wagon creaked and grated against a pile of rocks. Slowly the stones parted and slid into the roiling water, taking the wagon and Deke with them. Lashing currents whipped him into a vortex of tangled brush and branches carrying both he and the youngest Larsen girl downstream.

Stiles grasped her skinny frame and held on with all the strength he could muster. So intent on keeping a firm grip, his shirt caught on a jagged rock and jerked his arm free of the burden. Water surging around them, he grabbed a low-hanging tree branch and watched the current sweep the dead girl away.

James sprinted to the site where Deke had vanished. As he cursed the storm, the bloody murders and himself for not remembering to bring a rope, movement registered in his peripheral vision. It was Deke stomping up the muddy bank.

"I don't mind tellin' ye I was beginnin' to think we'd lost ye too."

"It'd take a hell of a lot more than a dunking in the river to get rid of me. I lost the youngest girl though." Deke shivered violently from the wind whistling through his drenched clothes. "We'd best get Borg untied and bury the family together."

They headed for the tree line where Borg Larsen was tied in a standing position. Beside one of the oaks, the lantern light revealed a recently used fire hole. Deke sniffed the air suspiciously. "Am I imagining it, or do I smell the leavings of a fresh fire?"

"Aye. I'm smellin' it too, and I'm not likin' it."

Hefting the lantern higher, the light glared on the extent of Borg's torture. Deke angrily slashed at the leather thongs that bound the Swede and cringed when the body thudded to the macerated earth. A feeble cry pierced the dark atmosphere.

Deke dropped to his knees beside him. "Borg! Borg! Can you hear me?"

The injured man's swollen lips parted. "I hear."

"Thank God! We thought you were a goner."

James opened the canteen and gave the man a few drops of water. He swallowed and choked. "They got..." Borg took a ragged breath. "Got. Family."

"Who's they?"

"Injuns. Pawnee. Two." Larsen coughed, determined to tell his story. "Kiowas...showed up. Ran...renegades off...passed out."

"Save your strength, Borg. We're going to make a litter. We won't be long."

After making Borg as comfortable as possible, the men moved as fast as they could in the muddy earth. James stumbled over a tree branch that had fallen in their pathway and picked it up. "We can be usin' this fer part of the stretcher."

"Yeah," he agreed as he grappled with another. "This one is just as big. Now let's get a move on."

"I don't mind tellin' ye I'll be glad when this night's endin'."

"We all will."

As they neared the wagons, Callie parted the flaps of the first one and peeped out. "What'd ye find, me dear?"

Without answering her inquiry, James spoke in a rush. "Be gettin' out a sturdy blanket, Callie, and we'll be tellin' ye while we're makin' a litter."

"And what'll ye be needin' that fer?"

"Do what I'm askin'. We're pressed fer time."

Callie procured a blanket while Bess laid out ropes and a sharp knife. Swiftly the men placed the branches they had gathered and spread the wool blanket across them. James rapidly explained the situation to the women as they wrapped the tree limbs in the covering. Bobby and Matthew silently watched as the four adults labored with the ungainly frame. The Indian boy observed Callie's frantic fingers trying to secure the heavy cord around one end of the blanket.

He clasped her arm and spoke to her for the first time since the grove incident. "Let me help you, Mother Callie."

Surprised, Callie gaped at Matthew. "Thank ye, me darlin'."

The child removed the narrow rope from her shaking fingers and completed the task with ease. Exactly as Great Eagle had taught him.

Wild Kat

After the men had gone, Callie and Bess began to make room for the stretcher in the middle of the wagon. They stacked boxes and clothes trunks on each side. Bess perused the contents in Sam's small traveling trunk.

"Look what I found, Callie." Bess waved a handful of kerchiefs and two blue woolsey shirts in the air. "I've been thinking that Deke could get some use out of these things. What do you think?"

"I'm thinkin' the kindness in yer heart's showin'." A series of grunts and curses reached their ears. "I hear the men comin' back."

"It's them all right," Bess acknowledged as she tied back the canvas flaps and moved to make room for the litter.

Bess sat down beside Borg and, through a blur of tears, began to bathe his face. The Swede opened his eyes and parted his swollen lips, but the words drowned in a garble of blood and saliva. Callie wept as she cleansed what was left of a butchered ear.

"Shhhh, me dear, there'll be time enough for talkin' when ye're more comfortable."

"Dying...followed your trail." Borg choked as the red spittle trickled out of the corner of his mouth. "Lost it...did it for Lissie."

Deke wiped his eyes on his buckskin sleeve. Privacy was what he needed and he found it next to a large oak tree a few yards away. Resting his head against the rough bark, he tried to wash away the pain.

The women worked over the tortured body, but it was futile; the Swede had lost too much blood. Bess laid a cool compress on his forehead. He tried to smile, but his feverish eyes glazed over as the death rattle died in his throat. Callie gasped and stood up. She wormed her way past the corpse to the back of the wagon and breathed heavily of the clean night air.

Rain had left a fresh fragrance in its wake. The moon and stars had come out en masse, adding a touch of serenity to the darkness before

Lydia Joe Cates

dawn. "This night is too eloquent to be claimin' another life," Callie murmured.

Bess shook her head. "Borg wouldn't have been happy without his family. I feel like he willed himself to die so that he could be with them."

"A sterlin' thought, Bess. I'll be rememberin' that from this night forward."

* * *

"It's as weighty out here as the death we're carrying," Deke commented, straining under their heavy load.

"Aye. A wee bit too still to my way of thinkin'." Without warning, James dropped his end of the litter and whirled around. "Who's that followin?"

"It's only me, James; I've been trying to catch up with you for five minutes," Bess sputtered, out of breath. "It's hard sashaying around in this mud."

Confused, Deke was still holding his end of the litter. "Don't sneak up on us like that, Bess girl."

She had a bundle in her arms and held it out to him. "I ran across this ducking that we use to patch the wagon covers. Use it to wrap the bodies, Deke. It'll be better than laying them in the mud."

"Thank you, Bess."

"You're welcome. It's about all we can do for them now."

"Go on back to the wagon. I'll watch you 'til you're safe inside."

"Do you want me to go the rest of the way with you and help bury the Larsens?"

"Naw. I don't want you to see what we've got facing us." He whipped out his tattered bandanna and had started to wipe his face when Bess snatched it away.

Wild Kat

"I've got something for you." Trying to lighten the moment, she reached into the pocket of her sweater and brought out one of Sam's fresh kerchiefs. "I'll wash the dirty one when you get me a new washtub."

"I'm grateful to you, Bess," he uttered as he ran the fragrant cloth over his face. It smelled of mint, of Bess. "I'd forgotten I let your tub float away, but you'll get a new one. That's a promise."

On her way back Bess's brain stewed with a mixture of emotions as she fought to keep her balance on the soggy river bank. Her life had been torn apart one terrible day last spring. Now a strengthening force in the name of Deke Stiles comforted her with security and hope.

She no longer felt disloyal to Sam. Amid the turmoil and suffering, it seemed as though she had lived a lifetime in the last few months. She had changed. Sam would want her to seek happiness again. Standing there on the bank of the Missouri, Bess Stone made a decision to do just that.

* * *

They had been working in silence until Deke came to an abrupt halt. "James, before we close the grave, I'm going to walk downstream a piece. You stay here."

Perplexed, James sat down on a rock to wait. He was becoming impatient when he spied Deke trudging back with something in his arms. As he grew closer, James recognized the youngest Larsen girl.

"When I was swept away by the water I didn't think of anything but getting back to the bank," Deke explained. "Then I remembered seeing a mass of brush farther down the river. I prayed it might have snagged her. Thank the good Lord it did. Somehow I just couldn't bring myself to bury the Larsen family without their baby."

James sniffed and wiped his arm across his eyes. "Ye're a good man, Deke. Now, lets be finishin' our task here."

* * *

Lydia Joe Cates

The Kiowa village was ablaze with activity. Long trenches, called pit ovens, were dug to cook food for the feast. Women and girls wore heavy mitts of buffalo hide, taking turns tending a sizzling fire where stones had been heating for hours. They removed a few at a time with a wooden scoop, then lined the cooking pits with them.

Others worked at a long table in the shade of hackberry trees, wrapping vegetables and fruits in green leaves and small animal skins. These were to be placed among the hot coals to simmer in their own juices throughout the night.

It was a beehive, Kat imagined, as she observed her new family swaying to the drum beats while making preparations for the festivities. The scene filled her with such fervor that it prompted her to join the action. She motioned to Bright Morning.

"Get me a pair of mitts like yours, little one. You can show me what to do."

"I see you have found a job to your liking," Ay-tah remarked on her way to the pond.

"I like." Katherine mimicked, tugging on the large buffalo mitts before gathering another load of hot stones.

"I am glad to see you wish to participate, Redbird; your help is greatly needed. There will be many cooking pits inside the circle of teepees before nightfall."

"Wait for me at the pond, Indian Mother. I will help you carry water when I am finished here."

Ay-tah nodded and smiled. "I will gladly wait."

*   *   *

Drenched in sweat from the long day's work, Ay-tah and Kat carried their pouches of water from the pond. They could hear a disturbance as they reached the crest of the hill.

Wild Kat

"Come, Redbird, walk with me to the main path."

"I wonder what the commotion is?"

"Can you not feel his presence?" She laughed happily. "It is your future husband and Ansote returning from Fort Riley."

Kat stepped up her pace. Her heart became a fist flailing at her chest. Why couldn't she compose herself? After all, Great Eagle had only been gone a day and a night. Kat slowed to a walk, conscious of Ay-tah and Cry Woman watching her.

Short, stubby Cry Woman elbowed Kat. "You blush at sight of our chief," she snickered, showing a toothless grin. "If you too tired to bed him, I not." She cackled and wiggled obscenely. Her flabby hips billowed like waves under her yellowed shift.

Kat pinkened and backed away from the shrewish woman. Ay-tah noticed Kat's discomfort. "Pay no attention to Cry Woman. Her husband died last year and she is in need of another. When a woman in our tribe is widowed, she must abstain from relations with a brave for an entire year. After that, she is free to marry again. This trial is known as *living clean*."

"Living clean!" Kat pinched the end of her nose and scowled. "Cry Woman needs a lesson in washing before she can do that. She makes me sick, Ay-tah. Does she ever stop babbling?"

"Cry Woman is an old gossip, but she does no wrong. I feel sorry for her, Redbird. Loneliness contributes to her inferior disposition."

Kat's attention shifted to Great Eagle's approach. He was close enough for her to see his grave expression. She experienced a pang of guilt mingled with a suffocating thrill as he rode up to her and smiled.

"Katherine, your appearance is that of a dirty waif. I'll take you to the lake for an evening bath."

Her mouth dropped open as he rode past and tethered Guo-la-te beside the lodge. "That's what you think, Indian!" Exasperated from not receiving a more romantic greeting, she raged, "I'll take a bath when I decide to take a bath!"

Ay-tah caught up with her before she had time to enter the teepee. "Do not fret, daughter. My son makes fun with you."

Kat remarked with sarcasm. "I'd like to lay a fist on that handsome jaw of his."

"Your chance will come," Ay-tah winked.

As they entered, Great Eagle squatted and stared into the fire pit. "There is no word of my son. The soldiers will send a runner if he is found. I have Colonel Beck's promise."

Sitting opposite the fire pit from her son, Ay-tah nodded and began slicing venison. Kat's head hung as she pulled up a low stool and sat down beside the Indian woman. Avoiding Great Eagle's stare, she began to pare potatoes.

She wanted to ease his grief, even if it meant endangering her family and the entire wagon train. She dared not glance in his direction for fear her eyes would scream **Your son is alive!**

Great Eagle sensed her agitation and studied her intently. "Why are you wearing a dress bound to your legs with knots?"

"It was too long. Ay-tah cut it off." Her face brightened. "I wore it to do my chores."

Disregarding her attempt at conversation, he flatly stated, "The moon is rising. It is time to muddy the lake with your dusty body."

Heart galloping like a herd of wild horses, the Indian acknowledged his symptom as inexplicable joy to be with her again.

In an arrogant tone. "I'll go to the lake when I'm ready, Indian. You could do with a bath yourself. You smell like Guo-la-te."

Ay-tah muffled her laugh with a cough as she glanced at the fire hole. Great Eagle's composure was less than stable as he picked up a light blanket and a wooden box from the cooking table.

Wild Kat

He clasped Kat's arm firmly. "Do you walk to the pond or do I carry you?"

Arrogant air. "Carry me."

Ay-tah lowered her head and smothered more amusement as her son tossed the blanket to Kat and lifted her without ceremony. "Wait! I must have something clean to wear back." She reached out and snagged a shift off of a peg. "I'm ready."

Great Eagle strolled along in silence as if he were carrying nothing more than a feather pillow. In a playful mood, Kat wound her arms tighter around his neck. An attitude of mischief burgeoned as she began to nibble on his ear.

"Are you proud of yourself, Katherine?"

"What do you mean, Indian?" she said between dainty bites.

"You build a fire inside me and act as if you do not know."

He set her down at the edge of the moonlit pond and drew her into a snug embrace. "Is this what you want, Wild Kat?"

His lips hovered over hers, then touched and slowly began to move. Her heart ceased to beat for a moment, but only for a moment, as his kiss deepened into one like no other. Dragging her closer to his rugged frame, his hands caressed her back, her hips and at last, a breast. Her only hope of remaining on her feet was to steadfastly cling to him.

His mouth was inches from hers when he spoke. "Are you afraid, my child who thinks she is a woman?"

"No," she gasped. A shuddering sigh shook her delicate frame as he began to lick and nip at her lips, her neck, until she thought that she would go mad from wanting him.

Kat stepped back and battled to catch her breath; all she could conjure was a feeble drone. "I will respect your place as a chief."

Great Eagle released her for fear that his passion would strangle what little willpower remained. He grabbed the wooden box, almost dropping it, and laughed outright at his boyish clumsiness.

He composed himself and handed her the box. "Use this to scrub yourself clean."

She opened it and made a face. "What is it?"

"Buffalo grease and wood ashes."

"I'd never use such a mess on my skin."

"That is why you are so dirty. Take your bath or I will be forced to bathe you myself." He left and sauntered into the pond, swimming upstream.

Kat laid her clothes on a large rock and stretched luxuriously. Her desire remained strong as she welcomed the touch of a faint breeze on her bare skin and compared it to his touch.

She shivered as she stepped into the cold water and dunked herself. With chattering teeth, Kat backed out of the water, took a handful of the chips and rubbed them into a generous froth. "I don't believe it; it really lathers." Her husky voice lowered as she mocked her future husband. "Yes, Katherine, it really works."

Holding her breath, she slipped back into the water and rinsed off. When she stepped back onto the rocky shore, he was there. Had he been watching her? Had he been listening to her childish prattle? She hoped not.

He silently draped the blanket on her shoulders and turned her around to face him. Moonlight glistened on the droplets of water dribbling down his brown, near naked body. She thought he was nothing short of magnificent.

Katherine sighed and raised her arms to the star-splashed sky, making no attempt to catch the blanket as it slid off of her shoulders and dropped to the ground.

"You have called me a child. Tell me, Great Eagle, do your eyes deceive you?"

In one swift movement he ground her into him, molding their bodies together in an embrace so intimate that she had the sensation of oneness. When she lifted her head for his kiss, she could see that the battle she had initiated was already lost.

Rigid with craving, his passion hotly denying his intentions, he allowed his arms to fall at his sides and huskily replied, "No, Katherine, I do not see a child standing before me."

Trembling as though she was a leaf in the wind, she asked softly, "Then why do you treat me like one?"

"You provoke me, Katherine. If I take you now, you will be considered unclean…unfit to become the bride of a chief. It does not matter that no one sees; I will know! Can you not understand honor?"

The many times she had teased and aroused him came back to her in a rush. Shame engulfed her. So that was it. Such a simple reason. She quickly retrieved her shift and slipped it over her head. With great tenderness she placed her hands on his cheeks.

"I've suffered many days and nights because I wasn't sure, until now, how much you cared. I needed to know if you wanted me as much as I wanted you." Kat ran her hands through his damp, ebony hair and kissed him with a gentleness born of understanding. "Yes, Great Eagle, I understand honor. Will you forgive me?"

Chapter Eleven

Deke watched Bess until she reached the wagon. After she climbed in, he picked up his end of the stretcher again. "I guess we'd best move along."

"To my way o' thinkin' Bess is a fair, fine woman."

Nonchalant. "It's crossed my mind a time or two."

"I'm guessin' she's a mite lonely with all the sorrow she's been carryin'."

"What're you getting at, James?"

"I'm surely thinkin' that it's no shame to be carin' about somebody if ye're intentions are honorable."

"I'm not doing a very good job at hiding my feelings these days."

"Aye, ye'd have to be blind not to be noticin'."

"My intentions are honorable, and when the time is right, I plan to let Bess know them."

The friends struggled the rest of the way in solitude, relieved that the rain had stopped. They labored with lessening strength for more than an hour, digging in the saturated earth.

James interrupted the silence and declared, "The hole's lookin' deep enough to me." He wiped his face with his shirt tail. "I don't mind tellin' ye I'm about sick," he complained as he helped Deke wrap the little Larsen girl in the last piece of ducking.

"I feel a bit queasy myself."

Sorrowful and spent, they plodded toward camp. Half-way there, Deke sat down on a boulder and sniffed the air. His intuition was

Wild Kat

usually right, and it was telling him that they were not alone. He shot to his feet and whipped around with the speed of a wild animal.

"Gawdamighty!" he roared.

Dawn was breaking and there was enough light to show the silhouettes of three Indians on horseback. One prodded his pony forward. He was followed by the other two who were leading the Larsen's four horses. Black and vermilion stripes decorated their high cheek bones, except for the one who appeared to be the leader. His entire face was painted yellow, the monotony broken by two wide white streaks across his forehead.

Under his breath. "For gawdsakes! I've had a sneaking suspicion all along that we weren't alone." Hoping that one of them could speak some English, Deke said, "What can we do for you, gents?"

Visibly shaken, James leaned against a tree. He was more than rankled by Deke's insolence. "Be watchin' what ye're sayin'. Ye're tone of voice could be gettin' us killed."

Deke settled down as the Indians maintained their frigid stares. One lazily dismounted by sliding off his horse and extorting Deke's weapon. The Indian tossed it to a brave holding a staff decorated with colorful feathers.

Stiles mopped his face, sniffing the fragrance of mint, and showed no emotion. He prayed that the women and the boys would see the uninvited guests and stay out of sight. Yet it was ridiculous to think that the Indians would overlook the prospect of more plunder by ignoring the wagons.

James shifted his position by the tree trunk and lost his footing in the mud. The action startled Yellow Face. He placed the point of his staff on James's chest and began to speak in fluent English. "It would be unwise to try anything foolish."

"I'll not be thinkin' of it." Bravely, James stared into the redskin's eyes as he slowly raised his hands in the air.

Deke eyed the situation with dwindling hope, itching to reach inside his pants for his gun. As if he had said the words out loud, a rotund savage…short, bowlegged and observant…jumped down from his horse. With a high-pitched cry, he slid his hand under Deke's belt and felt around his waist until he discovered the firearm.

The comedic dwarf, encouraged by the raucous laughter of his companions, chortled and danced. Yellow Face silenced them with one wave of his arm and glared at Deke. "Are you alone?"

"You talk our lingo right well," Deke commented.

"Answer!"

Acid rose in Deke's throat as his eyes became transfixed on an ornament around Yellow Face's neck. He snapped out of it as the Indian addressed him again. "Where are your people?"

"There's nobody left but us. The others died of the fever and we buried them along the way. I can lead you to the place."

As Stiles answered, he gawked at the decoration resting on Yellow Face's chest. Two bloodstained human teeth with crudely bored holes in them dangled obscenely from a leather thong. An image of the youngest Larsen girl, minus her buckteeth, left Deke clammy and sick at heart.

Yellow Face grinned maliciously. "I do not believe you."

When his eyes strayed to the Indian's chest, James squelched a look of horror. "Sure'n we're alone. Like me friend was tellin' ye, it's just him and me."

The explanation seemed to mollify the Indian's curiosity. Yellow face looked first at one, then the other. "You admire my ornament?" he asked as he fingered the human teeth around his neck. "It was a trade from a Pawnee who passed this way."

His two comrades sniggered, but the bowlegged man watched as James's head turned toward the wagons. The dwarf waddled over to the nearest one and investigated. Finding it empty, he dropped the flap and went to the other wagon. After searching it, he ambled back shaking his head.

"You speak the truth, white man. We will leave you now and I will keep your rifle as a gift." Yellow Face laughed and motioned to his followers. "This is a good firearm to show off at the Sun Celebration."

James and Deke exchanged knowing looks, astonished that the Indians would leave them unharmed and their belongings untouched. In guarded silence, they waited.

Suddenly Yellow Face grabbed the lantern beside James's foot. Another insane cry echoed over their heads as he targeted Bess's wagon. It grazed the top with a blaze and plunged to the ground. Using the stolen gun, Yellow Face held it by the barrel and smashed a deadly blow to Deke's temple. The brawny wagon master wore a shocked expression as he keeled over.

James lunged at the Indian and fell backward with a deep knife gash in his forearm. "Kill us and be damned!" he yelled, his hand holding the spurting wound together.

The heathen with the feathered staff straddled him, clutching James's hair, when a shot rang out. And another. The savage's large body slumped over James. The bowlegged Indian lay face down in a puddle of muddy water beside them.

Spooked by the gun shots, the Larsen's stolen horses bolted and galloped away. Taking advantage of the moment, Yellow Face swung himself onto his moving pony's back when the last shot was fired. Bess, carrying James's rifle, walked out of a thick cluster of trees. Callie followed with the boys. They watched the fleeing Indian, blood gushing from his side as he escaped.

Matthew glimpsed the yellow painted face. Darting past Bess, he screamed, "Howling Wolf! Whoooeeeyah! Eeeyah! Eeeyah!"

Yellow Face heard the familiar sound and pulled back on the reins. His horse reared as he nodded recognition and waved his arm in promise. The insidious howl of the wolf echoed from his lips as he bounded away.

Bess scowled at the black, smoking hole in the top of her wagon, grateful that it had been too rain-soaked to burn. She hurried over to Deke and sat down on the sodden ground. Holding him in her arms, she touched the bruised welt at his temple. His eyes were closed, but he was well aware of Bess and where his head rested.

She leaned close to his ear. "Deke, can you hear me? You mean more to me than I've been able to admit. But if you'll stay with me, I'll let you know how I feel."

He opened his eyes and tried to focus on her worried face. "I hear you, Bess girl." Deke took the liberty to brush hair away from her forehead with a twinkle in his watery gray eyes.

Bess hugged him close to her. Deke burrowed against the softness of her bosom. He raised up with reluctance and asked, "Where'd those red devils go?"

"Over here." James pointed to the water's edge. Both Indians lay stretched out on their backs, moccasined feet swaying in the raging river's current.

Frowning, Deke sat up straight. "Where's Yellow Face?"

As she tended James's knife wound, Callie's eyes darted to Matthew. The boy was sitting on a rock looking quite guilty when James said, "Sure'n that devil with the yellow face jumped on his horse and was gone before we knew it."

"Gawdamighty!" Deke's face turned the color of flour. "No telling how many of those painted injuns'll be swarming around us before nightfall."

Bess tried to calm him. "I doubt it, Deke. I shot the heathen in the side. Before he rode out of sight, I saw plenty of blood."

"You don't know Injuns like I do, Bess. They're hard bastards to kill."

Matthew sidled over to Deke. "Mr. Stiles, the one you call Yellow Face is Howling Wolf. He is my father's friend. I signaled him with the cry of our people and he waved his promise to come back. Now I am sorry that I did not wait, as Mother Callie asked me to do. Please don't be angry with me."

"Being sorry won't save the hair on our heads, Matthew. We've got to make some plans, and be quick about it."

Callie draped her arm around the boy. "What're ye meanin' when ye say ye're sorry, me dear?"

"Though I understand my brothers' ways, I could not bear it if something happened to you and Father James, or any of my friends here. I love you all. I should have believed you when you promised to get me back to my family."

"Oh, darlin', never ye mind. We love ye, too. We'll be findin' a way out of this flummox, ye'll see."

* * *

The sun was high when James and Deke reached a decision. Deke informed the women. "James's wagon is beyond repair without the proper tools–and we don't have a chance of making it to Fort Riley with one overloaded wagon. We'll make better time on the horses."

Callie dropped down on the wagon tongue, her face in her hands. James put his arm around her. "Don't be lookin' gloomy, me darlin'. It's the only plan that can be assurin' us a measure of safety."

"That's right," Deke added. "Our plan is to travel under cover of the forest. It'll be hard and slow blazing a trail through the woodland, but a lot safer than traveling in the open." Deke swabbed his face, dreading the rest of his speech. "We'll carry what we can on horseback and leave the rest."

"But Deke, everything we own is in our wagons."

"I know, Bess, but we don't have any choice. The redskins didn't get away with the horses. I'll tie all the belongings I can get on two of them. Bobby can ride on one and I'll ride the other. The Forsythes can do the same with their mounts." He smiled tenderly at Bess. "I want you to ride my bay."

He turned to Forsythe and said, "James, you'd best give Matthew a talking to. We don't want any more signals sent out, no matter what."

Bess forced a smile and began packing. "I'm reconciled, Deke. I ought to know by now that whatever you decide is the right thing to do for all of us."

"I appreciate your confidence, Bess. From now on we'll be traveling in the shelter of the woods, at least until we get within spittin' distance of Fort Riley."

James threw blankets over one of the less lively horses and tightened the girth. He smiled and held out his arms to his wife. "Come along, sweet Callie, it's time to be goin'."

She grabbed a tapestry bag and tied the handles to the strap with a rope. "I'm ready, me dear. I'm findin' it a wee bit hard to be leavin' what we've been collectin' through the years."

Deke stacked quilts on Bobby's nag and secured them with a leather strap. Matthew insisted on riding bareback and wearing his breechcloth. James handed him the pair of overalls that Bess had given him and, without a word, Matthew put them on and rode beside his friend.

Shaking his head, Deke stared at the two pack animals loaded with grain and flour sacks, bags of clothing, bedding and cooking utensils. He mumbled a silent prayer, slipped his work-worn hands under Bess's arms and lifted her onto his sprightly bay mare.

He waved to James, who was sitting on his work horse. "We'd best get moving."

Forsythe nodded and they were off. A motley crew on a perilous journey that sunny day in July as they began to blaze a new trail to Fort Riley, Kansas. Ignorant of the new dangers facing them, they forged their way into the depths of the woodland.

* * *

Wild Kat

Kat and Great Eagle strolled from the pond with a loving glance from time to time, but nothing more. Moments before, at the water's edge, she had covered her nakedness and asked his forgiveness. Kat now joined the chief in exhibiting patience. Until their wedding day.

When the couple came to the main path, she dropped behind him while the curious observed. Weeks ago she would have died rather than give in to such an absurd custom. Great Eagle's stride was long and Kat found herself falling behind.

"I accept this," she breathed heavily, "But my wish is that someday I may walk beside you."

"Speak up, Katherine."

"Never mind!"

He laughed softly, stepping up his pace. "My wild bride."

"What did you say?"

"You heard me."

"I want to hear it again."

Before entering the lodge, he abruptly stopped, turned to face her and gathered her in his arms. They clung together for a time. This alluring, animated young creature would soon be his own. She had such spirit, but he would not break it. It was a part of what he loved about her. He stepped aside and allowed her to enter the teepee first.

Pertly cocking her head, she told him, "You **can** be a gentleman!"

A soft laugh. "According to the white man's way."

Ay-tah greeted Kat and waved Great Eagle away. It was time for him to stay in separate quarters until the wedding day. The chief left expediently.

"Great Eagle is always disappearing. Where's he off to now, Ay-tah?"

"To my lodge. He will sleep there until the wedding night."

*   *   *

Lydia Joe Cates

Katherine stretched languidly and rolled over, feeling lazy and oddly content. Shouts of laughter and friendly chatter outside fed her curiosity as she peeped through the doorway. Excitement replaced prurience as she watched bands of Kiowa tribes drifting in one by one. Some had begun to pitch their teepees in a circle near the pond.

Inside the circle several braves had built a large, open enclosure of upright posts. In the center was one tall forked pole jutting from the ground. Kat knew what the structure was…an arena for a ritual of torture.

Tribal boys, fifteen and older, would participate in the ritual. If they passed the test, they would be proven men. It was one of the main aspects of the Sun Ceremony. Oddly, Kat had no qualms about watching the rite if she was called upon to do so.

Great Eagle had explained to Kat that the young men fasted and painted their entire bodies the day before the ceremony. After the color was applied, they danced from sunup to sundown, always facing the sun, in preparation for the next day's trial. When the sun rose the following morning, the older braves, having been through this rite, prepared the boys for their test by slicing four slits in their chest, two on each side. A leather thong was threaded through the slits and attached to the pole. The young men would hang there until sundown. At intervals during the day, a member of the family, a sweetheart or a friend were allowed to bring water to soak their parched lips and face. Some were blinded by the sun or, at the very least, scorched their eyeballs. At sunset, each boy would set himself free by tearing their chest skin from the leather thongs. The strongest would survive.

Kat pushed the horror story out of her mind and closed the flap of the lodge. She pulled a cedar box into the firelight. Great Eagle had made the chest for Ay-tah; however, the Indian woman presented it to Katherine as a gift in honor of learning to speak the Kiowa dialect so expertly.

Wild Kat

Stored inside the cedar container was a loose-fitting chemise sewn from deer skins which had been dyed a dark red color. Her future mother-in-law knew that it would be perfect for the evening feast and ceremonial dance. Kat slithered into it slowly, allowing the satiny texture to stroke her skin.

"Katherine like. Oh yes, Katherine like very much." She brushed her hair until it shimmered and permitted it to fall naturally, tying a dark red leather thong around her forehead. Kat retrieved yet another treasure from the chest. With a sliver of an old mirror she had found buried in the foothills, Kat surveyed herself a portion at a time. Pacified, she stored the fragment in her chest, thrilled with her new way of life. She wanted no other.

Hot coals smoldered under a crock of warm mush prepared by Ay-tah before leaving to fulfill her duties. As the chief's mother, she would serve as the official greeter. Kat could not eat. She could not wait to join the throng of new arrivals and to help with final preparations.

Leaving the lodge, she could see a constant stream of people. Some rode alongside the painted and befeathered young braves who would undergo the ritual of torture. Those on foot paused to greet old friends and relatives. The scene brought back childhood memories of a circus, without the usual nostalgia.

Above the blatant laughter and demented beat of the tom-toms her primitive side awakened, never to sleep again. This was her home and these were her people.

"Good morning, Redbird. You wake with the rooster."

"Good morning, Indian Mother." Kat spoke only dialect now. English had become too cumbersome for her tongue.

Kat and Ay-tah stood together observing yet another arrival. Kat noticed a lone straggler slumped over his horse's neck as the animal wandered at the fringe of the crowd. A cloud passed over Ay-tah's face. "Howling Wolf has come home alone."

Kat did not hear her. She became numb as she gaped in wide-eyed disbelief at a gaudily painted, potbellied Kiowa astride an Appaloosa. A lead rope in his hand was tied around a blonde woman's neck. She followed at a listless pace.

"Josie!" Katherine screamed. Before Ay-tah could stop her she was gone, rushing like the wind to meet the fiddler's wife.

Ay-tah matched a gazelle's grace as she ran after Kat, pleading with her. "Wait, Redbird! This is not our way." She was too late. Kat threw her arms around Josie and began to weep.

"Josie, don't you know me? It's Katherine Stone. From the wagon train."

The fiddler's wife stared straight ahead in a catatonic state. The sloppy Indian's belly jiggled as he slid off of his horse and jerked Kat away from the woman. Kat recognized him, even without his war paint, as the one who had taken Josie in the raid on the wagon train.

"My woman. Stay away," he grunted.

"She's my friend. Where's her little girl?" Stricken with panic, Kat saw that Josie's stomach was flat. "Where's her baby?" she screeched.

The fiddler's wife looked at Kat and spoke only once. "My children are dead and so am I."

Kat gasped as Ay-tah walked to her side. Composed, she disrupted the confrontation.

Dark Cloud scowled his disapproval. "Get rid of her, Ay-tah, before she annoys me further."

"You must forgive Redbird. She has not yet become acquainted with all of our customs, Dark Cloud. She meant no harm."

The Indian shot Kat a monstrous look. His eyes became two burning coals plugged with hate as they arrowed through her. "If she was not Great Eagle's chosen one…" he stopped and led Josie away.

Tears rolled down Kat's cheeks as she followed Dark Cloud, still begging to talk to Josie. Ay-tah caught up with her and gripped an arm with astounding strength. "Do not make more of a spectacle of yourself. You will shame Great Eagle before his friends. Cease your wailing, Katherine Stone!"

"Ay-tah! Please! Dark Cloud is a murderer."

"Go back to the lodge and wait for me there. I must go to Howling Wolf."

"Josie needs our help, Ay-tah. Surely you can see that."

"Do as I say, child. I will help you, but now is not the time." The Indian woman rushed to join two men who were attending the injured brave. "Bring Howling Wolf to my son's lodge."

Upon entering the teepee Ay-tah went to the fire pit, dusted the ashes away from the coals and balanced a crock of water on top of them. After examining Howling Wolf's wound, she was certain that he had lost too much blood to live.

The brave wallowed on the bed fitfully between two worlds. It seemed to the Indian woman that he was struggling to reach the surface of his delirium. He was trying to tell her something. "Do not try to talk, young son. Save your strength."

He ranted in agony. "Sleepi…Sle…Ra…"

"Yes. Sleep now," she crooned softly.

Ay-tah was so intent on removing the bullet lodged in the brave's side that she paid little heed to his ravings. She probed the wound with a long willow prong. Among torn muscle and tissue, she hit something solid. Grateful that Howling Wolf sank into nothingness, she chose tweezers made from animal bone and dug deeply to retrieve the bullet. When she tossed the piece of lead into a wooden bowl, the clattering sound arrested Kat's attention from across the room.

Ashamed of her earlier outburst, Kat lit a buffalo candle to shed more light on the wound. "Indian Mother, will you forgive me for ignoring your wisdom?"

Lydia Joe Cates

"All is forgiven, Redbird. Dark Cloud is a threat wherever he goes. We will accomplish more by waiting until after the feast, when he sleeps from a full stomach."

Kat planted herself beside Ay-tah and watched her smear a foul-smelling salve around the gaping hole before she bound the brave's side tightly with doeskin. Katherine began to make some sense out of Howling Wolf's ramblings. Panic engulfed her. "Do you think he will live?"

"I do not think that he will see another sunrise." Ay-tah continued to bathe his face until the last of the yellow paint was gone. "He's shaking with chills from the fever. Fetch a robe and cover him, Redbird."

Kat spread a blanket over him and sat by his side while Ay-tah disposed of his bloody buckskins. Howling Wolf began jabbering again. She leaned close.

My chief…am dying."

As the Indian woman entered the lodge, Kat informed her, "He is asking for Great Eagle."

Ay-tah bent over the ailing man and urged him to speak. "Tell me, my other son. I will take your message to our chief."

In a painful voice he whispered, "East of our… Sleepi…"

"I know you are sleepy. Rest for now." She turned to Kat. "Stay with him while I try to find Great Eagle."

Kat sat on a low stool beside the doomed man. His breathing had become more labored and shallow. Without warning, his eyes popped open, glistening with lucidity. "Found Sleeping Rabbit. Promised to go back for him." He sneered, "Your people have him, Flaming Hair."

Kat shrank from his wrath, but had enough courage to push him back on the bed. "Be quiet. I will tell your chief." With a blanched countenance, she moved away from the dying man.

Great Eagle entered the lodge minutes later. His face darkened when he saw that his friend was floating away on a fevered sea. Kat stood beside the chief, petrified that Howling Wolf would mention Sleeping Rabbit again. Her fear was well-founded.

As they waited, the dying man opened his eyes and stared at the familiar face of his chief. "Sleeping, promise. Sleepi…"

Great Eagle shook his head slowly, his sorrow apparent. "Yes, my brother, sleep." He turned to Kat. "I must prepare for the dance ceremony. It is my duty."

She followed him outside. For a brief moment she forgot Howling Wolf, as well as her fears, watching her love disappear into the throng. Again, she was burdened with guilt. She wondered where the Indian had seen Sleeping Rabbit. Had the three braves run upon the wagon train? Maybe they had attacked it. She pushed the repugnant thought out of her mind when Ay-tah beckoned to her from one of the cooking pits.

"Come, Redbird, the dancing will soon begin. I will go to Howling Wolf before I join you."

Warm and gentle winds rustled Kat's hair as she sat silently. Some eyed her curiously, while others pointed in her direction and smiled. She continued to search the mass for Great Eagle, but all the young men's identities were erased by colorful ceremonial paint. The disguises were innovative, not in the least as hideous as she had imagined.

Kat conversed with those who approached and took pride in speaking their tongue. Ay-tah appeared and held out a long bark tray. "Take a bit of each delicacy, daughter. Your palate is in for a treat. There are foods here that you have never tasted before."

Kat heaped her plate high with rattlesnake steak, venison, buffalo and golden potatoes, crisp on the outside and tender on the inside. Her mouth watered as she scooped up a corn cake sweetened with wild honey and a pod of acorn squash. Other choices were passed by for lack of room on her platter.

Ay-tah scanned her plate and laughed delightedly. "Come, we will sit in the designated area of the large circle."

Lydia Joe Cates

They sat on the ground near a huge campfire. After their meal, the Indian woman began to sway in time to the beat of the drums. Fascinated, Kat watched her. The rhythm showered her soul with a firestorm as she found herself mimicking her Indian Mother.

An exotic, trilling sound from eagle bone whistles shrilled and quieted the crowd. Seven young braves, led by Great Eagle, glided into the circle wearing nothing but their breechcloths. Their bodies and faces were painted with their own original designs.

Kat's demeanor beckoned to Great Eagle. He stood apart from the rest and her heart swelled with pride. When she caught his eye, the only sign of recognition was a sensuous half-smile. The red and black streaks across his cheeks were modest in comparison to the others. His forehead bore the symbol of a white star haloed in the same colors which adorned his face. A large white star embellished his chest.

The dance itself was creative but simple. Dancers merely rose on their toes in time to the blowing of the eagle bone whistles. Kat could not keep her eyes off of her future husband. Although she tried to take an interest in the others, it vanished when she witnessed the chief's long, sinewy legs moving sensually in time to the music.

Drums resonated louder, touching her subconscious and releasing latent, wanton emotions. She leaned over to Ay-tah and whispered in her ear. "Do they wear anything under those flaps?"

Ay-tah threw back her head in melodious laughter. "So you wonder, do you, Redbird? Yes, they do; it is something like your monthly sling."

Cry Woman's inquisitive nature was piqued by the whispering. The fleshy hag waddled over to them and inappropriately wedged herself between Kat and Ay-tah.

"You too little to be so strong. Scoot!" Cry Woman told Kat.

Kat wrinkled her nose in disgust, focused her attention on the dancers and spoke without looking at the squaw. "If you insist on sitting with us, then try to act like a lady."

Wild Kat

Cry Woman ignored her. "I bet you turn pink all over when you dance with chief."

"I've never danced with him, and furthermore, I don't know any of your Indian dances."

The squaw pushed on. "Wait and see."

Kat turned away and viewed the large audience. A stocky man with transparent blue eyes and a black beard sat among the honored Kiowas. He wore a bright red shirt and a black hat with colorful feathers in the band. Katherine had never seen him before, but decided that he must be of some importance to be sitting among the chiefs. Not long ago it would have given her hope to see a white man in camp. Now, it made no difference.

Ay-tah noticed Kat staring at the short gentleman. "After the dance, Redbird, I will introduce you to our friend, Trader Charley Bone."

"I'd like to meet the jolly little fellow," she acknowledged laughingly, when a new phase of the performance demanded her attention.

One by one each brave dropped out of line. He danced around the circle and stopped when he came to the maiden of his choice. He rose and fell on the balls of his feet with the rhythm while his fingers motioned to her. The routine was repeated until all the young women were taken and Great Eagle stood alone.

The chief began to dance, pausing every three or four steps. His scintillating carbon eyes roamed the audience, the calculated gaze of the hunter.

Cry Woman nudged Kat and pointed a chubby finger at Great Eagle. "He looking for pretty wife. See. He go to Laughing Eyes."

Kat watched closely as he lingered in front of a strikingly beautiful girl. The chief began to sway slowly and provocatively before her. When she reached out to him, he dodged the touch and danced to the next one. Great Eagle duplicated the charade until he came to Katherine.

Sensing her bewilderment, Ay-tah leaned across Cry Woman to instruct Kat. "This is the Betrothal Dance. It will tell our people who our chief chooses for his bride. Follow his motions."

Kat's forehead convoluted. "I don't know what to do, Indian Mother. What if I shame him before all these people?"

Ay-tah's warm expression eased Kat's tension. "Do as I say, Redbird. He will lead you well."

Great Eagle hunched down low, his torso swinging with the grace of an oak branch. Holding out his arms to Katherine, his fingers lured her to him.

Sitting cross-legged, consciously undulating her upper body, she took his hands and permitted him to lift her to her feet. He stood erect, pointed downward and rose upon the balls of his feet and toes again. His glint reassured her as he lowered his voice intimately.

"Walk my path, Tanguadal."

The feeling was exhilarating as the couple sailed around the campfire in perfect harmony, close enough to feel one's breath. They were absorbed in each other rather than the growing interest circulating among the horde.

A hair's breadth separated them. Eyes locked. Writhing rhythmically to the beat of the drums, Kat embraced her destiny. Gracefully, the chief spread his arms as though they were wings and began to undulate his lower torso slowly. Erotically. As if he had smoked a pipe of opium, he was drugged by her sensuality and chanted, "Show me your wild side, Wild Kat."

The compelling expression in his eyes and the warmth of his smile gave her the confidence she needed. Skin blushing hotly, Kat yielded to the dance. Although the flames of the bonfire licked out at her, she was oblivious of the heat as it sucked her deeper into a whirlpool of primitive desire.

Wild Kat

Perspiration shimmered on her forehead and trickled down her thighs as she pursued him with agile charm. Great Eagle's sepia body, glistening with oil, gyrated with hers. His arms raised and lowered, giving the illusion of gigantic wings brushing her hair ever so gently.

His erotic motion removed the last of her inhibitions. Their bodies grazed one another and the whisper of each touch magnified their cravings. The spark that had ignited them since the betrothal music began was ready to burst into flames. The chief's fiery gaze narrowed with passion. The muscles in his immense shoulders thrashed and knotted with anticipation as he became more conscious of her burgeoning desire. Kat dared to go farther. Swaying against his glimmering form, she matched his rhythm and began moving her lower torso with his.

Great Eagle's countenance was radiant when he summoned the end of the dance. He smiled down at her, dropped his arms and flattened his feet on the ground as a signal that the exhibition was over. They stood alone in the circle. Not a sound was uttered as the throng waited. With great fanfare Great Eagle swept Katherine into a close embrace and sealed the betrothal promise with a kiss.

Kat clung to him, vibrating from the powerful display that had taken over her mind, body and soul. The love Great Eagle had just professed for all the village to see was returned by the woman he had chosen. While their lips still touched he whispered, "You have become a woman, Tanguadal, but you will always be my Wild Kat."

"And you are my Indian, the great Great Eagle," she offered, tearing a resonant, delighted laugh from the cavern of his chest.

The older men in the crowd grunted and nodded their approval as Great Eagle raised his arm and sphered his hand into a fist as a salute to them. Wildly hammering tom-toms and music began again as the younger boys charged into the circle to offer themselves to the Sun Spirit. Their garishly painted bodies began the dance that would last until midnight. At first light they would undergo the torture.

Great Eagle held hard to Kat's hand as they strolled among the crowd of well-wishers. Ansote stood alone and waited for the couple. Great Eagle placed his hands on the old man's shoulders. "You were not in the circle, my friend."

"I have been with Howling Wolf. He is dying, my son."

Cursed with dread by the time they reached the lodge, Kat shrank from the sound of the frenzied man's voice. "He's suffering. Don't you have medicine that will ease his pain?" she asked Great Eagle.

"Yes, Tanguadal, Ansote has something to end his misery." In anguish, he turned to Ansote. "He is in your hands now, Second Father."

The old man left and returned shortly with a bag of rank-smelling roots. He tore several into bits and parted Howling Wolf's lips, placing the herb springs under his tongue. Only a minute or so passed before the drug began to take effect. The brave soon ceased his raving and lapsed into eternal sleep.

Great Eagle and Ansote carried Howling Wolf's corpse to a teepee set apart from the others…the death hut. Ansote broke the silence. "When the Sun Ceremony has come to an end, I will take our brother to the burial ground so that our people may honor him."

* * *

Katherine shed her sweaty dress, filled a basin with water and proceeded to bathe herself. Anxious about Josie, she reminded Ay-tah of her promise concerning the fiddler's wife. "The feast is over, Indian Mother. Will you take me to Josie?"

"I must find Dark Cloud first. Maybe his gluttony has lulled him to sleep by now."

Kat slipped on a shift and began to brush her hair when she heard a disturbance outside. The noise was drifting in from the guest camp near the pond. She peered through the open doorway and saw Great Eagle sprint by. Kat tossed the brush on the bed and ran after him.

"Wait! I want to go with you."

The chief halted, obviously disgruntled by the delay, and shook his head. "No, Katherine, there may be trouble."

"I can take care of myself," she argued.

Great Eagle whirled around. "Obey me! I sense an ill wind."

"Obey! That's a helluva thing to say after such an ecstatic evening. I hate the damn word!"

"Your swearing is tiresome, Katherine. Stay here."

Kat flopped down at the entrance of the lodge, sulking. Ay-tah appeared on the path in front of her. "I cannot find Dark Cloud."

"Josie needs me…I've got to see her, Indian Mother." Kat edged toward the pond. Torches had been erected along the pathways. Their flaming luminescence shed light on a group of people following the chief.

"Great Eagle is coming back." Kat squinted. "He's carrying a bundle or something."

Ay-tah shook her head as her son drew nearer. "His burden is a woman."

Blonde hair dripping with pond water plastered the head of the girl he held. The ghostly, bluish tinge of her scantily clad form told Kat that Josie was out of her misery.

"Where is Dark Cloud?" Ay-tah asked her son.

"He packed his belongings during the Love Dance and departed," Great Eagle answered crisply.

Kat wept bitterly as she walked alongside the chief. "She's better off dead. Dark Cloud is a murderer. If I were a man I'd go after him!"

"We will never see him again, Katherine. Dark Cloud left without knowing about your friend. He is suffering from a fatal disease and asked me to take care of Josie."

Great Eagle carried the dead woman inside the lodge. After laying her on the couch, Kat fell across the lifeless body sobbing. Spasms shook her slender frame as she stood and faced him, reverting to English.

"How could this happen?" Anger and confusion. "Leave. Me. Alone!"

Great Eagle picked up the fiddler's wife and said, "I will bury your friend in the white man's tradition."

*   *   *

It was the second day of the Sun Ceremony. Katherine could not bring herself to take part in any of the activities. Ay-tah strongly urged her to join Great Eagle, but Kat refused to leave the lodge. She was caught in a web of despair. Merrymaking and crude laughter rang in her ears along with regrettable mumblings about the two boys who did not survive the torture.

On the third and last day of the celebration Great Eagle arrived at the lodge early. He chose to overlook Kat's rude behavior. Even though she had disappointed him by not attending the second day's festivities, he was resigned. He had learned to compromise with his future wife in a way that his brothers could never accept or understand.

"This is our wedding day, Tanguadal. My mother will help you make ready."

Sullen. "There'll be no wedding, Indian."

He spoke slowly, enunciating each word. "There **will** be a wedding. When the sun is high, I will come for you." He turned to Ay-tah. "Make sure that she is ready."

Kat's nostrils flared as mother and son left the lodge. Ay-tah returned a short time later with an armful of wildflowers. She had gathered mauve columbine and white daisies for the bridal band.

"It is a fine day for your marriage, Redbird."

"I will not marry Great Eagle."

Wild Kat

Ay-tah, in her own inimitable way, quietly laid out the snow white doeskin blouse, skirt and moccasins. Tiny silver bells on the white leggings jangled when the Indian woman held them up for Kat's approval.

"They ring for you, daughter, as they did for me. By the time you finish dressing I will have your wedding crown ready."

Ay-tah's heart ached for Kat. She understood that the girl was torn between her deep love for Great Eagle and the Kiowa people, and her loyalty to Josie and the white man. "Sorrow passes with time, Redbird. You will be stronger when it fades."

With silent admiration, Kat watched Ay-tah's deft fingers weave the colorful flowers around the headband made from the delicate vines of blackberries. She remained fascinated by the woman's boundless patience and endless skills.

"Come, my daughter with hair of flame and laughing eyes the same."

A downy laugh escaped her lips as Kat proffered, "So you are a poet too."

Ay-tah laughed outright. The feminine equation of Great Eagle's rich voice lifted Kat's heart.

"You are a wise woman, Indian Mother. I love you."

"I love you, Redbird." With a less burdened soul, she unbound Kat's braids and brushed her hair until it gleamed like burnished copper.

Kat relaxed and admitted that she had been acting like a child again. Her love for Great Eagle had not changed; it had grown to such proportions that it was now rooted in her soul. With that revelation, she began to prepare herself for the marriage rites.

She dressed carefully in her wedding attire and openly admired herself in front of the full-length mirror that Great Eagle had salvaged from one of his raids. He had given it to her as one of her wedding presents. As she preened and paraded before it, she silently commended him on his choice of contraband.

Ay-tah was breathless, as she knew her son would be when he saw Katherine in her bridal dress. "It seems that my son has never been in love before."

"Nor I, Indian Mother."

Great Eagle stood in the doorway of the lodge unobserved while listening to the two women he loved most in the world. Kat's loveliness deluged him with joyous anticipation. He was consoled that his Wild Kat had tamed down enough to unite with him on their wedding day.

"Is this vision my bride?"

Ay-tah dabbed at her eyes. "Yes, my fortunate son. Now I must go. I will wait for you at the Council Lodge."

Kat's heart began its demonic pounding as Great Eagle took her hands in his. How handsome he appeared to her at the moment. His eyes were two black pearls shimmering in the early morning sun. She was speechless.

Chapter Twelve

Blazing a trail through growth as thick and foreign as a jungle was no easy task. Almost impossible with the lack of adequate tools. James stopped and wiped his face on the sleeve of his shirt. "I don't mind tellin' ye that I'm beginnin' to wonder if Fort Riley is a myth."

Deke slapped his sluggish nag's backside. "Take my word for it, James boy, it's there." He nudged the work horse's sides with his heels. "Giddyup, you danged flea bag," he grumbled and wiped a gnat from the corner of his eye.

"Bugs bothering you again?" Bess asked.

"Hell, yes! And a few other things too." Instantly contrite. "Sorry, Bess, I guess I'm just out of sorts."

"No need to apologize. We're all tired and edgy from scratching through this mess. It sure would be nice if we could stop for a while. I'm craving a good strong cup of coffee."

Her fatigued expression melted his resolve momentarily, but he knew that they had to keep going. Riding beside him, Bess patted his arm with a sigh. "Don't worry, Deke, I understand. I know we have to keep going until sundown."

They rode along in silence until the sun disappeared behind the horizon and blanketed the woods in darkness. The women were relieved when they stopped for the night.

James lumbered down from his nag, stretched his arms and flexed his shoulders. "Sure'n I'm glad to be stoppin'. I'll be diggin' a fire hole while

Lydia Joe Cates

Matthew and Bobby are workin' off some of their meanness roundin' up wood."

He was massaging his hips and backside when Callie crept up behind him. "I see ye're pattin' yer tush like when I'm kneadin' dough, James Forsythe. Maybe ye'd do well to be takin' some o' this paddin' o' mine." Callie laughed and smacked his backside.

James pulled her to him and said in a low voice, "I'm likin' the paddin' where 'tis, and I don't mind tellin' ye 'tis a little tirin' to be sleepin' with so many people around. I'm surely missin'…ye know damn well what I'm missin'."

"Just be rememberin', me dear, it'll be sweeter'n ever when there's no longer a full moon."

* * *

James took his turn at watering the horses and tethering them to graze. Deke untied the water containers from the animals and had started toward the river when Bess called to him.

"Wait, Deke, I'll walk with you." She was swinging two empty syrup buckets. "I dug these out of the food bag. They have lids and we can carry them for extra water." She was smiling as if the sun were shining."

Deke thought how gawdawful pretty she looked and wondered how much longer he would be able to last without her. Long months on the trail had never bothered him much. Once he reached a town, a romp in one of the bawdy houses held him until the next stop. That is, until now.

"There you go grinning like a satisfied tomcat again."

"I'm not in the mood for jokes, Bess." He pushed up the sleeves of his buckskin shirt and knelt to fill the water cans.

"I can tell you don't feel chipper, Deke. It's been working on you for the past two days. You got a bellyache?"

"Hell, no! It's not my belly that's aching."

Wild Kat

Bess recognized the signs of a man in need and dropped the subject. "I'd better see what the kids are doing."

"Bess, I-I'm sorry."

"Shush. We've got a long way to go, Deke. Save your apologies." She walked away with a heavy thought. By the time Bess got back to camp, she had reached a decision.

*   *   *

That evening everyone settled around the glowing embers as Callie told the boys their nightly ghost story. Deke interrupted, "I'm tuckered out. Since I've got second watch tonight, I'd best turn in."

James stretched. "I'll be takin' a catnap 'til it's lights out," he said, looking wistfully at his wife. "I'm not in the mood to be lettin' ye scare me witless tonight, sweet Callie."

"Shame on ye, me dear, but go on. I'll be wakin' ye when I come to bed."

The firelight stained her fair complexion. Slightly concerned, James stooped down and touched her forehead. "Ye're showin' a wee bit more color than usual. Are ye feelin' well, Callie?"

"Aye, me dear. Stop fussin' over me, I've been sittin' too near the fire." She told a fast tale, nonetheless spine-chilling, before she tucked the boys into bed. "Ye be goin' right to sleep, me dears, and I'll be thinkin' up a better story fer tomorrow night."

Giggling, the children settled down and closed their eyes. A shaft of moonlight fought its way into the tops of the trees as Callie sat down on a log beside Bess.

"Without seemin' to pry, Bess, could that frown ye're wearin' be havin' somethin' to do with Deke Stiles?"

"That it does, Callie. I think you know what's been on my mind and, well, I'm good and ready to do something that'd cause a scandal back home."

"And I'm sayin' go to it. There's nothin' more satisfyin' than a bit o' spice to liven things up." She squeezed Bess's hand. "I've seen it comin' ever since we left our wagons and took to the woods. Deke is a lovin' man and he needs a lovin' woman. Goodnight, me lovin' dear."

Bess sat on the log a while longer, tapping her fingers on her knees. After due consideration, she stood up and sauntered over to the boys' beds. Comfortable that they were asleep, she threw dirt on the fire and slipped across the camp. The moon had just disappeared behind a conglomerate of clouds. She knew exactly where Deke was and found him without a bobble. Sitting down on the edge of his bed roll she whispered, "Deke. You asleep?" As she scooted her backside against him, he tensed.

"Gawdamighty! I'm awake. What's gotten into you, Bess?" His brawny frame calcified. Deke grabbed for the gun under his saddle which was doubling as a pillow. "Did something scare you?"

She pushed him back down. "Goodness, no! I couldn't sleep. After the wind came up I got a little chilled." It was then that she felt the heat of his need, stirring her in a way that she thought was past reviving.

His low voice grated like sand on a smooth plank floor. "If you're cold maybe I'd best get up and build another fire."

"I could build my own fire if I wanted one." Her voice was so low and intimate that he could not mistake what she had in mind. "All I'm saying is that my heart could stand a little warming."

Deke held his breath until he was weak and let it go in one long sigh. Throat constricted, he swallowed hard as he lifted the corner of his bed roll for her. She slid in and felt the bunched up muscles in his rugged body tremble as he gathered her into his arms and kissed her. The kiss lapped his aching frame with the force of an ocean breaker.

Gathering her closer, his big, clumsy hands began to caress the beauties of her body that he never expected to see, much less touch. All this was done with the utmost gentleness. As ready as the cocked hammer of his shotgun, Deke hovered over her and prayed, for her sake, that he would last long enough.

She clutched his shoulders and silently screamed with joy as their passions rose and finally flowed. In a muffled tone Bess said, "I never imagined I'd feel like a girl again. But I do and I don't want it to end."

Deke hugged her and murmured, "You're my girl now, Bess, honey. I promise it won't ever end, not if I have anything to do with it."

*   *   *

Bess was settling down in her own bed near midnight when the horses began to whinny and stamp restlessly. An owl hooted from a nearby tree. Hearing a branch snap, she called out softly, "Deke?"

"It's James and me. We've got a visitor with us." The two men appeared, leading another man on horseback.

"I can see who's leadin', but I'd like to be knowin' who's ridin'," Callie chirped.

"Charley Bone at your service," the jovial voice rumbled.

Deke dropped the horse's reins. "You're free to get down, Mr. Bone, and tell us what you're doing here."

"I'm a trader by profession, sir." The short, black-bearded man wore a hat with colorful feathers stuck in the band and a red sacking shirt tucked into tan leather riding breeches. "I'm heading for my home in Leavenworth."

"Where're ye comin' from?" James asked.

"Bolton, Colorado, sir. I've been on the trail for weeks, except for a stop at Fort Riley and again at the Kiowa village of Chief Great Eagle."

Deke's eyebrows shot up. "This Great Eagle, he a friend of yours?"

"You can bet a bag of gold on it. I was sure sorry to hear the bad news about his boy."

"Bad news?" Deke queried.

"Afraid so. The young fellow's missing, could be dead."

"Too bad. Injuns have a knack of finding their way home. Maybe he'll turn up one of these days." Nervous sweat broke out on Deke's forehead as he thought about Great Eagle's son lying a few feet away from them.

Charley Bone spoke up in a raucous tone. "How 'bout building a fire? I've got some coffee beans and some prime whiskey to sweeten the taste."

"We've been doin' without a fire in the late evenin' in case there's redskins about." James grinned broadly and added, "But 'tisn't meanin' we can't be sharin' the spirits with ye. It has its own sweet fire."

Charley slapped his knees with gusto. "And you're welcome to it, sir, but there isn't an Indian within miles of here. You can take my word for it. They're all celebrating the Sun Spirit. I left Great Eagle's village after the first feast two days ago. He's getting married today to another white woman. His other one died a few years back."

"If Mr. Great Eagle is such a treasured friend, why didn't ye stay for the weddin', Mr. Bone?"

"Well now, Missus…"

"Forsythe, sir."

"Well now, Missus Forsythe, I wasn't invited." His infectious laugh rang out and Callie joined him in spite of herself.

Tensions eased and James built a small fire. Bess filled the coffee pot with water while the others gathered around to watch Trader Bone grind the beans. The children continued to sleep. Deke hoped that they were far enough away not to be disturbed by the commotion.

In a short while Bess announced, "Coffee's ready."

Callie filled the tin cups while conversing with the trader. "Ye're sayin' this Indian is takin' a white woman fer his wife?"

"Sure enough. He's getting hitched at high noon." Charley had their full attention and, being a bit of a showman, he proceeded to tell them, in detail, about his stay at the Kiowa village.

Wild Kat

"When I arrived Great Eagle insisted that I stay for the first day of feasting. Well, I tell you, I ate enough to see me back to Bolton." Laughing, he took a swallow of whiskey-laced coffee and continued.

"Great Eagle's bride is the prettiest young thing I've ever seen. Why, I was privileged when the chief allowed me to stay and watch them do the Love Dance. The sight was enough to get a dead man lathered up." He chortled gaily. "I'm not saying it affected me, but I'm sure looking forward to seeing my Myrtle again."

The affable little man had begun to feel the dulling effects of the whiskey when Deke asked, "What did the girl look like, Mr. Bone?"

"Like I said, she's a beauty," he slurred. "Not more than eighteen and hair the color of those dark red coals in the fire. About like yours, Missus Stiles. I traded the chief one of my last good pieces of jewelry for her wedding present.

Bess felt sick. The information Charley had just shared with them was a ghastly revelation. She did not bother to correct the man when he called her Missus Stiles. Her mind was too crowded with thoughts of her daughter. It **had** to be Katherine. Dizzy, Bess said, "I hope you'll forgive my bad manners, Mr. Bone, but I haven't been well and I need my rest."

Deke walked over to her and placed an arm around her waist. "I'll just tuck my wife in bed and sit with her for a spell."

"Hope you feel better in the morning, Missus Stiles. It's been a hoot chatting with you."

Leaning against the trunk of a large tree, Charley closed his eyes. Mouth gaping, a soft snore rose from the depths of his peaceful stupor.

When they were sure that he was sleeping soundly, James and Deke searched Charley's personal belongings for proof that would verify the trader's story. They found it. He was indeed a trader with very little merchandise left in his pack.

* * *

Lydia Joe Cates

Deke awakened before daylight and slipped over to Bess's pallet. "Are you awake, honey?"

"I haven't been asleep. The way Mr. Bone talked, it sounds like Katherine is getting married willingly."

"Yeah, it does. If everything Charley told us is true, she'll be a married woman in a few hours."

Bess began to weep. "Married to a savage."

Deke's hand closed over hers. "We'll find a way to get her back, Bess."

Her expression was one of hope. "When we get to Fort Riley, maybe the commander will be able to talk to Great Eagle; maybe even exchange Matthew for Katherine." Bess's guilt was apparent as she thought about Callie and her love for the boy.

Deke sighed, figuring that their chances were, at best, remote.

Charley Bone drained his coffee cup, thanked them and saddled up. The sun had risen high enough to brighten the sheen of Bess's hair. As they said good-bye, Trader Bone exclaimed loudly, "I tell you, Missus Stiles, you're the spittin' image of Great Eagle's bride. Your hair shines like a bonfire."

Bess smiled. "A lot of people have hair the color of mine, Mr. Bone."

"Maybe so. I'll tell you one thing, I've seen more redheads this past month than most people do in a lifetime. I saw one young fellow at Fort Riley with a thatch the hue of the setting sun."

Bess perked up and strengthened her grip on Deke's arm. "You told us that the boy was young. How old would you say he was, Mr. Bone?"

"In his twenties I'd guess, and you couldn't put a pin head where there wasn't a freckle. Well, folks, I thank you for your hospitality. Hope to run into you again sometime."

With that, Trader Charley Bone waved his befeathered hat and trotted off in the opposite direction from which he had come.

"Todd and Katherine are alive, Deke! I'm sure of it."

Wild Kat

Matthew was not asleep. Callie, who had instructions to keep the boys out of sight, noticed his atypical behavior and called to him as she packed. "Matthew, I could be usin' some manly help, me dear."

The boy came immediately and, as he helped with the packing, he offered, "I know the man, Charley Bone."

Callie cocked her head to one side. "How come ye're knowin' that jolly little man?"

"I have talked with him many times. He is one of my father's friends."

"And ye didn't see fit to expose us?"

Matthew eyed her seriously. "You made me a promise, Mother Callie. I saw no reason to put you and the others in danger."

She looked away and stuffed the last of the bedding into a flour sack. "It'll be tearin' me heart out when the time comes fer us to be partin', but ye're right, Matthew; I made ye a promise and I'm plannin' on keepin' it."

Deke avoided Bess's glances by filling the fire hole with dirt and sweeping up their tracks with a small tree branch. He did not want to embarrass her by being openly affectionate. He was not sure how she felt about last night in the brightness of day. A mixture of sweet memories scrambled his brain as he helped Bess mount. She nudged him in the chest with the toe of her boot; he looked up and smiled at her.

"I just want you to know that I'm not sorry for what happened last night, Deke Stiles. It was pure joy for me. The only ones we have to answer to are you, me and God. As far as I'm concerned, we're all in agreement."

Deke's limpid gray eyes caressed her with a loving touch. "I was hoping you still felt the same as me."

"You can bet your Sunday boots on it." Bess waved at the others. "Let's get on to Fort Riley. I'm getting itchier by the minute."

He rode past her and tipped his hat. "That's just what we're going to do, Missus Stiles," he joked. His cheery laughter split the air as the weary pilgrimage proceeded once again.

*   *   *

Kat's lips had been tinted with wild strawberries and the tangy sweetness was still on his tongue. The glint in Great Eagle's eyes contradicted his solemn tone.

"I have come for the woman Katherine Stone."

"I am that woman." She flirted as she told him, "You are the most beautiful man I've ever seen."

He chuckled and kissed the palms of her hands. "Beautiful? I do not believe that is the right word, Tanguadal."

Katherine was mesmerized by his handsomeness and allowed her imagination to take her places that she had not been before. The chief wore his finest attire–a white buckskin shirt and breeches edged with long fringe. Porcupine quills and intricate beading adorned the front of his shirt as well as the top of his white moccasins.

Kat reached up and touched his shining hair, which was seasoned with a pleasing scent. It was drawn back to accommodate the customary headdress of a tribal chief. White feathers, bleached for hours in the sun and spruced smooth with care, gleamed with the fluorescence of marshfire.

Kat's soft voice sounded timid as her hands glided over his shoulders. "I love you."

"You are my love, my only one."

He struggled to control the raging inferno inside of him and whispered as his lips moved against her cheek. "I am helpless with only your kiss. Do you know that you hold such power over me?"

Katherine knew, but she did not consider it a triumph. It was clearly a gift from the man she had come to revere.

Great Eagle led Kat outside. "It is time to say our marriage vows at the Council Lodge. Come, Tanguadal, the others are waiting. After the rites we will go to the wedding feast and after that…" His white teeth gleamed as he smiled openly at her. "Our wait is at an end."

* * *

Wild Kat

Wedding rites exchanged, Kat chose the last minutes of the feast to make a speech. With dignity, prouder than she thought possible, Kat raised her hand for silence. A hush settled over the people and a thrilling sense of authority seized her. She was acutely aware of the importance of her position.

At first the voice was not her own; it sounded thin and weak. Her legs quivered like jelly. As soon as she spoke her confidence swelled, and with it the strength of her tone. "From this day forward I will be known as Tanguadal. I will speak my husband's tongue."

Great Eagle stood and took her arm. Kat lowered her voice. "I'm not finished, Indian."

Beguiled, he remained at her side as she continued. "I will be a dutiful wife to Great Eagle, powerful chief of the Kiowa Nation. I will forever walk his path with honor."

Amid cheers, Katherine removed her maiden crown as the attentive crowd watched. For a moment she searched the audience, then found her mark and tossed the flower bedecked headdress to Bright Morning. This done, Kat smiled radiantly at her new husband and squared her shoulders to face him. "Now I'm finished."

Delighted and amused, Great Eagle bowed his head. "Come my little bag of wind, we will see how well you walk my path."

Their eyes met warmly as they brought the Sun Celebration to a conclusion, waiting while the throng offered wishes for happiness and prosperity. The last of the bands downed their teepees at sunset, tired and anxious to return to their own villages.

As the bride and groom strolled up the main path to their wedding lodge, Great Eagle stroked Kat's auburn hair. "It billows like a silken cape in the wind," he told her as he steered her into a garden of hack berries. When the gaily painted marriage teepee came into view, they saw several young girls emerge from the doorway, eyes downcast. They

Lydia Joe Cates

left a bowl of fresh berries and nuts for the bride to ensure conception if eaten on her wedding night.

Upon entering the lodge, Great Eagle closed the flaps and laced them together tightly. Drunk with anticipation, he had never felt more like a young buck at the height of mating season.

A buffalo candle flickered, casting deep shadows in the concave setting. Reality triggered a wave of shyness as Katherine realized that this was her long-awaited wedding night.

Sensing her bewildered state, Great Eagle tipped her chin and kissed her lightly on the lips. She leaned into him, winding her arms securely around his neck. "I have always been in love with you, Indian."

Hugging her breathless, he savored the redolence of her hair, still bearing the fragrance of her blossomed crown. "Always?"

"Yes, always. You came to me in a cloud of white smoke—a vision."

A mystical expression crossed his face as his mouth rested at her lips. "I promised that we would meet again."

His hand splayed across her spine, the other cupped the back of her head. Everything was new again. Provocative. His tongue slowly explored her berry-flavored mouth, the tip of it sliding in and out.

Her desire set off an erotic sensation that prickled through her body with devastating speed. As if it were the most natural thing, she sucked his tongue through her parted lips. He groaned.

"You are quaking, Tanguadal. The wind is howling through your virgin leaves."

She did not answer. Instead, she began grappling with the lacings on his shirt as he untied the thong at her waistband and caressed her skirt away. Kat helped him remove her blouse and the rest of her bridal regalia.

Naked, she lay down and watched the muscles of his bronze skin flex as he removed his clothing with the exception of his breechcloth. His face remained intense with passion as he tenderly smiled down on her and untied the thong which held his last garment.

Wild Kat

Kat gasped. The sight of his naked body challenged magnificence.

Blood surged in his veins with the power of a teeming river as his eyes roamed the milkiness of her skin where the sun had been denied. Deliberately, he sank down on the bed and took her in his arms. As he traced the swell of her upturned breasts, she closed her eyes.

"Look at me, Katherine," he murmured as he fingered the hardened nubbins of her breasts until they blushed. She opened her eyes and melted when he placed her hand upon his chest. "Can you feel my heart beating like a tom-tom, galloping with the speed of Guo-la-te?"

Her eyes were slits of ecstasy as she nodded and welcomed his warm breath against her skin. His hands and lips began to weave a spell of delight as they explored her. The moist, silken heat at the center of her passion urged him on and, in part, assuaged a hunger that only a man can know.

Undulating with his every touch, she perused his firm and corded muscles. Having the freedom to caress him wherever she pleased released a peculiar kind of thrill. She laced her fingers through his hair and felt the softness stimulate her. Currents of energy pulsed in private places as Great Eagle began to savor a breast.

The smell of her incited his wildest emotions. At first taste of her, he was overwhelmed with desire and knew that if he had to choose between Katherine or his rank among his people, she would be the chosen one. Not for the passion alone, but for all time—even when his groins had cooled.

Kat's urgent whisper rippled his ear. "I never imagined that making love would be so wondrous."

His mouth closed over hers as his seductive strokes quickened, maddening her into readiness. He hoped it would lessen the inevitable pain she might experience before the joy of the union.

Positioning himself over her, he lifted her hips and entered, then partially withdrew for a few moments when he encountered the fragile barrier.

Kat arched, wailing huskily. "Now!"

Swollen with desire, he shifted forward and whispered, "Remember, my only one, the bee stings only once."

Kat tensed, but she did not cry out as he buried himself and stalled. Restraining himself, Great Eagle remained immobile to allow her ache to subside. Perspiration sparkled her forehead as the overpowering pulsing sensation took control of her. She arched again and ground into him. The movement was charged with such strength that he knew that he no longer needed to contain himself. Fire coursed through his body, burning him with exquisite rapture incomparable to anything he had ever known.

Tremors soared from one to the other. Simultaneously, their bodies writhed in the mingling of need and fulfillment. At last Kat moaned and gasped in ecstatic surrender and collapsed in Great Eagle's arms.

His voice was low and husky. "My love for you is beyond my vision, Tanguadal."

Softly. "And mine for you."

They remained entwined long after the candle had sputtered and died. As they lay in each others arms, satiated, Kat understood the meaning of peace for the first time in her life. Her Indian love had filled the crevasse of her being and she saw him as a truly grand and gentle man.

*   *   *

Great Eagle awakened, aroused by his wife's contented cat-like movements. "Do you sleep, Tanguadal?" he asked as he lit a new candle.

She grinned and stretched in a languid manner. "No, my love. I am more awake than I have ever been."

"I have a wedding gift for you." He smiled and pointed to a red velvet pouch which lay nestled in the fluffy buffalo robe that Ay-tah had given them as a betrothal present.

Wild Kat

"A gift! But you have already given me the mirror."

He thought her exclamation endearing and child-like, but he could no longer call her a child. He adored the woman she had become.

Kat opened the sack and fingered a smooth object the size of a hummingbird's egg. It was an elegant black pearl attached to links of silver.

"Where did you get this?" She frowned for fear it had once adorned the throat of an old dowager who no longer had a head of hair.

Sensing her uncertainty, Great Eagle laughed out loud. "I made a trade with Charley Bone."

"The cheerful bearded one. I remember him." She embraced her husband with all of her strength. "I'll wear it always. Your eyes remind me of black pearls."

He smiled and playfully bit her ear. His lips began to wander. "Does this remind you of anything?"

She laughed and whacked him on his naked hip. "I have a surprise for you, too."

Still naked except for the necklace, she retrieved a bundle from beside the doorway. Before presenting it to him, she untied the leather thong that had once bound her wrists. She smiled as she shook out the doeskin shirt and held it up for his approval.

His expression was tender as he took it from her. "Did you make this, Tanguadal?"

Kat nodded. "With Ay-tah's help."

Great Eagle pulled the new garment over his head, showing his appreciation by examining the complex stitches and design with great care. He was conscious of the many hours she had spent to attain such suppleness of the skins.

"If you are pleased, show me how much."

Mischief loitered in his shiny gaze. "Have I taken a wife so bold that she speaks with the looseness of Cry Woman's tongue?"

"Don't compare me to that old witch."

Lydia Joe Cates

He chuckled. "You are beyond comparison, my Wild Kat."

As he lured her back to the marriage bed, he gently pushed her down and began to plant kisses and playful bites in favored places. He stole a look at her, saw the glimmer of approval and became bolder. Kat stretched and squirmed delightedly. Quite unexpectedly, she began to laugh. Great Eagle's brows shot up and a wicked smile crept across his winged lips.

"You find me amusing?"

"You are so very beautiful naked, but it brings to mind a question that I asked Ay-tah about your breechcloth. You see, I wanted to know what you wore underneath and she told me it was something like a woman's monthly sling."

Straining to keep a straight face, Great Eagle confessed, "I am better equipped when I go into battle, but on our wedding night, for obvious reasons, I chose less armor for our seductive combat."

His humor was not lost on her. A puckish gleam lit up her eyes as she pursed her lips and mounted him. In a frenzy of excitement she guided his burgeoning masculinity to her and deliberately slid down on him. The chief emitted a passionate growl as she moved swiftly, taking him with the speed of his prize pony.

Panting from the ride, Great Eagle regarded his gorgeous, energetic wife with awe. Silently he gave thanks to the Sun Spirit for making him a strong and virile man.

Chapter Thirteen

Another miserable week passed at the pace of a snail. The woods became so dense at times that it took hours to hack only a few yards. The stragglers yearned to be on the open plains, but the risk of running into renegades was too great.

Making matters worse, one of the pack horses blundered into a hole and broke his leg. "I'm not happy about having to shoot the old critter," Deke told Matthew and Bobby, "But I don't have any choice. You can see the poor thing's suffering."

Bobby patted the horse's head. "I wish you'd git on with it, Mr. Stiles. I hate to see 'im hurtin'."

Deke picked up his shotgun. "You and Matthew go on down to the river and catch us a mess of fish for supper." As an afterthought, he called Bobby back. "Son, you and Matthew can call me Deke. We're already old friends." He grinned. "That is, if you want to."

"All right, Deke, that'll be easier. Much obliged." The boys loped toward the water, but Bobby ran back again. "I seen you and Mama makin' eyes at each other, Deke. Just want you to know that I'm glad."

The brawny man shook his head, marveling at the wisdom of the young. Deke cocked his gun, pulled the trigger and walked away. A few yards from camp he dropped down on a log by a natural spring. For the past week he had been trying to rustle up enough courage to ask Bess to marry him. With firm resolve, he slapped his knees and muttered, "Today's the day." At least it would give them something to look forward to.

Lydia Joe Cates

Deke was anxious right down to his boot soles. Their horses were getting sicklier by the day. Grazing spots were harder to find and their provisions had reached a dangerously low level.

"You look mighty lonesome, Mr. Stiles."

"Bess. I thought you were picking blackberries with the Forsythes."

"I was. But I heard the shot and figured you might like some company."

"That's right sweet of you." Deke concentrated on the peaceful spring. "I've been thinking, honey. A man with a yen to settle down could make a fine living in this rich country."

"Sounds like you're talking about yourself, Deke. I was sure that you were a rambling man." She laughed softly and sat down beside him on the log.

"What I was trying to say didn't come out right."

She knew, but she needed to hear him say it. "Well?"

He wiped his clammy hands on his breeches before he took hers. "Bess, I've been a loner for a long time, eaten up with wanderlust. It's never bothered me 'til now."

She squeezed his hand. "We've been too much of a burden on you, haven't we?"

"Aw, for gawdsakes, that doesn't have anything to do with what I'm trying to tell you."

"No need to jump down my throat. Since you're so grumpy, Mr. Stiles, I'll just leave you alone."

He took a deep breath and spit it out. "Gawdamighty! Bess, will you marry me?" It was a cool September afternoon, but Deke was sweating profusely.

In her forthright manner, Bess smiled. "Yes I will."

The grin quivered on his lips as he glanced toward the river and spotted the boys fishing on the other side. No sign of the Forsythes. Sounds of the wilderness frisked their ears as he bundled her up in his burly arms and buried his face in her hair. He was a private man and his modesty moved her.

"I'm not much good at fancy words, but I do love you with all my heart, honey. As soon as we get to Fort Riley I intend to make you my missus."

Bess was radiant, her desire strong as he lowered his head to kiss her. His lips touched hers with a passion that only a man of his age can know, once he's fallen in love again.

*   *   *

Bess hummed as she cut out dough. "I'm about ready to drop my biscuits in the pan, Callie. I see the grease bubbling in your pot. Have you dabbed the fish in corn meal yet?"

"Just finishin' up. Sure'n I'm lookin' forward to such a grand meal. 'Tis a bit scary how low we're gettin' on provisions."

"Deke says not to worry. He thinks we're mighty close to our destination."

With stars in her sea-green eyes, Callie spouted, "Deke is sayin' this and Deke is sayin' that. Sure'n ye put a lot o' stock in whatever that big, goodlookin' man says."

Bess cocked her head to the side and retorted, "I guess I do; I'm going to be his wife."

Callie squealed and hugged Bess. "Oh, me dear, I can tell ye're not joshin' and I couldn't be happier fer ye. I knew in me heart that it was just a matter of time."

*   *   *

It was a peaceful evening as they sat around the small campfire and talked. Matthew and Bobby were tucked into bed before Callie would get out the blackberry cordial and pass it around.

"The berries we've been pickin' along the way would surely be makin' a keen and pleasin' wine." She winked at Bess. "'Specially nice fer toastin' a weddin'."

James looked up and said, "What do ye mean?"

"Just what I'm sayin', me dear, a weddin' fer our friends here."

Deke flushed. James's mouth dropped open. "Well, I'll be damned! So ye've popped the question, have ye?"

"That's right," Deke said. "And the lady said yes."

"Well, sweet Callie, be fillin' our cups again and I'll be makin' the finest toast ye've ever heard."

After a few cups of cordial, James noticed that Callie seemed to be feeling chipper after being under the weather for a few days. He welcomed the roses in her cheeks and could not resist the temptation to pinch her backside as she sat down beside him.

"It won't be long, sweet Callie, 'til ye'll be cookin' in a kitchen o' yer own again. Then ye can be makin' joy juice to yer heart's content."

"That I will, James Forsythe. But I'm thinkin' ye've had a wee bit too much fer now. Seein' ye're not too careful where ye're puttin' yer hands. And in front o' the others too," she scolded.

James ruffled Callie's hair and kissed her cheek. "I'm goin' to bed." Leaning close he whispered, "Be careful, mind ye, when ye crawl into bed. I've been savin' a few more pinches fer ye."

"Get on with ye, Mr. Forsythe. I'll be joinin' ye right soon."

"I guess it's time we all hit the hay," Deke professed, but he made no move to leave the campfire.

Callie looked knowingly at Bess. "Did the spirits make ye sleepy, me dear?"

"It's made me tipsy enough to sleep 'til morning. Thank you, Callie. I'll say goodnight now."

Wild Kat

Deke watched as Bess unrolled her bed and combed her hair with her fingers. He had been quiet all evening. "Are you ready for me to smother the fire, Bess?"

"Uh-huh. I'll be ready for bed in just a minute."

He stifled the fire with dirt and blew out the lantern. Pitch-black descended upon them. The moon had hidden its harvest head under a thick layer of clouds. While Deke waited for his eyes to become accustomed to the dark, he visualized where Bess lay.

"Goodnight, Bess. Sleep tight."

"And don't let the bed bugs bite," she answered with a trace of a slur.

He was there. Hunched down beside her. "It doesn't seem right if I don't kiss my intended goodnight before I hit the sack."

"I was wondering about that. Is everyone asleep?"

"By gum, I believe they are."

"Deke, honey, there's nothing wrong in wanting somebody, especially if you love them."

He conjured up the vision of the one time that they had made love. "I just don't ever want you to think that I'm putting pressure on you."

"You dear man. Here I am in a big bed roll that I'm willing to share and you haven't made a move. What are you waiting for?"

Under the cover of darkness he slipped in beside her. His robust frame trembled as she folded her arms around him and nestled him in the warmth and comfort of her bosom.

*   *   *

Great Eagle yawned. Eyes still closed, his hand reached out and touched the place where his bride should have been. His senses had awakened to a delectable aroma and informed him that Katherine had begun her wifely duties.

"Tanguadal, whatever you are cooking smells tempting, but I prefer something else." His deep voice wound its way into her soul as she cast the pan aside and went to him.

"Lie down beside me, Katherine. I have something to tell you."

Kat slid under the cover and fondled him. He groaned softy. "You are distracting me, to say the least."

"Exactly my intention."

"Your enthusiasm is enchanting, my only one."

"Are you teasing me?"

"No. I have something of grave importance to say."

Kat swooned from the tenderness in his voice. An almost sad tone. "You're my life, Indian. I want no other."

It was a phenomena for a woman to be that candid. It seemed like something of a miracle to Great Eagle. His heart raced as he read the hunger in her gaze.

*   *   *

The fire pit had lost its warmth. Breakfast remained in the pot, uneaten. Kat lay naked beneath the blanket, completely satisfied and drowsing. She lazily turned her head. "Give me your news, my love."

"I should have told you before now."

She propped herself on an elbow and looked down at him with a serious expression. "What is it?"

His preoccupation made her uneasy. "What I have to say is meaningful to both of us. Hawk Eye, the highest leader of the Kiowa, will go with the other chiefs of the Kiowa Tribes to Fort Riley one month from today.

"We are to sign a treaty that will give the Indian back much of what has been taken away by the white man. This means, among other things, that our people will be allowed to stay on their land in peace. It will enable us to fish, and to once again hunt buffalo when they are most plentiful during the summer months."

Then why are you troubled?"

"There are conditions. We have been instructed to give up our white captives."

She pondered the information. "I'm not a captive; I'm your wife. I'm a Kiowa."

She said it proudly, but a cloud settled over them as Great Eagle continued. "It has been ordered that **all** whites must be returned before the treaty can be signed."

Kat could not believe her ears. "I won't go! My place is with you. I will never leave you. Never!"

"I have given this much thought, Tanguadal. If my brothers threaten to banish me from the tribe, I will accept that rather than lose you."

"Would it mean that you would no longer be a chief?"

He affirmed. "We would be outcasts. Exiled. Our home would be the prairie, the forest or the mountains. Could you accept that, Tanguadal?"

"Yes!" she cried. "I will walk your path until death. You are my life."

He kissed her hungrily. A thread of fear began to wind its way around his heart. The strong determination that usually lit up his bride's eyes was missing. They clung together.

Their depression lifted after the morning meal when Great Eagle patted his stomach. "You will make me fat, cooking such delicacies every day."

She laughed and sat down on his lap. "It wouldn't bother me. I'd have more of you to love."

He was fascinated with everything about her. Laughing, he pecked her lips. "I have a surprise for you. I am making ready for a journey."

"That's a helluva surprise, Indian."

"You do not need to swear, Katherine. You are to come with me."

Thrilled, she asked excitedly, "Where are we going? Why?"

"We will travel east to a place where I have not searched for my son."

Kat lowered her head. So often she had wanted to tell him that his son was alive and in good health. "I'll pack our things."

"Ansote will come with us."

"Great Eagle…many times I've wanted to…" she could not finish. The burden of guilt would have to be carried for a while longer.

Disturbed by her anxiety and the fact that she so seldom called him by name, he embraced her and tried to soothe her. "You have wanted what, my dearest one?"

"Nothing. I am being childish again. Go now and speak with your friend, Ansote. I have work to do."

A terrible sense of foreboding descended on her as he left. If Great Eagle found out that she had deceived him all of this time, would he cease to love her? She could not bear the thought.

*   *   *

It was afternoon when Great Eagle boosted Kat onto Many Colors. The sleek paint pony was given to Kat as a wedding gift from Ansote.

"Let us begin our journey, my beautiful bride." The chief then made a running leap onto Guo-la-te's back. Ansote followed with the pack horses. The trio slowly made their way up the slope to the path that led to the edge of the woods. Kat inhaled the sweet, brisk autumn breeze. She silently prayed that her husband would be spared the anguish of her deceit.

As darkness fell, Great Eagle turned to Ansote and pointed to a small stream winding its way to the Missouri River. "This is the place I spoke of. We will camp here tonight. We will begin our search for any trace of Sleeping Rabbit tomorrow at dawn."

Ansote gathered the reins of Many Colors and Guo-la-te to feed and water with the other horses. Katherine stretched her arms toward heaven, swiveled her hips and writhed as if she were a sacrifice to the gods.

Great Eagle followed her movements with interest. "You tire of me?"

Wild Kat

"Why do you ask?"

"You sway as if you are pledging yourself to the Sun Spirit."

She laughed. "I'll never tire of you, Indian. I've ridden Many Colors so long that my rump went to sleep. I was just trying to wake it up."

He burst into laughter. She watched him, enjoying the timbre of his laugh as it rumbled over the quiet forest.

Kat wrapped herself in her new robe of white rabbit fur to ward off the chill. Warm and cozy, she flopped down by the fire to keep Ansote company. Her mouth watered as he spindled three fat squirrels on a green willow spit and anchored them above the fire with two forked sticks.

"Where is our chief?"

"He is gathering boughs for your bed."

An awkward silence followed. Then, "Ansote, Many Colors is quite a prize. I didn't know you liked me enough to give me a gift."

The old man was taken aback and responded in a hushed tone. "It saddens me to hear such words. I do not share my thoughts readily, but I have loved your husband since he was a small boy. When he captured you, I was certain that he was trying to replace White Doe. I was wrong. I have never seen a love so strong as his for you."

A corner of Kat's mouth curved upward. "You're being evasive, wise one. You've told me nothing."

His mottled hand reached out and patted her cheek. "I liked you in the beginning, my child. I see your soul when you look at my chief. I love you as a daughter, Tanguadal."

"My love is returned."

"Is my wife in love with another man?" Great Eagle stood before them, arms ladened with pine boughs.

She swept the branches from him and hugged him around the waist. "Only you, Indian. Come, I will help make our bed."

Great Eagle insisted on making the bed while Kat stayed warm by the fire. "It will be as before, when we were new to each other." Knavery flashed in his eyes as he added, "When I could not speak the white man's tongue."

"If you continue to tease, I'll be forced to sleep with Ansote." She spoke in English so that the older man would not understand.

Great Eagle roared with laughter. He finished their bed still chuckling, "My wonderful Wild Kat."

Ansote covered the coals and made his bed some distance from the newlyweds. Kat plunged beneath the warm buffalo robe followed by her husband. He folded his arms across his chest and closed his eyes. She smiled to herself. Just as before, when she was new to him.

"Are you camping because of me?"

"Yes, Tanguadal. The ride will be hard, but I wanted you with me." He held her close and stroked her hair, knowing that the sojourn would take less time without her. The Kiowa had been trained from early childhood to stay on a horse, sometimes for days, while families moved their camp to a new place for the winter.

"You don't have to stop for me. I can keep up with you."

He felt a rush of joy that this incomparable woman belonged to him. "Your chance will come tomorrow. We have a hard day of riding ahead of us."

"I'll be ready."

Her arms wrapped securely around him, he closed his eyes, confident that she would always be ready for whatever the future held.

* * *

An owl hooted. Another answered as the three broke camp and followed what seemed to be a fresh trail. Although they were ignorant of the fact, it had been blazed by none other than Deke Stiles and James Forsythe. Nothing escaped Great Eagle's scrutiny as they trotted along.

Wild Kat

A carefully disguised knot on a tree where a branch had been hacked away, a fire pit which had been filled and sprinkled with leaves, almost went undetected. Clever, Great Eagle mused. "This camp has not been dead long. What do you think, old friend?"

Ansote dismounted and examined the ground where people had obviously slept. He walked ahead several yards, stooped down and picked up something. Turning away from the stream, the old Kiowa waved a bandanna in the air.

Great Eagle examined the piece of cloth and, as he turned it, a whiff of mint assailed his nostrils. Kat looked in another direction, pretending to watch a covey of quail scurrying for cover in a nearby brush pile. Great Eagle eyed her sharply and held up the material.

"Do you recognize this?"

Her lips twitched nervously as she spoke. "I thought for a moment that it was one of Father's, but all white men either carry them or wear them around their necks."

He held it out to her. "Smell it." Moisture filled her eyes as she breathed in the cool, clean fragrance of mint.

"Well, have you swallowed your tongue, Katherine."

She flinched at the terseness of his words and hastily answered. "It may be Father's. Mother used to store dried mint in the bureau drawers with our clean clothes."

"Your white family must be somewhere on this trail," he snapped, watching her reaction.

"They couldn't be. They've probably reached Fort Riley by now. Why are you so angry?"

"Silence, Katherine. These people may have news of my son."

She was agitated now. Great Eagle had tangible evidence that white people had been on the trail they were following. Not only that, they could be her white family with the chief's son. Her tangled mind mulled over the possibility. What would they be doing in the woodlands? Yes, she was extremely distraught now.

Great Eagle called out arrogantly. "The trail is not cold. We will find them."

Having had enough of his rudeness, she fired back, "Then what'll you do, Indian, hunt them down and scalp them if they don't know anything?"

He snatched the kerchief out of her hand and stuffed it in the waistband of his buckskins. "I do not plan to hurt them, but I **will** track them down. They may have valuable information concerning my son."

They rode on. Kat squirmed with a back ache, but she did not complain. Great Eagle could not bring himself to rest. Ansote intervened. "We must stop, my son, while there is still light."

"Not yet, Second Father."

A stiff breeze had blown in from the east and Great Eagle grimaced as a foul odor drifted past. Ansote sprinted ahead to investigate and stopped about twenty yards ahead. He raised his voice. "A horse! Maybe two days dead."

Great Eagle scowled. "The wind blows in our faces. We must put some distance between us and the dead animal before we make camp."

Ansote used flint and tinder to light a small torch and led the way. The stench became unbearable by the time they passed within feet of the swollen carcass. The chief glanced over his shoulder at his wife and held out the bandanna. "Protect yourself from the ungodly smell."

Kat gratefully wrapped it around her face and ignored his smile. When they stopped, she slid off of her pony, waving away the help her husband offered. She was insulted by his early behavior and chose to sulk while the men set up camp. If the arrogant Indian expected her to work, he was mistaken.

Ansote built a fire while Great Eagle fished for their supper. He returned a half hour later with a rock bass for each of them. She watched her husband scale the fish for Ansote to cook over smoldering coals. Katherine had not spoken since their squabble. She huddled by the fire as her husband squatted behind her and nudged her with his arm. She faced him and refused his offering of a handful of berries.

"Eat it yourself, Indian. I lost my appetite somewhere between a mint-smelling kerchief and a dead horse." Kat yanked her robe tighter and buried her face in the fur.

Amused, he sat down beside her and began to eat. Ansote stifled his mirth with a cough and a complaint that the cool air stiffened his joints.

When it came time to extinguish the fire, Great Eagle tugged on Kat's robe. "Come, Tanguadal, it is time to sleep. Goodnight, Ansote."

"Let go of my robe! I'll sleep in it, thank you," she grouched and bowed her head, stomach growling.

Great Eagle picked her up. "You will sleep with me. I do not want a frozen wife."

For a time he stared up at the moon, deep in thought. If the white man had news of his son, they would tell him. With Katherine traveling alongside him, they would trust him. His mind at ease for the time being, the chief turned on his side, dragged his belligerent wife against him and cupped her body with his.

He whispered in her hair. "I will keep you warm."

She wanted to respond, but remained silent.

Determined to arouse her, he ran his tongue along the nape of her neck and an ear. When she did not stir he said, "You taste better than freshly-killed buffalo."

Willpower ebbing, she smiled in the darkness.

"I am sorry, my only one."

She turned to face him. "I accept your apology only because I cannot resist you for another moment."

Thrills coursed through his veins as their lips met as before, when they were new to each other.

Lying in his arms, Kat's conscience could stand no more. She gathered together all of her courage and attacked the subject without further delay. "I understand your concern for Sleeping Rabbit. I've watched you suffer long enough, my dearest one. Your son is alive and being cared for by white people."

She felt his body tense. He was too calm. "How do you know this?"

"I was the one who found him in the canyon. His arm was broken and he was starving. My mother set his arm and an Irish couple offered to take care of him. The boy is in good hands. Days after your son was rescued, you and your band attacked our wagon train. I kept it from you for fear of my white family's lives."

Stunned, Great Eagle shrugged her off when she tried to embrace him. "For months I have feared for my son's life. I have been insane with worry. And you have kept this from me," he stated flatly.

He sprang from the bed and dressed rapidly. His stance was wide and ominous as he stood over her. "You have betrayed me. Sleep well if you can. Tomorrow will be the hardest ride of your life."

"Where are you going?"

"To build a fire. My heart is cold."

"Please listen to me."

Simmering with fury he roared, "Speak!"

"In the beginning I was afraid that you would harm my white family. As time passed, I fell in love with you. Then I couldn't tell you because I was afraid you wouldn't love **me**."

The chief scowled and shook his head. "You have been a selfish child."

Crying, Kat took a deep breath and continued. "I was alarmed for fear you would trade me in exchange for your son."

Swiftly he turned and vanished in the darkness. Ansote arose from his bed and stirred the dying fire as Great Eagle approached.

"Your face bears the mark of a storm, my son."

Wild Kat

"Sit, old friend, I must talk." Great Eagle lowered his head in despair. He had believed that his son was dead. Because of her lack of trust in him, his wife had lied.

Chapter Fourteen

◯

Deke clawed his way from under the covers and pulled on his boots. Exposing what few coals were left, he worried them into a blaze. It would be comforting for Bess to wake up to a cup of strong, hot coffee.

"Where's yer apron, Mr. Stiles?"

"Shhhh, James boy, don't disturb the women's beauty rest."

"I don't mind tellin' ye one thing." He yawned and stretched his stout body. "I'm goin' to be mighty grateful when we get out of these blinkin' damn woods and back to where the sun's shinin' again."

Deke filled their mugs and passed one to his friend. "Amen! I'm not trying to dig up trouble, but I've got a peculiar feeling that we're being tracked."

James shook his head slowly. "Aye, I'm havin' the same feelin'; it's been gnawin' at me gut fer quite a spell."

"Guess we'd best keep a sharper lookout." Deke stole over to Bess with a cup of coffee. "Morning, Missus Stiles. It's time to start hacking our way out of this place."

"Morning, you dear man."

"Aw, heck, I'm far from dear. Here, I brought you a mug of java. I'll trade it for a clean bandanna."

"Thank you for the coffee. I'll trade you a clean kerchief for the dirty one."

"I can't find it, honey. I must have lost it on the trail."

"No matter. There's plenty more where that one came from."

Wild Kat

The days had grown cooler with Autumn's approach. The closer they got to their destination, the safer they felt. Provisions were all but gone and two more horses had died, but the determined group still had one pack animal left and a mount for each person.

By the grace of God they had managed to stay reasonably well. No snake bites, no sickness and they were not starving. Deke considered all of this and was thankful. But he was still spooked about being followed. He tipped his hat and gave Bess a meaningful smile.

Callie chortled. "Sure'n Deke's actin' like the cat that swallowed the poor little yellow bird."

Bess giggled. "He's on the bright side, all right."

"Don't be tryin' to fool me, Bess Stone. It's no sign I'm sleepin' as soon as me head hits the pillow, ye know. And last evenin' it sounded like such a good time ye were havin' that I almost woke me dear James." Callie bubbled over with laughter when she saw Bess's bewildered expression.

"I thought we were as quiet as mice, Callie."

"Oh, me dear, a teasin' I was. But I'll be tellin' ye straight that I'm thinkin' it's surely a grand thing that you and Deke discovered each other."

Bess's eyes spangled with tears. "Deke's such a fine man, Callie. I'll be so glad when we get to Fort Riley so that we can get married and I can start asking around about my children."

"It's good that ye're buryin' yer sorrow in the grave where it's belongin'. And right ye are, too. Ye've had enough misery to be lastin' ye a lifetime. Ye deserve to be happy."

*   *   *

It was nearing dusk when they spotted a small clearing. Callie trotted over to Matthew and Bobby. "Ye know, me dears, it'd be fun to race, but seein' how the poor horses look, it's be a shame to be puttin' 'em through it.

Lydia Joe Cates

So, here's what I'm proposin'. We'll be startin' off together and see whose horse can walk the fastest. Once ye break into a trot, ye lose."

They lined up and began to walk their nags. Giggling, the boys could barely contain themselves. Callie purposely lagged behind, the wind in her hair trailed like a pony's mane, as she watched the children maintain their speed. They reached the clearing together and laughed when they saw how far behind they had left Callie.

"Ye're not ones to be lettin' a woman get the best o' ye, I see." She laughed. "Not that I thought ye would."

Squirrels were plentiful along the way. James and Deke trapped seven for supper. They turned the rodents over to Bobby and Matthew, who skinned them with the expertise of seasoned hunters.

On the surface there was an air of serenity, but Deke sensed otherwise. He looked over his shoulder intermittently as he chopped wood. Finally he said, "We've got enough to build a small settlement. I'm quittin'."

James chuckled, dropped the head of his ax on the ground and leaned on the handle. "I'll be tellin' ye one thing, I was ready to be quittin' before we began. Ye still feelin' qualmish, Deke?"

"Yeah. Can't shake the feeling."

*   *   *

Great Eagle threw a blanket across the back of Many Colors and tightened the girth while he waited for Katherine to join them. When she did not get up, he went to the bed and shook her. He was exuberant now that he knew his son was alive.

Impatiently. "We ride, Katherine." His anger toward her had not lessened.

She sat up, rubbed her swollen eyes and slipped into her soft doeskin riding pants that Ay-tah had made for her. Kat quickly tied her hair back with a leather thong, recalling Great Eagle's delight when she had shown him her pants. He had referred to her as his beautiful boy. She shrugged. In his current state of mind, he probably wouldn't notice if she jumped on her pony naked.

Great Eagle rode as if he were a statue. Staring straight ahead. Disregarding Kat's presence. Anger boiled below the surface of her cool exterior as she, in turn, ignored him. She wanted to crumble the wall that separated them, but his expression of indifference told her that any attempt to make amends would be futile.

They rode hard when the crude trail was wide enough and slowed to a walk when it narrowed. Kat jogged along behind her husband with Ansote bringing up the rear. When they began to get whiffs of the dead horse, she turned her head toward the old man and wrinkled her nose.

Ansote chuckled and rode up beside her. "The animal should be ready for roasting by the time we reach him."

"Give my part to the sulking Indian."

They laughed together and, as the merriment vibrated in his ears, Great Eagle frowned at them. "You both are of good cheer this morning. Allow me to contribute. We will ride through the night."

Ansote shook his head. "Why do you drive yourself so hard, my son?"

"The ones we hunt may be days ahead. I feel Sleeping Rabbit is near."

"We know by the fresh tracks and the dead horse that they cannot be more than two days away."

The chief softened his tone. "I feel my son's presence growing stronger with each mile."

Ansote had always respected his chief's uncanny predictions. He was usually right. "Your wife has told you that the boy is safe and travels with a wagon train."

Great Eagle's brow furrowed. "I have no wife. Come, we are wasting time." He nudged Guo-la-te in the sides and cantered away.

Kat poked Many Colors into a trot with Ansote keeping up with her. "Will he forgive me, Ansote?"

"He is a benevolent man. In time, Tanguadal."

*   *   *

Kat was queasy and laid her head on her pony's neck. Ansote noticed and rode ahead to alert Great Eagle. "We must rest; your wife is exhausted and I fear she is ill."

The chief stole a glimpse at Kat. She heard Ansote's plea and lifted her head so high that her chin jutted out as she spoke. "We cannot spare the time."

Ansote was astounded at Kat's display of spirit. He rubbed his chin thoughtfully. His second son had met his match.

Great Eagle's gaze darted back to Kat again. A hint of distress was evident. He waved to his companions to halt. "We will stop here for a while."

Kat's face turned the color of fury. "Dammit, Indian! Don't stop on my account. I'm not a child!"

"Your profanity is boring, Katherine. Remind me to teach you something new."

She wanted to roll her fists into balls and pound the daylights out of him; instead, she issued a blatant sigh of relief that she had not grown to her pony's back.

Kat passed the reigns of Many Colors to Ansote after experiencing the luxury of walking on solid ground again. She reached into her pouch for some pemmican and sat down on a blanket to chew the jerky.

A blackberry bush nearby caught her attention. She gathered a handful of the plump, ripe fruit to snack on and stuffed several into her mouth when Great Eagle slapped her between the shoulder blades. Berries spewed out of her mouth, splattering her treasured riding pants.

"Dammit to hell, Indian! Are you trying to choke me to death?"

Wild Kat

"Examine wild berries with caution before you gobble them down. They could be poisonous." With that, he spun around and stalked off, wrapping himself in a blanket to lay down and rest.

While her husband slept, Kat washed the berry juice off of her face at the stream and removed most of the stain from her pants. Ansote was also asleep. Kat dragged her covers over to the chief and cuddled up to him for warmth. The ache inside of her subsided when she felt him bundle her in his arms as he slept.

*   *   *

Deke reached into his hip pocket and pulled out a creased, sweat-stained map. Conscious of its worn condition, he spread it out carefully on a flat rock and set the lantern beside it for light. His gnarled finger traced a faded, uneven black line stretching across the parchment and stopping.

"That's Fort Riley," Deke explained. "Don't mention to the others that we're this close, that is, until we know for sure."

"I've been noticin' the woods thinnin' fer the past two days and I'm agreein' that that's it."

"I'm going to leave at first light, James, and I'll ride to see what's on the other side of that hill." His finger moved along the line and tapped the map. "Right about here."

"What will ye be tellin' the women?"

"I'll just say that I'm going to scout the countryside for the day. No need to get their hopes up in case I'm wrong."

*   *   *

Deke mounted his bay and rode away. Bess and Callie coerced James into taking the boys fishing. By noon, Matthew and Bobby had caught a mess of rock bass and left them on a stringer in the stream.

Lydia Joe Cates

After much cajoling, they finally wheedled James into helping them gut and clean the fish.

"Sure'n that's a fine catch, men. I'm guessin' it won't be killin' me to be cleanin' a few, as long as the ladies are doin' the rest o' the supper."

He cut off the head of a two pounder and began to scale it, but his mind was on his friend. If their calculations were correct, Deke should be back by nightfall.

Bess lowered the fish into hot grease, listening for the sound of a whinny or approaching hoofs. "James, isn't it about time for Deke to be coming back?"

Rebraiding a frayed rope, James looked up at Bess's convoluted forehead and answered with nonchalance. "I'm thinkin' it'll be a while longer, Bess. Deke had a long stretch to be coverin'."

Mollified, Bess roasted coffee beans, crushed them and poured them in the pot while Callie set out sorghum molasses and hardtack. "We've enough flour fer two, maybe three more meager meals and that's the endin' of our staples," Callie remarked.

"Callie, the good Lord says to live one day at a time and I'm intending to do just that. I don't care to hear any more about how low our larder is."

"Very well, me dear." Then she put her hand on Bess's shoulder. "Sure'n it's a natural thing fer ye to be frettin', but that big man o' yers is smarter'n any Indian. He'll be ridin' in soon. Mark me words."

No one had an appetite. Their thoughts were focused on Deke and the hope that he would wander in at any moment. Time dragged on and still no Deke.

*   *   *

Wild Kat

The discouraged group sat around the campfire washing down leftovers from the night before with bitter coffee when a gravelly voice rang out. "Anybody home?"

Bess dropped her cup on the ground and ran to the stream. "It's Deke and…" She cut herself off and stared open-mouthed as he trotted up the middle of the stream followed by four men dressed in blue uniforms with yellow kerchiefs tied around their necks.

Deke wore a broad grin as he waved. "I brought you an escort to Fort Riley, Bess girl."

"United States Cavalry at your service," Sergeant Spivey announced. "And this here is Corporal Pinkerton, Private Sheffield and Private Stone."

Bess stepped back. Tears trickled down her cheeks in a steady stream when a lanky, freckle-faced boy with hair the color of a ripe apricot slid off of his horse and ambled toward her.

"Mama, don't you know me?" Todd wound his skinny arms around Bess and tried to comfort her. "It's all right, Mama, we're gonna be a family again. Where's Papa and Sis?" He grinned and craned his neck. He had already spied his little brother and waved a hand for him to join them.

Todd squatted down on his haunches and held out his arms. "Come on, Bobby, and gimme a hug."

Bobby lunged into his brother's arms and buried his face in Todd's scratchy blue cavalry uniform. He had given up trying to be a man, for the moment, and let his brother hold him close.

Linc Sheffield trotted his horse forward, his eyes darting to each face. He was looking for just one. "I'm glad to see that you're well, Mrs. Stone. Where's Katherine?"

"She's not here, Linc."

His frown increased. "Is she de…?"

"No. She's not dead, but she might as well be."

"What're you talking about, Mama?" Todd searched the familiar faces again. "Where's Papa and what about Kat?"

Bess led the two young men aside. For an hour she explained, starting with Katherine's abduction and Sam's death, and ending with the horrors and hardships of their journey. The death of his father came as a grievous shock to Todd. His tears of grief turned to anger when Bess told him that the Indians had kidnapped Kat. After he calmed down, Linc began his line of questioning.

"You say Kat is alive…how do you know?"

"A trader spent the night in our camp, Linc. He told us. If he was telling the truth, Katherine is now married to Kiowa Chief Great Eagle."

Linc was stunned into silence and collapsed on a huge rock. He put his head in his hands, and without looking up he said, "We'll get her back, Mrs. Stone. I promise you, we'll get her back."

Todd spoke softly. "We know what the Indians do to whites, Mama. Linc and I were captured, but we escaped before they could get us back to their village. We traveled for weeks and dang near starved before we got to Fort Riley." Todd put his arm around his mother's shoulder. "I'll get Sis back from those savages if I have to ride into their camp and kill every damn one of them."

Linc agreed. "I'll be right alongside him, Mrs. Stone. I want to marry Kat, if she'll have me. That's all that's kept me going."

Sergeant Spivey raised his voice. "Be ready to leave for Fort Riley at the break of dawn."

Todd shot a quick look at Matthew. "As soon as we get back to the Fort we'll set up a trade with Great Eagle." He glared at Matthew. "This Indian in exchange for my sister."

The following morning troops and stragglers alike mounted and moved out. The last leg of their arduous journey had begun.

*   *   *

Wild Kat

Great Eagle felt the auburn hair covering his bare arm. He opened his eyes and studied his wife's face. She had unnatural coloring for a redhead. Instead of the usual freckles, she had the brown hue of an acorn. Kat possessed the soul of an Indian. There was no doubt. He swelled with pride, remembered the reason for their estrangement and removed his arm. It was a matter of principle.

The chief was up and out of sight before Kat was awake. As she gathered her gear, she was painfully reminded that her body was still stiff. She could hardly bear the thought of the ride facing them. She asked for Great Eagle's help in mounting Many Colors.

"I'm deeply sorry I've hurt you, Indian."

He ignored her affectionate attempt with a shake of his head and jumped on Guo-la-te's back. "It is time to go."

Katherine climbed onto Many Colors in pain. They rode all night, only stopping to water the horses and fill their pouches. At noon the following day, his tolerance at an end, Ansote shouted an abrupt halt.

"Tanguadal is pale and weak from exhaustion and so am I. I will stop with her so that we may rest. We will catch up with you before nightfall."

Impatience darkened Great Eagle's face. "What have you become, old friend? A nursemaid?"

"You are driving us like cattle. Tanguadal did what she thought was right. She told you that your son is alive and cared for. Have you not punished her enough?"

Great Eagle's nostrils flared. "Your temper is far from your nature, Second Father."

The old man held his head high. "Search your heart, Chief Great Eagle. Your benevolence has faltered these past days."

The chief rode to Kat's side. "Are you ill?" He was emotionless, but concern wrinkled his brow as he took note of her rosy cheeks against the ghostly pallor of her skin.

"If I could sleep for a while it would help."

He dismounted, lifted her from the pony and laid her on the blankets that Ansote had spread on the ground. The chief placed his hand on her forehead. Dread clouded his expression as he turned to Ansote.

"We will stay here until her fever is gone." He squatted beside her and stroked her hair. "Rest, Tanguadal."

The sound of his voice repeating her Indian name brought tears to her eyes, rolling out of the corners and dampening her hair. "I love you, my Indian."

"I cannot share my love with you until my anger subsides."

Resigned. "I understand. I will never hide anything from you again, as long as I live."

Recalling Ansote's advice, Great Eagle spoke gently. "I am elated that my son is alive and well. Thank you for telling me."

*   *   *

Later that afternoon the chief rode in with a small doe lying across his lap. "We will eat royally tonight, Ansote." For the first time in days he managed to exhibit a good nature.

Katherine sat by the fire wrapped in her rabbit robe, sipping a bowl of bitter broth. "Drink it all and it will kill your fever, daughter." Ansote's kind eyes smiled at her.

Kat drank it down without stopping. "Ugh! What is this?"

"It is a medicinal herb. It is good for the stomach, the head and the heart, even the heart, daughter."

Great Eagle rushed back from taking a bath in the river and stood by the fire swishing a blanket over his glistening brown body. Shivering, he dropped down behind Kat and positioned her between his thighs out of habit. His arms embraced her as he whispered in her ear. "Are you hungry?"

Wild Kat

His action surprised her. Maybe her punishment was coming to an end. She turned her head and looked into his eyes. His anger was gone. She took heart in this observation and risked a quip.

"Yes, I'm hungry, for more than food, my dearest."

Ansote noted what he hoped was a reconciliation and said, "I will see to the horses before it grows darker."

As soon as the old friend led the animals to a grassy clearing to graze, Great Eagle stretched out close to the fire to warm himself. He put his head in Kat's lap, looked steadily into her eyes, and spoke in a voice rich with tenderness.

"Tanguadal, after days of pondering, and with the help of Ansote's wisdom, I understand your actions. In your place, I could have done the same."

He turned on his side and slipped his hands between the folds of her robe, untying the lacings of her blouse. "I have missed you."

His lips were hot as he captured a swollen breast for a moment, then kissed each one. His rage had ended and left him free to say, "I love you, my Tanguadal."

As Ansote approached, Great Eagle wrapped the blanket of fur around Kat again and wedged her between his thighs. They stayed that way, content to hold each other while their souls mated in silence.

*   *   *

Another day in progress. The trio rode into yet another newly abandoned site. Great Eagle bounded off of Guo-la-te before the horse had completely stalled. It was noon when he ran through the lifeless camp scraping his moccasins across trampled leaves and dirt. His eyes flashed brightly as he knelt on the ground and touched the earth around the fire pit.

"It harbors warmth." He raced to the stream and halted where the tracks of many horses had trod. His eyes strayed to Kat. "We are not far behind the white ones, Tanguadal."

"You say they're white. How do you know for sure?"

"The white man leaves many signs. Their horses wear shoes of iron, and they have yet to learn how to cover tracks."

Ansote offered, "It will be an easy task to follow them." He raised a bony finger and pointed upstream. "Fresh prints at the water's edge. They crossed only hours ago."

Great Eagle took a running jump onto Guo-la-te. His hands landed precisely on the horse's rounded rump as his powerful arms lifted him onto the sleek red steed's back. The chief opened his mouth and liberated a deep, resonant cry. "Whoooeeeyah! Eeeyah! Eeeyah!

Energized by the frenetic yell, Kat prodded Many Colors and galloped to Great Eagle's side. They trotted together across the stream and through the thinning trees. When they reached the clearing, greeted by the warmth of the sun, another war cry exploded in the air. The sound was just as strong, just as vigorous as the previous one, but the tone bore a distinctive feminine quality.

Chapter Fifteen

☙

It was October 18, 1865. A sentry on the lookout bridge of Fort Riley sighted horse soldiers leading a group of people toward the fort. The motley crew had, at last, reached their destination safely. The suffering was over, but not the sorrow.

A depressed Deke Stiles rode alongside Bess. "Well, we made it."

His cheerless tone stuck Bess like a needle. She eyed him sharply. "What're you looking like a walleyed calf for?"

"Gawdamighty! I figured you might have second thoughts about me making you my missus. Now that we're here."

"Well, if you still feel the same about me, then everything is still dandy. If you're worried about Todd, don't. He'll get used to the idea."

"You mean you told Todd about us?"

"Bobby beat me to it. That's why Todd's acting like his nose is out of joint." Bess leaned over and patted his shoulder. "Just remember this, Mr. Stiles, I love you. That'll never change."

Deke's face bloomed. "It'd be near to impossible to explain my feelings for you, honey."

"Then quit acting puny. There's nothing else to be said."

The Forsythes rode up beside them. "Well, Deke Stiles, I don't mind tellin' ye that ye're the one to be given credit that we're here. If ye hadn't seen fit to be leavin' the wagon train, I'm doubtin' we'd be ridin' in today er any other day."

Deke shook his head and mumbled, "Don't go talking like that, James. I'm too damn old to be a hero."

Todd caught up with Bess and shot Deke a stony glare. "Come on, Mama. You and me and Bobby are going to ride through the gates of Fort Riley like a family is supposed to do. Mr. and Miz Forsythe, you and Linc are welcome to ride along with the Stone family."

Bess felt a pang of sympathy when she saw Deke's hurt expression and Matthew's bowed head. "Well now, Mr. Todd Stone, I've been fooled all this time thinking your papa and I raised you to be a gentleman. Did you leave your manners back on the trail?" Bess took a deep breath. "It won't be long, young man, 'til we're members of the Stiles family, so you'd better get used to the idea right now. And you can start by offering Deke and Matthew an apology."

Uncomfortable, Deke interrupted, "It's all right, Bess, I understand. Go ahead and ride in with your family."

"Pish-posh, I'm not going anywhere without you from now on." She waved to the Forsythes, Matthew and Bobby to ride with them. "Come along, Deke, the head of the family rides up here with me." She smiled at her eldest son. "Are you and Linc coming, Todd?"

The young man nodded and reflected on what his mother had encountered. The wilderness, the loss of his father and Katherine. All had made his mother a stronger woman, if that was possible. Deke Stiles must have had something to do with her survival. Todd relented and decided that he would give the wagon master a chance.

* * *

Howling winds blew across the prairie that afternoon. Kat's white family would have called it a *norther*. She draped her rabbit robe over her head and across her face as she waited patiently for her husband and Ansote to inspect fresh hoof prints.

Wild Kat

Buried in the darkest reaches of her soul, an uneasy feeling began to gnaw at Kat's insides like a rat chewing on a sack of grain. She somehow knew, as she drifted into sleep, that she was facing a sorrowful reality in the new day.

* * *

Dawn broke crisp and crystal clear. Ansote and Great Eagle were not in sight. Kat scooted to the fire to warm herself. Tightening her robe around her, she decided to take a walk. Dew prickled her ankles like tiny spears of ice as she tiptoed to the crest of a small knoll. She was peering over the peaceful prairie when a feeling of desolation engulfed her once again.

Kat sensed his presence before his arms encircled her from behind. As he drew her to him, she laid her head against his chest and listened to the rapid beat of his heart. "I am frightened."

"Do not fret, Tanguadal, we are safe. The soldiers at the fort are good friends."

She turned and threw her arms around his neck, burrowed her face in the hollow of his throat and wept. Lightly massaging the middle of her back, the power of their love consumed them. Jagged energy pulsed through them as the wind swept clouds over the morning sun.

They clung to each other on the lonely hilltop. The tang of tears moistened her lips as they met his with an eagerness born out of uncertainty. They fell to their knees in the tall, whispering grass. Great Eagle parted her robe and gently laid her down. He removed his buckskins and pressed his body to hers. The verdant haven surrounding them cradled the lovers in the pink-tinted morning.

Their eyes met and held as Kat told him, "I cannot live without you."

"We will always be together, my Tanguadal. This, I promise."

* * *

It was past noon when the three Kiowas spotted Fort Riley in the distance. Great Eagle held out his hand to Ansote. "Give me the flag, old friend."

The old Indian handed him a square of white sack cloth. Great Eagle slid off of his horse to retrieve a thin tree branch and began tying the fabric to the end of it. He watched Kat intermittently, his concern unabated.

"Our home is one day from the fort, Tanguadal. We will return as soon as I have made my inquiries." he assured.

Katherine could only nod. A delicate thread of ripening maturity was weaving an acceptance of the situation to come. For the first time in her life, Kat cared more for another's happiness than for her own.

"The time has come." Great Eagle motioned to Kat. "Please ride beside me, my only one. Ansote and I will walk our horses so that the soldiers will know we come in peace." He held the white flag high so that the wind could tease it into movement.

Chapter Sixteen

Corporal Pinkerton opened one side of the huge fort gate wide enough to slip through. He was a rangy, owl-eyed young man and looked a bit frightened as he carried a wooden bucket of slop and a burlap sack full of dry trash to the ravine to bury.

On his way back, the corporal glanced across the bleak prairie and spied the Indians. The cold winter wind watered his eyes and blurred his vision, but he was able to make out the figures. Great Eagle and Ansote walked their horses at a slow pace as Kat rode Many Colors beside her husband. The soldier could not tell whether or not the people were red or white, but he was relieved to see that they carried a white flag, the symbol of peace.

Pinkerton's lean frame paused before he bolted for the gate. "Heeeey, Saaarge! Some drifters are inchin' their way to the fort."

"Saddle up!" Sergeant Spivey hollered. "I'll advise Colonel Beck."

Deke happened to be in the commander's office when the soldier reeled off his news. Colonel Beck made a hasty exit motioning for Deke to follow and led him to the open gate.

"What's it look like to you, Stiles?"

"A peace mission, I'd say, since they're carrying a white flag. There's no battle going on right now, so it's not a surrender."

The bullnecked Sergeant took two of his men and rode out to meet the visitors. He exchanged a few words with Great Eagle before escorting the small entourage to the fort.

Deke's mouth fell open as he watched them approach. The sun's rays lasered through Kat's hair, coughing out glints of copper sparks as she rode proudly beside her husband.

"Colonel Beck, I know that girl."

"The hell you say, Stiles. I can see she's white. Who is she?"

"She's Miz Stone's daughter, the one I told you about last night. If my old eyes aren't fooling me, that injun with the flag is Kiowa Chief Great Eagle."

"That's him all right. There's no mistaking that devil. He's a shade more civilized than his brothers, and a good friend too."

Callie and James had already joined Deke at the gate when Bess arrived panting. "What's all the fuss about?"

"Get a grip on yourself, Bess." Deke grasped her hand. "I believe that's Miss Kat riding beside her Injun husband."

Bess gasped and jerked her hand free. "I'm going to meet her."

Deke's arm shot out like a whip and grabbed her. "Stay with me, Bess girl. Injuns get skittish if you move too fast."

Bess waited anxiously, holding Deke's arm as the small group neared. "She's dressed like an Indian. What have they done to her?"

Kat stopped in front of them and stared blankly at the crowd. Bess was frantic. "A redheaded Indian!"

"Keep your voice down," Deke reminded Bess.

As they entered the fort, Great Eagle and Ansote mounted and rode slowly. Katherine, already past the line of onlookers, looked straight ahead.

Bess sobbed, "Kat acted as if she didn't even know me."

Deke's heart knotted. "Maybe she's just doing what's expected of her. We don't know what the girl's been through."

Callie was pale as she watched the striking appearance of the proud Indian Chief. A blizzard stormed inside her brain, cold and killing. Great Eagle had come to take her son away. She bowed her head and watched the moisture from her eyes drop on the dusty road.

James draped an arm around her shoulders. "Don't cry, sweet Callie. We've been knowin' all along that Matthew wasn't ours to be keepin'."

"I know, me dear. But me love fer Matthew just won't stop growin'."

Colonel Beck ushered the guests into his office and, after what seemed an eternity, the commandant exited and bellowed loudly from the wide plank porch. "Stiles, come in, and bring Mrs. Stone and the Forsythes with you."

Deke scanned the countryside to see if Bobby and Matthew had returned. They had been making rounds of the compound with a special detail. The group was still gone.

Following the Forsythes into the small office, Bess sagged heavily against Deke. Great Eagle admired her. She was, indeed, the mother of his wife. Bess saw only her daughter, dressed in tribal garb with skin the color of an overdone wheat muffin.

"Katherine, don't you know your own mama?"

Kat raised her head and eyed her mother without emotion. "I know you, Mother, but I'm not Katherine Stone anymore. I'm Tanguadal, wife of Chief Great Eagle."

Refusing to believe what she had just heard, Bess asked, "The Indian's holding you against your will, isn't he Kat?"

"No, Mother." Katherine's attention was fixed on Deke, then Callie and James before her gaze returned to Bess. "Where's Father?"

Anger roiled in Bess's mind and formed words of venom. "The Indians killed him!" Bess held hope when she caught a flicker of pain cross Kat's cool countenance. "You don't have to be scared, Kat, you're safe now." She held out her arms. "Come to me...please."

Kat allowed her mother to embrace her, but Bess received no response as she kissed her daughter on the cheek. With an aching heart, Bess could smell the fragrance of wood smoke as she fingered the softness of her daughter's doeskin clothing. She imagined that she cuddled a small, wild animal in her arms; one that would flee as soon as she released her hold. It came sooner than she expected when Kat disengaged from her mother, stepped back and took her place beside Great Eagle again.

Deke clasped Bess's arm and led her to the hall outside Colonel Beck's office. "Don't worry, honey. Why, Miss Kat'll warm up to you as soon as she realizes there's nothing to be afraid of anymore."

"I'm not so sure about that, Deke. And you aren't, either! Katherine is different."

The Forsythes joined them, feelings engraved on their faces. "Bess, me dear, I'm feelin' pain fer the both of ye." Her lips quivered. "I see Matthew and Bobby comin'."

The children ran up the steps laughing and poking each other playfully. Both boys wore yellow kerchiefs tied around their necks and metal crossguns pinned crookedly to their coats. Deke took them aside and knelt down in front of them.

"Bobby, your sister is in Colonel Beck's office and Matthew, your pa is..." Before Deke could finish, Matthew cried out in the Kiowa tongue.

"Father!" The boy flung open the door, his eyes blazing with joy as he shouted, "Father, I knew you would come!"

Deke and the others watched from the open doorway as Great Eagle dropped to one knee and folded the boy in his arms. After the touching moment, Bess straightened and marched into the room.

"Chief Great Eagle, in case you haven't been told, we're not handing over your boy until you give Katherine back to us."

The chief's face froze, his nostrils flared as he shot a deadly look at the commanding officer. "What does this mean, Colonel Beck?"

"It means that you are to exchange the white woman for your son, or the treaty will not be signed by our government."

The Indian's face radiated hell's fury as he took a step toward the officer. Ansote clasped his friend's arm. "This is not the time, my son." Great Eagle recognized the wisdom of the old man's words.

Wild Kat

Regaining his composure, the chief said, "The trade you ask for makes no sense. Katherine is a Kiowa now. I expect you to return my son on the honor of our friendship."

"I know, I know, Great Eagle, you can take your son, but without the white woman. The treaty that's to be signed within the week prohibits white captives from being held by your people."

"As I said, Katherine is not a captive." Kat edged closer to Great Eagle as he spoke. "Remember this, my friend, your people want this treaty, as mine do." His eyes leveled with the Colonel's and held a deadly glint that was both composed and intimidating.

A chilling silence followed and dangled in the air as Colonel Beck reviewed the situation at hand. He knew that the Indians might stall and it was his job to appease them until the agreement had been signed and stamped with the government seal.

Backing down as gracefully as possible, the officer said, "You're right. We still have almost a week to get everything in order. It's a fine treaty, Great Eagle, and we want to afford your nation every privilege."

"Privilege?" Great Eagle scoffed. "The right to hunt our own lands and fish our rivers? Forgive me, Colonel, I sometimes forget the fairness of the white man."

Colonel Beck's pernicious blue eyes squinted as sweat dribbled down the sides of his round face. "You're free to take your son and go, but I advise you to leave now."

Great Eagle made no move. Kat came forward and took her place beside him. She looked up at the face she adored, then at the officer, who had summoned two soldiers into the room with drawn rifles. They stood at attention waiting for the command that only Kat had the power to prevent. She could not risk losing her husband or his son to a soldier's gun. The room had quieted to the likeness of a tomb. Kat's eyes fell on Sleeping Rabbit. The child's face was stricken with fear, giving her the strength that she needed. She approached the boy while unclasping her cherished wedding gift. She secured the black pearl attached to links of silver around her Indian son's neck, grasped him by the shoulders and spoke softly.

"Wear this, my son, as a symbol of my love for you and your father. Someday I will return to our village. This is my solemn promise."

In reflection, Kat knew that her premonition had been true. Her life with the people that she had come to love was fading before her eyes. She addressed the small assembly in English. "I am Tanguadal, wife of Great Eagle. I married him of my own free will. So deep is my love that I would gladly die for him."

The chief held on to her hand, surprised to find it cold and clammy. He whispered close to her ear. "This is not the time for speeches, Tanguadal."

Unheeded tears coursed down her cheeks as she gazed into his bottomless eyes with all the love her soul possessed. "I'm not finished, my love." She turned to Beck. "I have seen my husband grieve too long for his son. Give him back his flesh and blood and I will stay."

Two soldiers came forward and escorted Great Eagle from the room. Katherine walked beside him to the courtyard. When he saw her look of desperation, he spoke to her in their native tongue.

"I will come back for you, my only one," he promised. "I will not forsake you."

As Great Eagle and Sleeping Rabbit joined Ansote at the gate, a tear-filled, feminine voice rang out. "Matthew, me darlin', a kiss before you go." Callie beckoned and fell to her knees as the boy ran back. "We'll be thinkin' of ye, Matthew, with all the love a son's deservin'."

She turned her cheek for his kiss, but his small hand came up and stroked it, then he kissed her on the lips. "I will remember you with love, Mother Callie, and you, Father James. Thank you for keeping your promise to me."

Wild Kat

Tears streamed down their faces unchecked. "We'll not be fergettin' ye, Matthew. "'Tis a fact ye stole our hearts away, and we're hopin' ye'll be rememberin' us kindly," James professed.

Bobby stood beside them and slapped at angry tears as if he were swatting flies. His Indian friend approached him. They said nothing. Matthew reached for Bobby's hand and placed a set of new willow sticks, polished to a sheen, in his palm. Bobby took the only thing of value he possessed, his leather sack of marbles, and handed them to Matthew. Without hesitation or embarrassment, the friends embraced. Good-byes consummated, Sleeping Rabbit turned and joined his father who was waiting at the gate with Katherine and Ansote.

For the last time Kat embraced Matthew, then Ansote. When she went to her husband she was dry-eyed and smiling. They kissed softly and stepped back, hands clasped. Great Eagle voiced his conviction. "The mills of the gods grind slowly, but exceedingly fine. I am leaving you for no longer than it will take to make my plans, Tanguadal. This is my promise."

"I will wait, my Indian."

Great Eagle moved closer to the Forsythes who were standing nearby. "You have my gratitude. The gods will bless you for taking care of my son. Mark my words, for they are true."

The chief's tortured mind raged as they rode across the prairie. When they reached the hill that would take them into the woods, he swung around and raised his fist in promise.

The small figure in the distance waved back as her husky voice lilted over the land, strong but effeminate. The war cry escaped with vigor from the top of her lungs.

"Whoooeeeyah! Eeeyah! Eeeyah!"

* * *

Chief Hawk Eye was dead. Word reached Fort Riley only two days before the signing of the treaty. A new date was set for the middle of November, leaving ample time for another personage to be selected and approved by the Kiowa Tribal Chiefs. In a recent dispatch Colonel Beck received the good news that Great Eagle was appointed the new high leader of the Kiowa Nation.

*   *   *

Kat grew increasingly despondent as days stretched into weeks. November arrived on a swift cold wind. She wandered near the barracks hoping to hear news of her husband. It was useless. The soldiers either clammed up or went about their duties without so much as a nod.

Humiliated by Kat's appearance and sullen attitude, Bess began to encourage her to wear civilized clothes. "You've dressed like an Indian long enough, Katherine. And please don't call yourself by that silly name anymore."

"I'm Tanguadal, wife of Great Eagle, whether you like it or not."

Bess sighed with frustration. "You may as well paint your face like a savage."

Kat fumed. "Don't ever use the word **savage** in my presence again!"

Bess was astonished by the tone of her daughter's voice. "I don't know you anymore, Katherine. Maybe I never did."

Scorn still in her eyes, Kat slipped on her rabbit fur, tied a leather thong around her forehead and started for the door. She stopped and said, "No, Mother, no one ever really took the time to know me."

"Katherine, it's dark outside. Where are you going?"

"To sit in the orchard; at least it's peaceful there. While I'm gone, don't put my damn mattress back on the bed like you always do. I prefer to sleep on the damn floor."

"If your papa was here he'd smack you a good one for cussing, Kat."

Wild Kat

"Father isn't here. I believe he might find it hard to understand what's going on between you and the wagon master so soon after his death."

Terribly hurt, Bess shook her head. "Your papa would want me to go on living. I'm a lonely woman and Deke Stiles is a good man. There'll always be a place in my heart for your papa, but I love Deke and we're going to get married as soon as the preacher passes through."

"I hope he's scalped before he gets here."

"Oh, Katherine, what a horrible thing to say." Bess grabbed a kitchen chair for support. "You don't sound human."

"I don't feel human. How can I, when part of me is gone?" she asked bitterly and lunged through the door, slamming it behind her.

Todd admonished Kat for her behavior, so she chose to ignore him. Linc tried to talk to her on more than one occasion, but she turned a deaf ear. Bobby was the only one who understood her desolation.

Linc decided to try again and dropped by her cabin one morning during breakfast. Bess opened the door, delighted to see him.

"Linc! What a nice surprise. Come in."

"Is Katherine up, Mrs. Stone?"

"Yes. I'll tell her you're here."

Bess went to Katherine's door and knocked. "Kat, you've got company."

"I'm not dressed."

"Linc's here. We'll have a cup of coffee while you make yourself presentable."

Kat appeared minutes later wearing her doeskin pants and shirt. Her hair was braided into two ropes and a dark red headband hugged her forehead.

Bess sighed. "Katherine, all your nice clothes are in the trunk in your room."

"I'm more comfortable in these. You don't mind, do you, Linc?"

"Certainly not." His manner was stuffy, not at all as she remembered him.

"Good. Let's have some breakfast." Kat did not miss Linc's look of disdain as she filled a bowl with mush. "Will you join me?"

"No thank you, Kat. I've already eaten."

"Well I'm starving," she twittered as she flopped down cross-legged on the floor and proceeded to use her fingers as a scoop.

"Katherine Stone! Don't you have any pride left?"

Kat shrugged. "My name is no longer Katherine Stone. I am here to ensure my husband and my son's safety."

Linc shifted uncomfortably on the straight back chair. "Let me have a minute with Kat, Mrs. Stone."

Bess flung a wool cape around her shoulders. "Maybe you can talk some sense into that hard head of her, Linc. I'll go out for some air."

As soon as the door closed behind her, Linc turned a suspicious eye on Kat. "You're quite an actress, Katherine, but the part you're playing is rather inappropriate."

"I don't give a damn what you think; furthermore, I have told you on more than one occasion that my name is Tanguadal, wife of Chief Great Eagle."

Linc studied her for some time. He had always thought of her as pretty, but now she possessed a beauty that was ethereal. "Kat, you're the most desirable woman I've ever known. I still want to marry you."

"I'm already married! Can't you get that through your thick skull?"

Throwing aside what remained of his dignity, he grabbed her roughly and hauled her into his arms. "Don't be a little fool! You're no more married than I am. A heathen ritual is not a marriage ceremony."

She pushed him away and kicked his boot. "You sonofabitch! I'm Tanguadal, wife of Chief Great Eagle. We've made love together. I want no other."

Her copper eyes locked with his. He knew he was staring at a stranger. She removed her knife from its sheath at her waist. "Get out. Or I'll be forced to relieve you of your manly power."

Wild Kat

Linc backed off and glared at her. "How revolting. I won't bother you again, Katherine."

Bess walked in and cried out when she saw Kat's drawn knife. "Oh, dear Lord! Linc, I do apologize for Kat's heathenish behavior."

"I was just leaving, Mrs. Stone."

Bess closed the door and draped her cloak over a chair. "I love you, Katherine. I would rather accept you as you are than lose you all over again."

Shocked, Kat softened and said, "Thank you, Mother, for understanding."

* * *

Deke arose early. It was the day of the treaty signing and he wanted to have a cup of coffee with Bess first. He knocked and called from the porch. Bess opened the door with one of her sunshine smiles.

"I hope I'm not butting in too early, Bess girl."

"No, Deke, we've been up for a little while. Come on in." She nodded her head toward Katherine sitting on the floor by the stove. Kat ignored both of them as she wrapped her rabbit robe around her shoulders and walked outside. She stood on the porch looking eastward to the sun peeping over the horizon. The morning was bone-chilling and her tears came close to freezing as she made her way to the pecan grove. Her sanctuary.

Bess handed Deke a mug of coffee and smiled. "I hear tell the parson's due any day now."

Deke's face lit up. "Who told you about the preacher coming?"

"Colonel Beck–just yesterday. We're free to tie the knot. Bobby is tickled pink about having you for a pa. Todd will adjust and Katherine doesn't care about anybody but that blasted Indian."

Deke sobered. Bess thought that he seemed a little sad. "Have you ever noticed how Miss Kat's face softens when she talks about that Injun?"

Lydia Joe Cates

"I've noticed."

"You know, Bess, it's not easy for you and me being separated right now. Can you imagine how Miss Kat feels? Maybe she's as tormented as we are. Even more, being younger and all."

"I-I never looked at it like that before, Deke."

"It'd bear thinking about, honey." He kissed her and stepped back. "I'd best go. You taste so good that once I get started I don't want to quit."

Bess was hugging him when Kat walked in. Deke smiled and made a feeble attempt at conversation. "I haven't seen near enough of you since you came back, Miss Kat."

"No, you haven't, Mr. Stiles, but you've been seeing a lot of the lady standing beside you. That's what you do when you're in love, isn't it?"

Bess had raised her hand to slap Kat when Deke caught hold of her wrist in midair. "Simmer down, Bess girl."

Kat did not bat an eye. "I've been robbed of the most precious thing in my life. I can feel myself dying day by day."

Bess's face was chalk-white and her body seemed to fold as she lowered herself onto a chair. "You're right. I don't know why I've been so blind. You are Tanguadal, wife of Great Eagle, and I think it's about time you went back to him. I'm going to talk to Colonel Beck."

The wicked expression disappeared from Kat's eyes and her spirit soared with her mother's declaration. A vapor of mist shrouded the ordinary kitchen and the Indian rose out of it, signing his promise before the apparition vanished.

Deke watched Kat intently, startled by the transformation taking place before his eyes. Katherine's face softened. She smiled at Deke and her mother and went to the bedroom, softly closing the door behind her.

Moved by the sight he had just witnessed, Deke asked, "Could you find it in your heart to part with Miss Kat again, Bess?"

"I already have, honey. I'm on my way to speak with the commander and see what can be done."

Wild Kat

Deke whirled around at the sound of clomping boots on the plank walk outside. A quartet of soldiers raced past the open doorway amid shouts and bellowed orders.

He stuck his head outside and yelled, "What's going on, Private?"

"Go see for yourself, Mr. Stiles, you won't believe it."

Deke hustled across the courtyard and up the ladder to the catwalk. Before he reached the steps to the lookout tower he cast his eyes across the prairie and swore. "Gawdamighty!"

A wall of Indians lengthened across the horizon as far as the eye could see. Bess and the Forsythes were hurrying toward the gate when he hailed them. "There must be a thousand Injuns out there. Take a gander from this catwalk."

Colonel Beck rushed out of his office still strapping on his holster. He rounded up four of his best men and commanded, "Saddle up!"

A crowd gathered to watch the pow-wow as the officer and his entourage rode out of the fort. Great Eagle presented a majestic figure in his white feathered headdress as he sat proudly atop Guo-la-te. Bare from the waist up, chest oiled, he shimmered like bronze in the morning sunlight. The chief waited until Colonel Beck and his men trotted out of the fort. He then raised his staff as a signal to Ansote and three other braves to accompany him to meet the soldiers.

The cavalry officer came within a few feet of Great Eagle and reined in his horse. Colonel Beck waggled his head and waited for the chief to speak.

"I have come for my wife, Colonel Beck. There will be no trouble if I am allowed to take her back with me."

"Dammit! Have you lost your mind, Great Eagle? Today is the signing of the treaty. It's just hours away, when the sun is overhead."

"I am well aware of that, Colonel. Look around you. You will see the chiefs who are to sign the pact along with me. You will also see many of our braves."

Colonel Beck observed the solemn expressions of Little Bluff and Strong Buffalo, who nodded to him. The officer's beady eyes squinted in the brilliance of the morning when he surveyed the impatient masks of Gray Fox and Red Cloud.

"I'll go back to the fort and speak with my advisors. I trust you'll give me the time I need."

Great Eagle warned, "You have until the sun is overhead. If you send an escort the chiefs and I will follow to make our marks on the agreement...and to take my wife. If you do not send an escort, we will attack."

Red-faced and sweating, Colonel Beck took a deep breath. "I understand." He prodded the animal with his heels and galloped back to the fort.

As he dismounted, Beck tossed the reins to Private Sheffield. "Tell the captain to get in here on the double. Come with me, Sergeant Spivey." As they stepped onto the porch, Beck spied Deke with a group of soldiers and called out to him. "Stiles, meet me in my office! Bring Mrs. Stone and that daughter of hers with you."

The group gathered according to Colonel Beck's orders and waited for the brusque man to speak. He paced back and forth behind his desk, sweating and cursing. "I'm sure you know that we have a war party breathing down our necks." The officer glared at Kat. "The treaty signing will go according to schedule if we agree to Great Eagle's ultimatum," he barked.

"What's the Injun demanding?"

"He wants his wife, Stiles. As an officer of the United States Cavalry and Commander of this Post, I can't legally turn her over to him, even if she does insist that she's a blasted Indian!"

Kat listened intently. Bess observed her daughter sitting cross-legged on the floor next to the chair she had refused. Beck glared at Kat with an air of irritation and turned to Bess. "Mrs. Stone, I've been considering what you told me this morning. If you still agree to let your daughter go back to Great Eagle, I may have a solution to our dilemma."

Wild Kat

"I'm willing. The girl isn't happy and she won't be until she's with her husband again."

The sparkle returned to Kat's eyes. Back straight, she listened to the unbelievable exchange between her mother and the commander.

"Excellent!" Uncomfortable with his position, Beck cleared his throat and glared at the serious faces trained on him. "Is it clear to all of you what I'm proposing?"

All nodded as the officer outlined his plan. "One hour from now we'll send an escort for our 'guests'. The gates will be open to welcome them. After the treaty is signed and the chiefs have departed, the gates will remain open until the guard change. If Mrs. Great Eagle were to escape during that interval, there's nothing I can do about it." He looked each individual in the eye with raised eyebrows. "Understood?"

The small group acknowledged as Kat walked over to a chair and sat down beside her mother. Deke suppressed a smile and Beck's eyes widened. "I see you **do** know what a chair is for, young lady."

The portly man went to his desk drawer and withdrew the treaty. "You may 'escape', Katherine, but you must wait in the pecan grove until the pact is sealed. There'll be ample time for you to slip out during the guard change."

Kat stood and gingerly approached the officer. "Do you speak the Kiowa dialect, Colonel?"

"Some."

She began to speak rhythmically in dialect, using hand signs to make her speech more impressive. "I want to thank you from the bottom of my heart. I don't know if you have ever loved deeply, but if you have, then you know the joy in my soul at this moment."

"Well I'll be damned if you're not the most eloquent Indian speaker I've ever heard." He allowed himself a small, nervous chuckle as Katherine stood on tiptoe and kissed him on the cheek.

Beck sputtered with embarrassment. "Well now, let's see. Oh, yes. Sergeant Spivey, wipe that infernal grin off your face and bring my horse around."

Colonel Beck cantered out alone to talk to Great Eagle. The chief took his cue from the officer and waved Ansote away, then rode to meet with Beck in private. When their exchange came to a conclusion, the chief offered the man an unusual gesture. He shook hands in the white man's fashion. In turn, Beck raised his arm and gave the Indian sign of peace. Great Eagle removed a red pouch from his waistband and placed it in Beck's hand with a few words of instruction.

The chief returned to wait with his followers until the appointed time. He was anxious to convey the good news.

*   *   *

Kat wiped away tears of inexplicable joy as she fastened the black pearl necklace around her neck. Colonel Beck had even smiled when he presented it to her. She tied her bundle of belongings with a leather thong and waited by the open door dressed in her fringed longshirt and berry-stained riding breeches, hair flowing free in the wind–for the favor of her husband.

The sun was high when the colorful assembly of Kiowa chiefs rode confidently through the open gates of Fort Riley. Colonel Beck in full-dress, white gloves and all, saluted the impressive group.

Every nerve in Kat's body screamed out to Great Eagle as he rode past her cabin. A table had been set up in the courtyard with chairs arranged in a semicircle for those who wished to witness the important event. One by one the chiefs made their mark. Great Eagle was the last to sign in the place of honor, befitting his position as the new high leader of the Kiowa Nation. Proudly aware that he was the only chief who knew how to write, he did so with great flourish.

*   *   *

Wild Kat

Kat viewed her mother with compassion and said, "Please love me for who I am now."

Weeping, Bess cuddled the girl in her arms. "I'll never stop loving you…Tanguadal."

Kat kissed her white mother for the last time, picked up her bundle and slipped out the door. Her excitement grew as she entered the small pecan orchard at the far corner of the yard. She spied a tree nearest the entrance and hunkered down to wait. The moment she heard Colonel Beck's congratulations in sketchy dialect, she began to watch for the chiefs to leave. As the last one trotted away from the fort, she crept out of the grove and skimmed through the gates unobserved.

Kat tumbled into the nearest ravine and waited for the fort to be secured. It was sunset when she heard the hinges squeaking and the grating of the gates closing. Cotton-like clouds interspersed with dark gray ones formed overhead as a light fog rolled in and settled over the prairie.

She was free!

Kat rose from her cramped position in the ravine. As her eyes scoured the edge of the woods, she ceased to breathe. A short distance away she could see Great Eagle rising out of the mist, leading Guo-la-te and Many Colors. She stood motionless as the vision became clear.

Katherine scooped up her bundle and flew the last few steps to her husband. She tossed her burden on the ground, tears of happiness coursing down her glowing cheeks, as his arms completely enveloped her.

His breath was warm and sweet as he murmured over the top of her head. "My Tanguadal, my only one." He continued to hold her in a close embrace and stroked her auburn crown. The moisture on his handsome face remained unseen.

Their bodies blended with intimate grace as they touched. In a voice humbled by their separation, Great Eagle softly and simply said, "Let us go home."

Lydia Joe Cates

With an exhalted surge of energy, Kat broke into a run and leaped high in the air, placing her hands precisely on her pony's rump and swinging herself up on top of the grand animal. Great Eagle's deep, resonant laugh echoed over the prairie as he mounted with the same precision. They rode like the thunder that calmed them both until they were swallowed up by the woods.

* * *

Fog had changed into a light rain as Bess and Deke, along with the Forsythes, hurried to their cabins. "It's getting colder," Bess remarked, "But I'm glowing inside. Funny, I don't feel sad. I guess it's because I know Kath…I mean Tanguadal…is finally happy."

Deke held her hand tightly. "You know, that Great Eagle kind of stands alone. What I mean is, he seems different. You know, honorable."

"I'm catchin' yer meanin', Deke, and sure'n I'm thinkin' the same," Callie agreed. "I'll be tellin' ye one thing though. That Mr. Great Eagle is a beauty, and I'm bettin' a hot-blooded gent fer sure."

"Sweet Callie, ye're not talkin' like a lady."

"Maybe it's the untamed frontier that's doin' it to me, James, me dear."

Without warning, mist became a downpour and the foursome rushed to Bess's cabin. As they crowded onto the small porch she said, "I've got a bottle of fine blackberry wine. Come on in for a spell."

When the wine had been passed around, Callie spoke up. "Let's be makin' a friendly toast to Deke Stiles fer all he's done fer us." The four took a sip and waited. Smile widening, her green eyes met her husband's as she announced, "I've one more fer the health of the wee one that'll be comin' to the Forsythe home in early summer."

Glasses stopped in midair and Deke grinned his usual grin, but the look of adoration that James bestowed on his lovely wife was a sight that would not soon be forgotten.

Wild Kat

"Ye've waited long to be a mother, sweet Callie. I'm thinkin' what a lucky babe it'll be."

"Aye, and to have a father like ye, me dear. I'm rememberin' Great Eagle's words as he was takin' Matthew away. 'The gods'll bless ye fer takin' care of me son', he told us." She smiled through tears. "I'm thinkin' we've been blessed."

* * *

A loud knock on the door awakened Bess. "Who is it?"

"Your intended," a gravelly voice roared.

"The door's not bolted," she called out.

Deke marched in supporting a new washtub on his shoulders. "Here's your wedding present, my dear, and guess who rode in a few minutes ago?"

"Thank you for the tub." She laughed and said, "Parson Tilley is here."

"How did you know?"

"You brought me a wedding present, silly, and I haven't seen a grin like you're wearing since the morning after we sinned the first time."

Deke screwed up his face with indignation. "Bess, I'd sure as hell appreciate it if you'd stop calling what we did sinning."

She patted his cheek and ignored his remark. "Suppose you get out of here and go fetch the preacher."

* * *

Deke and Bess stood before Parson Tilley that very afternoon and exchanged vows with James and Callie witnessing the modest event. When the preacher told Deke to place the ring on Bess's finger, James handed him a wide gold band.

"Where'd you get the ring, Deke?"

Lydia Joe Cates

"Trader Charley Bone. I've been toting it around ever since he stumbled into our camp in the woods."

Parson Tilley frowned and wedged into the conversation. "I now pronounce you man and wife. You may kiss the bride."

Deke pecked Bess lightly on the lips and said, "Howdy do, Missus Stiles."

*   *   *

Kat rode double with Great Eagle while Many Colors trailed behind. She wrapped her arms tightly around her husband's waist and rested her cheek against his back. Closeness had become a necessity.

His hand splayed over hers as he recalled the time he had whisked her away from the wagon train. "Our camp is not far from here, Tanguadal."

"Where are our people?"

"They have returned to their own villages."

"We'll be alone?"

"Yes, my Tanguadal. It will be as before, when we were new to each other."

As if they had coasted on the wind, they soon reached a small clearing. Great Eagle dismounted, lifted Kat in his arms and set her down in front of a fire pit glowing with lively coals. A freshly-cut green willow spit skewered two fat rabbits roasting over the embers.

Kat scanned the forest. "Is someone else here?"

"No, my dearest. Ansote is the considerate one. He left after preparing for your return."

"Did Ansote do all this?" She made a sweeping gesture with her arms.

Great Eagle smiled at Kat's awe when she spied the elaborate bed of pine protected by a canopy made of deer hide. "Ansote did everything except the covering. Your Indian Mother sewed the skins."

Wild Kat

"My dear Ay-tah," she crooned, fingering the soft animal skins. "I've missed her so." She looked up and touched his face ever so gently. "Are you a vision, my Indian?"

"Let us find out, Tanguadal."

Heart plundering his rib cage, the chief carried her to the bed of pine and undressed her slowly. He laid aside her shirt and suckled her breasts with tender hunger until she shivered with anticipation.

Trembling, he untied the waist thong that held her pants and dropped down on a knee to slip them off. The chief shuddered as he kissed the swell of her belly and felt her fingers comb his hair. With a joy he had not known since they parted, he showered her with kisses on her supple skin, beginning at her ankles. Hands and lips caressing along the way, he paused when he reached the auburn thatch of her womanhood, pulled her closer and kissed her deeply. Kat moaned as he laid her on the bed of pine.

Great Eagle shed his clothes and sank beneath the covers with her. As he wound his arms around her she whispered, "I know the strength of your love, my Indian. It feeds the hunger in my soul."

No longer contained, groins aflame, Great Eagle hovered over her for only a moment. A primitive sound erupted from his throat as he burrowed within her. Kat matched his movements until they lapsed into another dimension, their bodies pulsing with ecstasy. At last, their moans of irreverent delight echoed in the still night as he released the heat of his passion.

In the early morning hours, bodies intimately entangled, they spoke of empty days and nights. Kat anticipated their future and reflected on the past, hoping to reconcile the two one day. Great Eagle hugged her with the contentment of peace. "You are full of talk, Tanguadal."

"I am **far** from finished."

"You walk my path well, my Wild Kat."

Solemnly, she turned to face him. "I always will, my Indian…my only one."